FOR OLD CRIME'S SAKE

DELANO AMES

Also available in Perennial Library by Delano Ames

MURDER, MAESTRO, PLEASE

FOR OLD CRIME'S SAKE

DELANO AMES

PERENNIAL LIBRARY
Harper & Row, Publishers
New York, Cambridge, Philadelphia, San Francisco
London, Mexico City, São Paulo, Sydney

This book was originally published in England under the title *Lucky Jane*; first U.S. publication by J.B. Lippincott Company in 1959. It is here reprinted by arrangement with John Farquharson, Ltd.

First PERENNIAL LIBRARY edition published 1983.

LIBRARY OF CONGRESS CATALOGUE CARD NUMBER: 82-47790

ISBN: 0-06-080629-X

83 84 85 86 10 9 8 7 6 5 4 3 2 1

TO PAUL HORGAN

FOR OLD CRIME'S SAKE

Chapter 1

DAGOBERT WAS DEEPLY moved when my premium bond drew a fifty-pound bonus. Money so simply come by opened up new vistas. Far too many people, he decided, underrate money; and to acquire more of it momentarily displaced his current passion for Mudéjar architecture.

Knowing my husband's aptitude for getting what he wants, I stirred expectantly. He grew pensive, giving the problem fuller consideration. In an effort to be helpful I said that some people made money by going to work. Dagobert who is always open to fresh ideas at once went out and bought the morning newspapers.

I plied him with coffee as he ran a hopeful eye down the Situations Vacant column.

"There are all sorts of things," he said in surprise. "The Government of Nigeria, for instance, is looking for a driller. Or, nearer home in Slough, Tracers and Estimators are urgently required. Bee-keepers . . . no, it's book-keepers. Coffin-maker . . . Write," he added, discouraged, "stating experience. How about 'Tool-makers for fascinating prototype work with own canteen and generous superannuation scheme'? Or here we have 'Night-shift vacancies for Hand-Fed Platen Minders.' "

"I like the hand-fed part."

But I sensed his enthusiasm was waning. He scowled and shook his head.

"No," he said. "You'd hate that."

"What?"

" 'Previous training unnecessary, good pay while you learn, rapid advancement—for intelligent young woman.' "

He turned the page before I could see it. "We mustn't rush these things," he said, feeling that enough had been done for one morning. "It may take us a day or two." He paused to admire a photograph of Henry Howard Hutton Junior's yacht at anchor in Tabarca harbour. "Meanwhile—between jobs, as it were—I was wondering if a carefree month in . . ."

"On fifty pounds?"

He saw my point. "If you're dead set against Tabarca—wherever Tabarca may be—there are 'budget holidays' in the Peak District with rucksack, rope and grappling irons. Just the thing, it says, to set one up for the winter—help you tackle that new job with new keenness."

"I'm not looking for a job," I said.

"Oh?" He shrugged affably. "Then it must have been me."

We changed papers. He found the financial page and noted that money was jittery. Zinc, however, had eased; reassured by this he settled down with an article entitled: "The New Polyester Laminates: Useful Do's and Don't's." I read the caption over the picture of Tabarca: "Time Stands Still in Europe's Tiniest Principality"—and debated whether to have my new shoes stretched again or give them to the landlady's dwarf daughter.

"Who," I asked idly, "is Henry Howard Hutton Junior?"

"H. H.?" he said, as though they rubbed shoulders daily at the Stock Exchange. "Just another captain of industry. Which reminds me—what in your opinion ought I first to cultivate: a smart and prosperous appearance, or the ability to bring out the best in my employees? It's a competition," he explained before I could point out that I was his only employee. "You arrange these qualities in order of desirability and then, let me see, name in block letters, a postal-order value one shilling and . . . there you are!"

"Where?"

"Out of the rut! Free from the dreary routine of working for others. It says: 'Win our fascinating competition and BE YOUR OWN BOSS.'"

"You already are," I said. "That's what's worrying us."

"True," he said and changed papers with me again.

I saw him examine the photograph of Tabarca with revived interest. He had just noted the Time Stands Still bit and read that Tabarca, inaccessibly located somewhere between Corsica and Minorca, was not to be found on normal-sized maps—details I should have known would be irresistible.

"Hello," he exclaimed. "It says H. H. 'has bought the island, together with feudal rights dating from the eleventh century. Plus—rumour has it—the hand of the lovely Princess Juana, only daughter of Jaime the Fat, nineteenth Prince of Tabarca, with whose recent death the direct male line of the house of Branza became extinct.'" He read on: "'Although the date of the marriage has not yet been fixed local society can talk of nothing else, and already the simple islanders affectionately refer to Henry Howard Hutton as Prince Enrico El Loco. Today Prince Enrico (Plain Mister Hutton, to you!) flies his own semi-royal standard from the ancient fortress of Tabarca, mints his own coins and issues his own postage stamps' . . . I wonder," he broke off speculatively, "how you go about a thing like that?"

I had already skimmed through this doubtless highly coloured description of Tabarca's new owner.

"It's quite simple," I said, paraphrasing what it said of Mr. Hutton's career. "You start life as a ragged urchin selling the *Evening Gazette* in the streets of Quebec. You save, penny by penny, until suddenly one day you own the *Evening Gazette*. Then you pick up a few railways, an oil well or two, some factories and a string of pulp magazines, glossy periodicals and horror comics, always remembering to give the public exactly what it wants: crime, sex, sport, and a chance to get something for nothing."

"Why sport, I wonder," Dagobert murmured, wandering over to the bookcase. "Now, let's see, with fifty pounds . . ."

He took down an atlas. I don't know whether he was looking for Tabarca or for a similar island with a view to making an offer. Fortunately an advertisement in the *Daily Mail* distracted him.

"A thousand pounds in cash," he said with awe, " 'and NO entry fee. All you need do is enclose six gay labels from the handy new zip-open packets of Vito-Caff, the coffee-like beverage that's BETTER than coffee and SO VERY MUCH BETTER for you! Put them into a sealed envelope together with a ten-word description of why you love VITO-CAFF. Here are some useful tips for competitors: "Its creamy consistency—ummm, so good! My doctor endorses it because it's brimming with vitamins and free from harmful caffeine! Its tangy, tingly, *different* flavour." ' "

Tempted as much by this as by the thousand pounds in cash Dagobert went out to the grocer, leaving me to rough out ten words in praise of Vito-Caff. He returned with six handy zip-open packets and an armful of periodicals. All, it appeared, were eager to give away money. My fifty-pound premium bond seemed a very modest beginning.

"The *Daily Sketch*," I said, catching his optimism, "offers to double our income."

He considered the proposition. After a quick mental calculation he decided the sum involved wasn't worth it. "We want to aim higher," he said. "For instance we could quite easily be among the Lucky Seven."

"Who are they?"

"I'm not quite sure," he said, "but the woman at the newsagent's is very excited about it. You have to buy a weekly called *Home Truth* which explains the competition. It comes out this afternoon. I've told her to save us a copy. Meanwhile there's much to be done: slogans to write, crossword puzzles to solve, hats to match with dresses, favourite T.V. stars to— What on earth," he gasped, "is this?"

"Vito-Caff," I said.

"They're right about the flavour being different," he said, pouring it into the wastepaper basket. "We'll work on the creamy-consistency angle."

I left him with a pair of scissors and a book of synonyms, sharpening pencils. Dagobert, I realised, had found a job.

When I returned late that afternoon he was still hard at it. The place was strewn with magazines and papers. He had forgotten lunch and smoked two packets of cigarettes. He had worked out that by winning, say, only a quarter of the competitions he had already entered our earnings would be in the region of a hundred thousand pounds.

He stopped worrying about the income tax situation which would be thus created when he saw my new shoes. They had tall heels which resembled toothpicks.

"They're called 'Stiltees,'" he told me. "I've just rated them first in *Modern Miss*'s Shoe Competition. It's for a bungalow in Peacehaven. How did you manage to walk home on them?"

"I took a taxi."

"I hate to think of your having to take taxis, Jane," he said. "I want you to have what other women have—a long silver Rolls-Royce with your own chauffeur in green livery." His glance strayed again to the copy of *Home Truth* on the table. On the cover there was a portrait of Her Highness Princess Juana of Tabarca who presumably had these things. "Champagne, orchids, a wild-mink coat to wear . . . Does that sort of thing appeal to you?"

"Very much."

"Really?" he said in astonishment. "You wouldn't rather be the envy of your neighbours and own a Dream Kitchen?"

I said I was quite happy with our gas ring and teetered across to the harpsichord in search of a cigarette. He urged me to accept one of his, glad of the excuse to open a new packet. The brand was unfamiliar to me. They were called Breeze.

"King's size," he told me. "Men of distinction, like Henry Howard Hutton Junior, smoke them. With the new scientifically planned filter-tip, Breezes are fresher, cooler . . ."

A blast of ice-cold menthol caught me in the throat.

"See what I mean?" he said. "Wait till you reach the filter-tip."

"Why? Do you get a prize?"

"Breezes distribute their profits in the form of coupons," he said, "thus making every smoker a shareholder in the firm. When we've saved a thousand, for instance, they send us a Smoker's Companion in rolled gold and ormolu."

"By that time we'll need a companion," I said, "preferably with hospital experience."

By the end of the week we had rather sinister coughs, but we'd collected enough coupons for a set of coloured pencils in a plastic case. It was, as Dagobert said, a comfort to feel there was something solid behind us while we waited for our bungalow in Peacehaven.

Somehow we didn't win the bungalow, or even the Morris Minor which had seemed such a sure thing. Our mistake, Dagobert decided, was not sending in a sufficient number of entry forms. To avoid this in the future he trebled all newspaper subscriptions.

Nothing very dramatic happened during the next few weeks except the bill we received from the newsagent. Dagobert's thoughts were reverting to Mediterranean islands where newspapers did not exist when again we struck lucky: an honourable mention in the *New Statesman* competition and a book token.

Heartened by this he worked with renewed zeal and, by solving a crossword puzzle in *Hearth and Hobbies*, very nearly won a useful electric lathe with simple instructions on how to make your own machine tools at home.

I realised how hard Dagobert had taken this setback when next morning I found him reading a pamphlet entitled: "Choosing a Career." He dropped a half-smoked Breeze listlessly into the last of the Vito-Caff, too disconsolate even to fill in the football pools.

My heart bled for him as he went off in his clerical grey suit, black and white silk tie, rolled umbrella and deer-stalker to keep an appointment with a man named Jenkins who was starting a motor-scooter factory in the North Circular Road.

He returned that afternoon in better spirits; the factory had openings for keen young men with ideas who were eager to get to the top. The openings would not be available until next month.

To celebrate this Dagobert had bought me a dozen roses, a box of liqueur chocolates and exchanged his book token for a volume called *Documents in Mycenaean Greek.*

That evening at the Load of Hay around the corner I learned a great deal about Linear B. I didn't learn what Linear B was exactly, but I gathered that in the controversy raging over the subject Dagobert's views were strictly anti-Minoan. A child could see that the clay tablets excavated at Knossos were inscribed in a form of archaic Greek. If I remained unconvinced he would (and did) show me illustrations of the ideograms which had helped epigraphists to crack the script.

In brief, life had returned to normal.

Next morning the motor-scooter factory telephoned to present Mr. Jenkins' compliments and to inquire who Mr. Dagobert Brown's hatter was. Mr. Jenkins wanted to buy a deer-stalker. We cashed in our Breeze coupons, settling for a chromium toast-rack. In Stoke Newington we ran down the Japanese film we'd missed when it was showing locally. Dagobert brushed up his archaic Greek at the British Museum and in response to an advertisement urging him to make writing his hobby *now* he began to make notes for a best-seller on pre-Gregorian plain-song. I renewed my search of the Brompton Road for a plain neutral brown twin-set.

I limped back to our rooms in Roland Gardens one evening, carrying a thing in hot-house scarlet poodle-wool with the new ostrich neck, to find a long silver Rolls-Royce parked in front of the house. A chauffeur in green livery stood beside the car. There was a wild-mink coat over his arm.

I wondered who the visitors were and found my keys. At the front door a hatless young man with fair curly hair was studying the names over the doorbells. He wore a shaggy Harris tweed suit with a plaid waistcoat and carried a spray of orchids. He found the bell he wanted and pressed it. It was our bell.

We both waited tensely, but there was no answer.

"No one at home?" I suggested. "I mean, who, or rather whom . . ."

"The lucky name is Brown," he said.

The name struck a chord. "Brown? Yes. My n-name is Brown."

"Not *Jane* Brown!"

"As a matter of fact . . . er, yes."

His cheeks dimpled and his blue eyes twinkled merrily.

"I bring glad tidings, Jane," he said.

He stooped to pick up the parcel I dropped on the step and handed me the orchids.

"How much?" I said hoarsely.

"Two of our competitors fainted," he confided. "You're quite sure you are Jane Brown?"

I no longer was, but I took a chance and nodded. "What is it?" I whispered. "Oh dear—the Dream Kitchen!"

He looked contemptuous, then brisk. "No more drudgery of that sort for you, Jane," he said. "But first a few simple formalities: proof of identity, a signature or two. Then half a dozen photographs in the mink coat while the chauffeur holds the door of the Rolls-Royce. Finally a few words to *Home Truth*'s less fortunate readers saying what it feels like to be—one of the Lucky Seven!"

Chapter 2

It felt terrible. I said:

"There may be gin upstairs." Memory stirred vaguely. "Wasn't there something about champagne?"

"Rest assured, Jane, *Lucky Jane*," he soothed me, "that nothing will be spared to make the next fortnight the most memorable of your life, even if we can't absolutely guarantee the wedding. Champagne, nothing. Bobby Marcovitch will make himself personally responsible for this." He showed even white teeth in a boyish smile. "I am Bobby Marcovitch."

I said how do you do and then: "Whose wedding? What fortnight? Not—not the one with grappling irons?"

He was plainly used to dealing with the mentally arrested and he politely ignored the interruption.

"But of course we are already friends, aren't we? All readers of *Home Truth* are Bobby's friends." He held the smile, as though for purposes of identification, and wagged a reproving finger from which flashed a sapphire. "All, that is, except those who have something to hide. Editorial page," he prompted, "Bobby's Fireside Chit-Chat. You *do* read *Home Truth*?" he said doubtfully. "But enough of me. James! Madam's wild-mink coat."

He clapped plump manicured hands. The chauffeur, who plainly resented being called James, approached with a sullen expression.

"He's upset because he isn't coming with us," Bobby confided.

The chauffeur held out the coat as though it smelled. It did actually, of mothballs.

"Mine?" I asked.

"For the next glorious fourteen days," Bobby nodded gaily. "The orchids, of course, are your very own to keep, while the Rolls-Royce we all share. I can't wait, can you?"

"I'd feel more impetuous," I said, "if I knew what was coming—apart from the orchids, and a seat in the Rolls-Royce."

Bobby's patience showed signs of strain. His voice rose plaintively and East End vowel sounds infiltrated his Commercial T.V. English. "Fun's fun," he said, "but I'm a busy man. Did you fill in winning entry form Number 11,326, or didn't you? Where is it? Here." He spread the half page cut from *Home Truth* on the flap of his briefcase. "Brown, Jane," he read. "Roland Gardens, 9. Is that you, or isn't it?"

I said it was.

"And your signature, stating that you've read the rules and understand the competition and will abide by the decision of the judges? Do you recognise it?"

Dagobert's forgery was excellent and I said I recognised it.

"Well, then," he said, placated. "What are we getting excited about?" He grinned apologetically. "You had Bobby worried there for a moment. I'm glad you're one of us, Jane. Wait till you see some of the others! Now, as I've said, we cannot absolutely guarantee the royal wedding. These things, like the weather, depend, may I say, on the will of God." He paused for a moment to lend the words solemnity. "But the rest of the good things, the fun and romance and luxury are all yours."

"What royal wedding?"

He appealed to the chauffeur. "She asks *what* royal wedding! I'll put that in tomorrow's Chit-Chat. But no, perhaps not," he concluded more soberly. "I don't think somehow that Henry Howard Hutton Junior would be amused."

"What's Mr. Hutton got to do with it?"

"H. H. is our publicity-shy bridegroom."

"The one who owns that Mediterranean island?"

"And, at the moment, fifty-one per cent of *Home Truth*," he said thoughtfully. "Enrico El Loco. I looked up *loco* the other day in a dictionary. It means crazy." He recovered his buoyancy. "Ah well, perhaps a little madness is what this drab world of ours so badly needs. But now a photograph or two. We go to press at midnight. Standing, perhaps, at the door of the Rolls while James hands you in. A smile—do you think you could manage it? I always say, er, 'Shee-shee.' It shows the teeth to advantage. Like this."

I hadn't noticed the press photographer who, like the chauffeur, took all this with a certain lack of enthusiasm.

"He'll touch you up afterwards," Bobby promised as I blinked at the flash-bulb. "Now one reading your copy of *Home Truth*. No, don't hold it upside down."

It had begun to drizzle and the knot of people who had gathered round hoping it was a street accident began to put up umbrellas.

"This time one with *me!*" Bobby cried, slipping his arm possessively around the fur coat. "There! Shall we try it again?"

The onlookers decided it was an elopement. "I 'eard 'im say," one woman confided to her neighbour, " 'e couldn't guarantee no wedding." "*He's* cute," a girl in a plastic mackintosh commented. Mrs. Petherbridge, our landlady, regarded me from the steps of the basement area as though she had long suspected that something of this sort would occur. Bobby said:

"Finally a few details for our readers who will want to know all about you. Age: shall we say twenty-six?"

"Yes, let's," I said.

"Jane, then, is a piquant brunette with shrewd laughing eyes," he improvised. "Nose, retrousse, rather impish, deliciously pert. Her hair is blue-black and her mouth is generous. There is the suggestion of a dimple on her finely moulded chin."

My public followed this fanciful description carefully, trying to discover a resemblance between it and me. The person who listened with the closest attention was Dagobert, whose deer-stalker had appeared over the heads of the crowd. He must have recognised me suddenly, for he made an instinctive move to hide the parcel of long-playing records—doubtless Ambrosian and Mozarabic plain-chant—which he carried under his arm.

"Jane dresses with a certain chic," Bobby continued. "She is very feminine and in her manner there is a hint of wilfulness, perhaps even of stubbornness. Jane is the sort of young woman who gets her own way. Now her vital statistics: I should say about 35–22–35. Is she pretty?"

He paused while we waited with bated breath.

"*Interesting* would be the better word," he said disappointedly. "Though there *is* an indefinable something about her which could be called beauty."

Dagobert looked pleased at the concession. Mrs. Petherbridge who had joined the group shook her head, not seeing it.

"A touch of mystery," Bobby enlarged. "What could it be?" He glanced at me with earnest inquiry. "Love life . . . ?"

"Lurking beside the lamp post," I said, "with gramophone records he hopes to smuggle into the house without my seeing."

"Love life!" Mrs. Petherbridge echoed. "She hasn't any love life—she's a respectable married woman."

"Ah yes, of course," Bobby said. "Dagobert."

"Do you know him?" I asked suspiciously.

"Bobby knows everybody," he smiled. "And *almost* everything about everybody. It is his job to know—as readers of Fireside Chit-Chat sometimes find out to their chagrin."

I stared at Dagobert. He seemed as bewildered by this ominous aside as I was.

"You didn't by any chance cook this up between you?" I said.

But Bobby was again addressing his audience. "Jane," he said, "feels only one small, lingering regret. How to leave her tall, handsome husband even for two brief weeks—that was Jane's problem."

"How did she solve it?" I said.

"She suddenly remembered that Dagobert too—like the rest of you—can follow her adventures and share her joy, simply by making sure to order well in advance the Special Holiday Competition number of *Home Truth.*"

"I missed the beginning of this," Dagobert apologised. "Where's she going?"

"Nowhere," I said impatiently.

"Your wife, sir, is a very lucky person—one of the seven luckiest in England."

"It's that wretched competition," I explained. "You filled in my name and now . . . now it's raining," I concluded lamely.

"In Tabarca," Bobby smiled, "it never rains."

"Tabarca?" said Dagobert. "Don't tell me she's won that trip—"

"With all expenses paid," Bobby nodded. "Fourteen thrilling, out-of-this-world days in Europe's most romantic island principality. Jane is going to Tabarca."

"I'm going indoors before I get wet."

"But this is wonderful," Dagobert exclaimed. "She's had her heart set on Tabarca for months. It's been a dream of hers."

"A nightmare," I admitted.

"When does she leave?"

"On Monday morning, bright and early."

"I tell you what I *will* do," I put in desperately. "I'll settle for the fur coat. Or, better still, Dagobert can go in my place."

Bobby's public-relations smile became a little fixed.

"That would never do," he said. "The, er, decision of the judges . . ."

Dagobert nodded gravely. "I shall miss her. But of course I'll have my Special Holiday Competition number. . . ."

"They can't make me go!" I protested.

"It's a nice legal point," Dagobert said. "There's your signature on the entry form and . . . I'll re-read the rules carefully."

"Besides, the list has already been approved," Bobby said. "We got the okay from Tabarca this morning."

"In that case," Dagobert shrugged, "there's nothing else for it."

"You did this to me!" I accused him hysterically. "Fur coats and champagne, chauffeurs in green livery! Orchids!"

I pushed the orchids at him and fled.

"The change," I heard him assure Bobby as I opened the front door, "will do her a world of good."

Chapter 3

Aunt Osyth was of the same opinion. She rang up next morning to congratulate me. She had seen my photograph in *Home Truth* and instantly observed that I needed a change.

"A most extraordinary journal," she digressed. "The nice theatrical couple next door showed it to me. It has a mission, they tell me: to expose corruption and castigate the morals of a degenerate society. I shall order it at once. How very kind of the editor to offer you this delightful holiday. I was in the West Indies once myself and I rather think we called at Tobago, or it may have been Tabasco. When bathing one must be especially cautious of sharks and barracuda. And what will Dagobert do during your absence?"

This was what Angela Simpson, who rang up immediately afterwards, also wanted to know. Angela and I were at school together and she has always worried about how I look after Dagobert. Although she has a perfectly good husband of her own named Bill, she feels she ought to help.

"I'll pop around," she promised, "and cook him something he likes, and listen to his records. Monday, I think it says."

She had recognised my name with something of a shock; *Home Truth* not being, she imagined, the kind of magazine one expects to find one's friends mentioned in. Had I read the article about the so-called nursing home for tired businessmen in Eastbourne? And that photograph of Lord Paddington—with *friend!* No wonder W. H. Smith and Sons refused to distribute the paper. Bill thought it a damn' scandal the thing was allowed through the post. Still, a fortnight's holiday—which I so obviously needed—was not to be sneered at, no matter who paid for it.

By the time I had received two anonymous telegrams abusing *Home Truth* and me for reading it I was dying to go out and buy a copy. During our competition epoch we had been much too busy filling in forms to read what was in the papers.

The telephone continued to ring and there were more telegrams from people I had never heard of, mostly asking for a small loan. The boy from the greengrocer's called with a list of Tabarca postage stamps he particularly needed. Mrs. Petherbridge came up from the basement to tell me her daughter had been on a Polytechnic tour to Tabarca last summer, though it may have been San Marino or Liechtenstein—anyway one of those places.

She hadn't thought much of it. "Lots of motor coaches, of course," she conceded. "Coca-Cola and neon lighting. And cultural, if you like that sort of thing. Churches. But not a decent cup of tea to be had for love nor money."

She showed me a postcard her daughter had sent. It was of Andorra.

"Tabarca," Dagobert informed me as we walked round to the relative quiet of the Load of Hay, "is a volcanic island situated about a hundred and fifty nautical miles north-northeast of the Balearic group, with which some geographers claim it has marked affinities. . . ."

"Where have you been all day?" I asked.

"With Mr. Jenkins in the North Circular Road . . . Its population, which speaks a degenerate form of Catalan, was at the last census in 1920 two thousand six hundred and one. Known to the Phoenicians, settled by the Ionian Greeks . . ."

"How did Bobby Marcovitch happen to know your name?"

"They vet the list of winners, I imagine, before announcing them. . . . Destroyed by an earthquake in 44 A.D., conquered by the Counts of Barcelona in the twelfth century, Tabarca has frequently been a bone of contention—"

"Angela Simpson wants to cook you steak and kidney pie."

"The Saracens sacked it in the thirteenth century, slaughtering every man, woman and child. In the early days of the eighteenth century a British fleet bombarded it by mistake and—"

"And listen to your records. Angela's been wild about plainsong ever since she saw Gary Cooper in *The Plainsman*, especially about the one that starts 'Out on the Prairie.'"

". . . and in the Treaty of Utrecht it was mislaid, due to a cartographer's error which placed it among the Lipari Islands. The House of Branza for centuries maintained the quasi-independence of the principality thanks to the mutual jealousy of Tabarca's more powerful neighbours. It was also too poverty-stricken to be worth quarrelling about. No one knows exactly how many millions Henry Howard Hutton has poured into the island treasury or whether his marriage to Princess Juana will give him a legal right to assume the title of . . . But I wonder if I am holding your attention, Jane."

"I'm not going," I said.

He pressed my arm sentimentally. "It's like you, darling, to say that. Sometimes I almost wish one hadn't spent so many hours on that competition, invested so heavily in stamps and postal orders. But no, I can't let you make this sacrifice for me."

"But I don't want to go."

"I know exactly how you feel," he sighed. "I'll miss you too. You'll write to me every day, won't you? How have you got on with your packing?"

"Monday is quite out of the question—nothing will be back

from the cleaners and I've a hundred things to do: your waistcoat to finish, or at least to start. And—I know—my passport's run out."

He produced it from an inner pocket and put it into my handbag. "I had it renewed today."

"Besides, what would you do?"

"Me? Oh, I'll jog along," he said bravely. "I may be fairly busy."

"Buying gramophone records to play to Angela?"

"What I really had in mind was Mr. Jenkins. He's worried about the new motor-scooter they were about to put into production. It's developed a very peculiar wobble."

"Speaking of peculiar wobbles," I said, "isn't that Angela with—good heavens! Could it be her own husband?—just in front of us?"

We found Bill and Angela occupying bar stools in the Load of Hay and entertaining the company with page thirteen of *Home Truth* which contained a picture captioned: HOW JANE TOOK THE GOOD NEWS.

"Did I," I said to Dagobert before we joined them, "did I make it quite clear that I am not going to Tabarca?"

"In that case," he gave in cheerfully, "there's nothing more to be said about it, is there? What are you having?"

Bill greeted me with good-humoured envy. "Some people," he grumbled, "have all the luck. You off on Monday to the Mediterranean, me off to Manchester."

It was a detail Angela hadn't mentioned on the telephone this morning.

"How boring of you, Bill. Must you?" she murmured, still pondering Bobby's description of me. "*I've* never noticed a dimple."

Angela had dimples herself and resented the intrusion into her domain. She was fair and plump, playful and at the same time maternal. Her technique of fussing over men while giving an impression of vague defencelessness seemed to enjoy a wide success.

She patted the bar stool beside her to indicate that she had been keeping it all for Dagobert and waved an unlighted cigarette with a gesture of helplessness as though she didn't know how to light it herself.

"I suppose by 'retrousse' he means turned-up," she said, pointing to the relevant passage in *Home Truth.* "Though I will say—and I've always said it—Jane does look 'interesting.' Even in that picture of the school hockey team taken—let's face it—some years ago."

Dagobert and I were looking at the photograph. It showed few signs of the 'touching up' that had been promised.

"It's good of Bobby," Dagobert said, and began rather thoughtfully to read the part about "Jane being the sort of young woman who gets her own way."

"What," he asked absently, "are vital statistics?"

"These, old boy," Bill explained, graphically outlining his idea of what female curves should be. "Angela's been measuring herself in front of the mirror all afternoon."

There were several comments I could have made on this, but I let it pass. I was feeling more charitable now that I had finally and definitely decided against going to Tabarca.

I left Angela at the bar trying to persuade Dagobert to eat something ("Jane is bound to have forgotten your dinner in her excitement") and took *Home Truth* over to a chair beside the fireplace. I tore myself reluctantly away from the page devoted to me to see what Bobby said about the others.

Of the seven winners the judges (who, I wondered, were the judges?) had chosen, four of us were women and three were men.

Mrs. Margaret Penrose was about fifty. She lived in Reading and eked out a small private income by helping in a local lending library. She had grey hair, rimless spectacles, no make-up and no jewellery except a plain old-fashioned wedding ring. It was hard to imagine Mrs. Penrose as a subscriber to *Home Truth*.

She had, Bobby reported, received the news with disbelief and at first flatly refused to let him enter her neat bed-sitting room. "I had," he wrote, "some difficulty in persuading Margaret it was not some fantastic practical joke. When at last she understood she turned away and I heard her murmur in a strange voice: 'How *amused* George would have been.' I asked her who George was, but she didn't hear the question. I saw that her gentle grey eyes were misty, and I didn't repeat it. But at the library they told me Margaret Penrose has recently come from a village in the West Country. Her husband, they think, died in circumstances she does not care to discuss. So let us leave her to the privacy of her grief. Who was George? What was his tragedy? Let us probe no further, trusting that the next fortnight will bring oblivion and comfort."

The photograph was of Bobby administering comfort. He had his arm around her in a big-hearted, protective way and on his face there was a nauseating expression of filial devotion. Mrs. Penrose, I thought, looked distinctly uncomfortable.

Ninette Nixon was, in Bobby's words, our starry-eyed teenager. For Ninette, Tabarca was an enchanted island. At the Granada in Wolverhampton where she worked as an usherette, she had once seen a film of Henry Howard Hutton's steam yacht in the harbour of Tabarca (during the visit of Princess Grace of Monte Carlo) and she had pictured herself on deck in a wide floppy hat sipping cocktails. When she learned she was one of the Lucky Seven she had fainted.

In the photograph Ninette was quite as pretty as Bobby said she was. She clutched her mink coat around her as though afraid it might be torn away before the allotted fourteen days. Bobby leaned elegantly over her hand which he was about to kiss. There was a suave smile, half mocking, half flattering, on his lips as though he had just murmured some Olde-Worlde gallantry destined for her ears alone.

The third picture was of a family group on the verandah of a semi-detached villa in Lathomstowe. Bobby again was the centre of interest as the others crowded round to hear the good news. He was in his genial, Father Christmas mood and showed a great deal of white teeth.

"To bring joy to homely folk like this," he wrote, "is a rare privilege. How excited the kiddies were to hear that Mum was one of the Lucky Seven! And Hubby too—how proud and pleased he looks!"

The prize-winner herself, Mrs. Florence (Flossie) Martin, appeared in an apron at the edge of the photograph, as though as an afterthought. You could not make out much of her face which was averted, but she looked plump and agreeable.

Flossie, Bobby wrote, "was thrilled at the thought of seeing the world though she dreaded to think what Jim and the two kids would get up to while she was away."

Instead of mink coats the men who won the competition received Leica cameras. Bobby was pictured with Derek Upjohn demonstrating the automatic view-finder.

Derek Upjohn was a pleasant-looking young man with a ginger guardsman's moustache. He was dressed in dirty corduroy trousers and a vast sweater ravelled at the elbows. He described himself as a "sort of vet" and was surrounded by mangy dogs of uncertain breed who made a friendly background, though perhaps not a very good professional advertisement.

Derek, according to Bobby, had forgotten he'd entered the competition. Winning it surprised him only mildly. He enjoyed an occasional flutter and had always been a lucky type.

If with Derek Upjohn Bobby achieved an all-boys-together look of bonhomie he managed to appear almost deferential in the photograph taken with Hugo Warrington.

Colonel Warrington—"only a courtesy title, dear boy,

though I did manage to help Monty a bit in the desert in ways which certain laddies in M.I.5 still don't want talked about; just call me Warrington"—Colonel Warrington, as Bobby nevertheless called him, was a tall, thin man who almost absurdly looked the part which Bobby (or perhaps Colonel Warrington himself?) sought to create. In his middle sixties, he wore shabby but well-brushed tweeds, had jutting eyebrows and a military bearing.

Hugo Warrington lived quietly near Dorking and looked forward to a spot of sun and a dip in the Med. He was delighted to have won a trip to Tabarca—"never been there actually, though I used to know old Prince Jaime slightly, raced together at Cowes once, the Princess Juana only a nipper with pigtails and freckles at the time, probably won't remember me."

"I won't pretend I'm not grateful," Bobby quoted him. "Rum way to travel perhaps, but nowadays . . . what with currency restrictions, don't you know . . . ?"

Bobby assured the Colonel that he did indeed know and said: "An honour, sir, to have you with us."

The photograph showed him shaking hands with a firm, respectful grip.

There was no photograph of the seventh competition winner. He lived in Glasgow and Bobby had only been able to interview him over the telephone. His name was Juan Roig.

"And," Bobby wrote in a flutter of excitement, "you'll never guess how capricious Dame Fortune can be! My mathematical friends tell me the chances against *this particular* winner ran into I don't know how many millions. For Juan Roig was born, believe it or not, *in Tabarca!*"

Dagobert, who read this over my shoulder, was even more excited when he heard that Juan Roig was a "hand-fed platen minder."

Juan Roig had left the island of his birth many years ago and was now a British subject with a Scottish wife and three bairns. She, Bobby reported, had done most of the talking; for the news of his amazing good fortune left Juan Roig speechless and bewildered.

Juan Roig was still bewildered and almost speechless the following Monday morning as, early if not bright, he sat huddled on the back seat of the silver Rolls-Royce, dourly clutching his Leica camera. He was, as a matter of fact, huddled next to me.

I made a halfhearted attempt to engage him in conversation but it was heavy going. Was he not, I asked, pleased at the prospect of seeing Tabarca? He said he had already seen it and preferred Glasgow.

We lapsed into silence as the car crept through the early morning mist along the Old Kent Road towards Lewisham. At Maidstone I tried again: Hadn't he been surprised at winning the competition? He said, yes—he had thought it was a competition for an electric dishwasher. Then why, I wondered, as we entered Ashford, had he come? He said his wife reckoned the change would do him good.

This plunged us both into a brood until we reached Dover. Juan Roig and I evidently had something in common: a streak of feeble-mindedness which allowed us to be talked by our spouses into leaving home.

The car ferry was half empty in late October and beyond the spray over the harbour breakwater you could see grey-green waves heaving morosely. I ignored the professional heartiness of a steward who tried to lure me into the dining room and retired to a cabin.

It was one of those channel crossings which get into the evening papers and I hoped Dagobert would feel guilty when he read about it. When over an hour late the ship at last reached Boulogne most of us were more dead than alive.

We were not, however, as dead as Juan Roig who didn't reach Boulogne at all.

Chapter 4

WE ARRIVED IN the dense fog which had persisted ever since Dover. In the prophetic words of the hymn with which Flossie Martin sought to enliven us we were to "know each other better when the mists had rolled away."

Derek Upjohn's ginger moustache twitched; it had wilted during the voyage. "Could somebody, do you suppose, stop her singing that?" he muttered.

Ninette Nixon smiled courageously, trying to look happier than she was. "Are we there?" she asked and held a crumpled handkerchief tight to her mouth.

Hugo Warrington stood very erect outside the purser's office on B deck where the loudspeakers had directed us to gather. His face was the colour of an ancient document preserved in the War Museum. "What's the delay, I wonder," he said, gripping the brass rail as though the ship were still rolling.

Mrs. Margaret Penrose had suffered least from the crossing and reported that excellent coffee had been served in the lounge.

"Where," she asked with unexpected tartness, "is our shepherd?"

I found him up in the bar having a swift whisky and soda. Like everybody else Bobby Marcovitch looked unhappy. He had had, I learned later, a bad session with the ship's captain and the port officials.

"Have a Scotch on the expense account," he said.

"Your little flock," I told him, "is getting restive."

"Oh, they've heard about it, have they?"

"No. About what?"

He ran distracted fingers through fair curly hair still moist with sea spray. "It makes swell publicity, doesn't it?"

"What does?"

"When the Lucky Seven reach France there are only six of them."

For the first time I remembered that Juan Roig had not been among the group on B deck. I pushed away the whisky the steward had put on the bar and said: "What happened?"

"How would I know?" His voice rose querulously. "He's disappeared."

"Disappeared? Have you looked for him?"

"What the hell do you think everybody's been doing all this time? They've turned the ship upside-down. There's no sign of him."

"Could he have . . . fallen overboard?"

"Either that or jumped overboard."

"But why?"

"Don't keep asking questions. People have been asking me questions for the last hour. How do I know why he jumped overboard? Maybe he just felt like it. God knows he was a gloomy so-and-so. Maybe he did it just to annoy me. What was he doing up on deck anyway?"

"Who saw him on deck?"

"Only a lunatic would go out on deck during a crossing like that. You had to hold on to things to keep upright."

He regarded his wet suede shoes glumly and drank my whisky

neat. "The point is," he added, "what does Bobby do next? The stiff upper lip and reassuring smile—in other words, carry on? Or call the whole damn' thing off?"

"Call it off," I said.

But he was practising the stiff upper lip and reassuring smile in the glass behind the bar. He turned reluctantly from this congenial occupation to give me his blue-eyed, bewildered-boy look.

"I wish I knew what to do, Jane. Unfortunately," he sighed, "we have to think of others in moments like this, haven't we? Of Ninette, for instance, who has set her simple heart on the trip. Of poor Margaret Penrose to whom the next two weeks could mean so much. Even of the Colonel, hiding his bitter disappointment beneath a bluff soldierly scowl. Of Derek Upjohn, Flossie . . . No, Jane, I can't do it. Anyway I want to have a look at Tabarca myself."

"Haven't you ever been there?"

"Between ourselves I've never been east of Southend. Christ!" he broke off irritably. "He had his Leica with him too. Another fifty quid down the drain."

"Why should you care?" I soothed. "That's H. H.'s bad luck —or even Juan Roig's."

He overlooked the sarcasm and ordered two more whiskies. "Fifty-one per cent of it is H. H.'s bad luck," he said practically. "The other forty-nine is Bobby Marcovitch's."

"Oh, do you own that much of *Home Truth*?"

"How do you think I eat?" he said simply. "Juan Roig's all right. He was insured. We took out a two weeks' policy on each of you. When Saunders of our legal department gets in touch with Glasgow he'll be able to add that a fat cheque, in fact five thousand pounds, will be forthcoming as soon as Roig's death is satisfactorily established. If I may say so, damn' smart of me —and, er, a great consolation for that poor widow and her three little ones."

It seemed to console Bobby too. He chose one of the four fountain pens from his breast pocket and scratched calculations in his notebook. Absently, under Entertainment Expenses (Supplementary) he jotted down "six whiskies."

"Yes," he said a little wistfully, "ten thousand pounds."

"I thought you said five."

"Five for the deceased," he explained, "and five for ourselves —to cover us against possible complications. Let's hope there won't be any."

The loudspeaker repeated its appeal to the *Home Truth* group to gather on B deck. Bobby rose. The whisky had fortified him.

"This may not be the moment to look on the bright side," he said, "but I've just worked out that five thousand pounds will nicely meet all our expenses."

"I've worked out something else," I said, beating him this time to my whisky. "If anyone else gets, er, mislaid, you could show a clear profit."

He looked shocked and said: "Do be careful with your cigarette! That mink coat is hired. Thank God none of us knew Roig. In fact I was able to convince the authorities that not one of us had ever seen him before this morning. On the whole they were pretty co-operative, even the Frogs. Anyway they've consented to let the party proceed. Shall we keep all this to ourselves, Jane?"

He gave me a warm trusting smile as he bustled down below to apologise for the delay. He found the party still in a depressed mood, but more aggressive.

"I make it an hour and a half behind schedule already," Colonel Warrington said, glancing at his watch.

"We'd about come to the conclusion you'd jumped overboard," said Derek Upjohn, looking as though it were a pity he hadn't.

"Roig seems to be missing too," Colonel Warrington pointed out.

Margaret Penrose said: "He went up on deck when we were about halfway across the channel. But of course!" she remembered. "You were with him, weren't you, Mr. Marcovitch?"

"Please call me Bobby," he appealed to her. "Otherwise I feel so out of things. Yes, Juan Roig. I, I'm afraid I have disappointing news about Juan. That's why I've been so long. He's changed his mind—and suddenly decided not to come with us."

"Whatever for?" Flossie demanded.

"Can you," Ninette began, "I mean—is it possible—to change your mind? I mean, if—suddenly you wanted to go home . . . ?"

"Where is he?" Derek asked.

"So many questions all at once!" Bobby protested. "I'm afraid we'll be even further behind schedule if we stay here chattering. Now, down to the car deck everyone. Jane, you lead the way!"

Margaret Penrose hesitated. "I'd rather like to say goodbye to Mr. Roig."

"I'd like to ask him what made him change his mind," Derek said.

"It does seem silly, doesn't it?" said Flossie. "But cheer up—there'll be less of a squash in the Rolls-Royce."

Bobby was arranging us in the car, re-seating everyone so "we should remain one big family party instead of breaking up into cliques." He put Flossie Martin and Margaret Penrose in the back seat where they could "share" the Colonel between them.

Derek and Ninette, "our young couple," were given the folding seats. At hearing themselves so described they glanced at each other and fell silent. A moment later I saw Derek surreptitiously combing up his moustache.

The chauffeur, having served his purpose as photographer's model, had been left behind in London. Bobby drove and it was my turn to sit in front beside him.

Passports and car papers had already been dealt with on the boat. Customs formalities were cursory and luggage was not even examined.

According to our souvenir programmes—written in Bobby's best manner—we should have been served a substantial four-course luncheon on board ship. Tea would be at the Coq d'Or in Rouen—"our first sample of the French patissier's art—with an opportunity of exploring the ancient capital of Normandy with its many historic associations and quaint sights: the Church of St. Ouen, St. Maclou, etc., etc." Then dinner at Chartres—"where rooms are engaged at the famous Grand Cerf and mine host, the chef, awaits us with his mouth-watering specialties: Poulet Grand-Roy, Souffle Creole, etc., etc., champagne, coffee, liqueurs . . ."

These details still made revolting reading as we bumped through the side streets of Boulogne, following signs which with Gallic insouciance announced: *Toutes Directions*. It was after two o'clock when we found ourselves on Route Nationale Number 1.

The fog had begun to lift. An autumnal sun sent shafts of pale gold through the leafless rows of poplars and hitch-hikers that lined the road. Already we could make out faded blue *Pernod* advertisements and soft sodden fields of beetroot. The thought of Poulet Grand-Roy became more supportable.

"At any rate," Bobby called back gaily as he dodged a man with a knapsack who was trying to thumb a lift, "we're still seven. I'm the seventh myself!"

This for some reason dampened attempts to revive general conversation. I wondered if the others too were still inwardly pondering Juan Roig's absence. The subject had been allowed apparently by common consent to drop.

We bowled along the almost deserted grey ribbon of road as though we could leave the thought of Juan Roig physically behind us. Before we reached Abbeville where the road forked right for Rouen everyone was chattering again.

Ninette described the personal appearance at the Wolverhampton Granada of the film actress whose autographed photo she treasured and whose "hair-do, tempest-tossed" she copied. Hugo Warrington interrupted Flossie's description of her own appearance in a bathing suit—"a bright pink baby hippo, beginning to peel,"—to reminisce about Alexander Korda—"a dear chap, great friend of mine, irreparable loss to the film industry." Derek Upjohn was offering round the box of duty-free Senior Services he had bought on the boat and looking rather handsome and superior in his dark glasses and sports jacket with leather-patched elbows. He and Ninette had recovered from their initial shyness.

Only Margaret Penrose remained withdrawn. I caught sight of her reflected in the driving mirror. Her face was composed and told me nothing of her thoughts. Perhaps they were of George who would have been "amused" at the thought of her winning a *Home Truth* competition—George, whose tragedy Bobby had generously decided not to probe.

Mrs. Penrose did not observe that I was studying her in the driving mirror, for she was staring fixedly at the back of Bobby's curly head.

Bobby himself was in bubbling spirits. I heard him chuckle as he stepped harder on the throttle.

"I was thinking over that little joke of yours, Jane," he said.

I could not remember having made even the smallest joke and I asked him what he was talking about.

"About Juan Roig and the insurance money," he said. "You know—that if anything should, er, happen to anyone else—how it would show a clear profit."

I nudged the steering wheel, reminding him of the eccentric

French habit of driving on the right-hand side of the road. He remembered it immediately and swerved skilfully past a wavering farm cart, screaming out his favourite and almost sole French phrase: "*Sale cochon!*"

The farmer recognised it and shouted back: "Bloody, goddam, blimey limey."

I glanced round in admiration and saw we were not the only G.B. plate on Route Nationale Number 1. A motor-scooter also weaved past the cart. I wondered if it was the new type of motor-scooter Mr. Jenkins of the North Circular Road was having trouble with; there was no doubt about the peculiar wobble.

"Speaking of insurance," I said to Bobby, "you remember those complications your share of the money is supposed to cover you against? Don't look now, but one of them is just behind us."

Chapter 5

THERE WERE, IN FACT, two: there had been a pillion rider on the motor-scooter. The thought flashed through my mind that it was Angela, but a second glance reassured me. Dagobert had picked up one of the hitch-hikers we had ignored in Boulogne.

We didn't see much of the ancient capital of Normandy, though Bobby pointed out the distant tower of what he took to be St. Maclou. Tea, he decided, would only make us late for dinner and, ignoring Flossie's loud protests, he drove ruthlessly past the half-timbered façade of the Coq d'Or.

That was the last I saw of the motor-scooter. Dagobert, sticking to our programme, had evidently gone in to sample the French patissier's art.

"Anyway," Bobby said, "we've shaken off that motor-scooter. It's been on our tail ever since Boulogne."

It would, I imagined, reappear at Chartres where the chef of the Grand Cerf awaited us with his mouth-watering specialties.

The Poulet Grand-Roy was, in an obscure way, one of the reasons I was on my way to Tabarca. Last night, inspired by Bobby's prose, Dagobert had looked up the recipe for Poulet Grand-Roy in *Larousse Gastronomique*. This led by gradual stages to Angela Simpson's steak and kidney pie. A note of warmth had begun to creep into the discussion when the telephone rang. It was Angela herself to say she would bring her collection of rock 'n' roll tomorrow to play on Dagobert's gramophone. It would, she felt, console them both for being deserted.

After she rang off the conversation grew more animated, branching out into subjects like matrimony and separate holidays. By midnight I was against the former and all for the latter. By two o'clock Dagobert, who had complained of a busy day in front of him, was fast asleep, while I was rapidly packing. By dawn when the Rolls-Royce arrived I was on the doorstep waiting.

I liked to think of Dagobert, waking up this morning to find me gone, seized with terrible remorse. I pictured him leaping impulsively onto the motor-scooter to chase desperately after me.

There were, however, a couple of things wrong with this theory; the motor-scooter must have been provided with foreign touring documents well in advance, and Bobby had plainly expected me to be waiting on the doorstep in spite of repeated assurances that I wasn't coming.

In brief, all had gone according to plan—Dagobert's plan.

I ought to have felt annoyed. All I felt was relief, not unmixed with the pleasant reflection that at this hour Angela would be ringing our doorbell with an armful of rock 'n' roll records. The familiar sight of the battered deer-stalker had so cheered me that I could think of nothing else—not even of Juan Roig.

Dagobert missed the Poulet Grand-Roy. But he did appear in time to see the head waiter set the Souffle Creole alight. I caught a glimpse of him through the dining-room window. He was peering through a gap in the curtains and wistfully munching a dry roll.

Ninette noticed him too. "Poor man," she said. "He looks so hungry."

Dagobert vanished, but the sight of him so affected her she refused the souffle. She became aware of Derek Upjohn's cool brown eyes upon her and coloured, ashamed of what she had said.

"Silly?" she asked uncertainly. "Oh, all right. *Oon pitty poo,*" she told the waiter. "Only it doesn't seem fair to have *all* the luck."

Derek smiled vague assent. He hadn't seen the starving apparition at the window and had no idea what she was talking about. Derek had been looking at Ninette purely for the pleasure of looking at her.

It was the pleasure of watching a colt or a kitten or a lamb who is graceful no matter what it does. Gestures which would irritate in a creature less lovely—the refinement of her table manners, the gentility with which she handled what she called her serviette—even these were a delight to the eye.

It probably didn't cross Derek's mind that the pink net dinner dress she'd put on would be more in keeping at a Palais de Danse. You didn't notice it any more than you notice a cheap vase which holds a perfect rose. Ninette was quite simply irresistible, and if Derek was struck dumb with admiration you couldn't blame him.

Everyone else was talking about food which seems to be the chief thing the island race, once recovered from the channel crossing, talks about.

Hugo Warrington, who knew André Simon, spoke of early days at the Wine and Food Society and entertained us with reminiscences of pre-phyloxera vintages. "You won't find their like today," he added sadly, glancing at Flossie Martin. "It's all body, no bouquet."

Bobby, stung, began to study the wine list. He consulted the little card he carried in his wallet with vintage years handily marked with stars. He nearly ordered a bottle of '21 Chateau Yquem—five stars—until he looked again at the price.

Flossie Martin thought that Continentals mucked up their dishes with a lot of sauces and things in order to disguise inferior ingredients.

"Hey!" she called to the waiter, in the slightly transatlantic accent she had developed since the champagne. "Where do you think you're going with that?"

He brought back the remains of the souffle which, like the poulet before it, she finished with unabated greed. The gastronomic discussion continued. There were the usual patriotic reservations about a "properly matured Stilton" and Cox's orange pippins "when you can hear the pips rattle"; but on the whole it was agreed that the French, though deficient in sanitation and morals, knocked spots off us in the kitchen.

Only Margaret Penrose dissented. "I'm from Cornwall," she said, "where we consider our cooking as good as anyone's. On the other hand our sanitation is certainly no better than what I've seen in France, and as for our morals—I think Mr. Marcovitch will agree that they are often much, much worse."

She looked at Bobby for confirmation. She polished her rimless spectacles in order to see him better. Her grey eyes may have been misty—as Bobby had once reported them—but they were not gentle. Bobby said we'd have coffee in the lounge.

"*And* liqueurs," Flossie, who knew her souvenir programme, reminded him.

As we left the table Bobby asked me: "What's eating Margaret?"

"I think you are," I said.

He sighed, hurt at being apparently unloved by Mrs. Penrose, whom he had cast in the role of the group's "mother-figure." He retreated with a martyred air into the writing room to swot up what his guidebook had to say about Chartres.

Ninette, our "starry-eyed teen-ager" was playing her role of pretty ingenue more satisfactorily. She had captured Derek, our juvenile lead, and borne him off to a sofa in the corner where, a willing prisoner, he listened to her prattle. She loved dogs, she said, but not cats. Horses, too, when they weren't too big. Derek listened in a dreamy state of hypnosis. His good-looking features, rather melancholy in spite of the ginger moustache and eyebrows, would light up occasionally in a quick smile, to indicate he followed what she said.

I saw Colonel Warrington pass sugar to Margaret Penrose and light Flossie's cigarette. They glanced at me with the predatory expression of people who see a possible fourth for bridge.

I decided to skip coffee and walk up to the cathedral. What I actually decided was to walk out and find Dagobert.

Not finding Dagobert, I walked up towards the cathedral anyway. The town was already half-asleep, though there were still a few people in the cafes reading newspapers and playing dominoes. I glanced through the steamy windows of an occasional bistro advertising *plats du jour* at economical prices, but Dagobert wasn't in any of them. He too might have gone to see the cathedral. It was the first thing we always did in Chartres —or what we always meant to do.

I came upon the west front from a narrow cobbled street at the same moment that the moon broke from a ragged bank of clouds. The twin towers, one earth-bound, solid and Romanesque, the other soaring, fanciful and Gothic, revived memories of the unresolved debate that has been going on sporadically for years between us as to which is superior. I think Dagobert defends the fanciful North tower while I prefer the one that is down to earth—or it may be the other way round.

I moved round to the south side to see the Last Judgment. The elongated figures flanking the portal seemed to be on the verge of movement in the moonlight. Then, as I glanced up at the tympanum, where the souls of the blessed and the damned are being weighed and divided, a figure not far from me did move. The moon plunged instantly into the clouds and the high stone walls became a dark formless cliff, whipped by fresh gusts of wind.

Footsteps sounded on the porch. The building would normally be locked at this hour, but a door creaked—evidently a door which had been overlooked, or perhaps the person who had just gone in was part of the cathedral staff.

Obsessed with the notion that it was Dagobert, also on a sentimental visit, I tried the door myself. It opened and I stood in the south transept, feeling small and insignificant beneath rising stone piers which vanished miles, it seemed, above me in a dim, half-imagined foliage of ribbed vaulting. The rose window in the opposite transept glowed with soft opalescent fire as though outside the moon were dodging among the clouds again. There was a solitary red flicker from one of the chapels in the apse—a sanctuary lamp. On the floor before it I saw the kneeling figure of the person who had come in before me.

It was a woman and she wore no hat. I could make out the small white square of handkerchief which covered her head. In any case it was not Dagobert and I began on tiptoe to retire.

My shoes squeaked and she glanced quickly around. There

was something furtive in the action, as though she were afraid of being caught there. She rose to her feet, confused, apparently abashed, like an intruder who had no right to be kneeling before the altar.

She made a hesitant sign of the cross and clattered precipitously on high heels across the pavement towards the door. I drew back into the shadows. The precaution was unnecessary; she hadn't seen me and she continued her flight. She wavered for a second at the holy water font, but did not dip in her plump fingers with the blood-red varnished nails. The door creaked again and banged behind her.

I jumped at the sound. Flossie Martin's nervousness had been catching.

She still did not see me as I reached the porch. She was staring up intently at the figures in the Last Judgment. In the moonlight her face was a white blur. She shivered in her mink coat and crossed the road. I in a similar mink coat was shivering too; for the wind whistling around the corner was sharper than ever.

I heard Flossie ask a man who had stopped to light a cigarette the shortest way back to the hotel. I was about to join her, but she had already hurried on. I began to follow, but paused, wondering what it was that had puzzled me during her brief exchange of words with the man at the street corner.

Then it struck me: Flossie Martin had addressed him in what sounded like fluent French.

I said to him in my own far from fluent French: "Madame speaks French well, does she not?"

"*Que voulez-vous?*" he shrugged, less impressed than I. "Since —in a way—she is French."

"*Is.*"

"*Eh bien*, at least French Canadian."

Chapter 6

I DON'T KNOW why this should have startled me. At dinner I had noticed Flossie's transatlantic accent. There was no reason why she shouldn't be Canadian, or even French Canadian.

And if she had walked up to the cathedral, so had I. Both of us had been awe-stricken by its vast unlit interior. Doubtless I had exaggerated the furtiveness of her movements and the sense I had had of someone under nervous—I almost said spiritual—stress.

Yet it was out of character for Flossie Martin to be there at all. She should have been watching the television in the lounge of the Grand Cerf or playing cards with Colonel Warrington. She should have been sipping *creme de menthe* and being the life and soul of the party instead of kneeling alone on the cold stones of Chartres Cathedral and, at the creak of a footstep, starting like a guilty thing surprised.

And it was out of character that she should speak fluent French: no one had heard a word of French out of her all day. Flossie Martin was a jolly, uncomplicated North London suburban housewife who at the age of thirty was putting on weight and had two children, and a "hubby" in the building trade.

That was the picture readers of *Home Truth* had of her and there had been no reason until now to question it. It was Bobby's picture of her and Bobby knew everything about everybody.

Or, to quote him fairly, "almost" everything about everybody.

There would seem to be flaws in Bobby's omniscience. He had not, for instance, even spotted Dagobert—which reminded me that I hadn't either; and again I began my patrol of the bistros. I looked into five without seeing him. In the sixth I found Derek Upjohn.

It was a modest place in one of the narrow streets which lead down to the square which the Grand Cerf faces. It advertised *casse-croûte à toutes heures* and announced that here one consulted *le Bottin.* Inside two workmen in blue jeans were playing at the pin table. Behind them the proprietor was getting down to a soup tureen and a copy of *France-Soir.* Derek was the only other customer.

He was building a kind of pagoda with match boxes, dominoes and lumps of sugar. He was so intent on the task he didn't see me in the door. I watched him balance a domino on the top tier of the crazy structure and admired the steadiness of his hand, the controlled movements of his strong, bony fingers. They were like precision instruments.

A gust of air from the open door toppled the pagoda and at the same instant Derek saw me. He jumped to his feet.

"What the devil are *you* doing here?" he scowled. "You ought to be in bed."

He sounded furious but at the same time pleased. Puzzled by this ambivalence I said I was taking a walk.

The scowl faded. His face which had been pale and tense slowly flushed. I realised he had mistaken me for someone else. He covered his confusion by fumbling in his grey flannel suit for the dark glasses he affected. The cafe was wretchedly lighted but he seemed more at ease when he had put them on.

"A walk. Yes, of course," he stammered. "Fresh air—just what the d-doctor ordered after a dinner like that. I was doing, er, much the same thing."

He indicated the marble-topped table with a vague gesture.

Aware that the smoke-laden atmosphere could hardly be described as fresh air, he smiled.

"And having a nightcap. Why don't you join me, Mrs. . . . er, Brown?"

"But aren't you expecting someone else?"

There was a bottle of Calvados on the table but only one glass. He shook his head and said:

"No, she won't come now. She's silly, but not—let's hope—*that* silly. I mean, to chase through the night after . . ." He flushed again. "Well, to chase through the night."

He was holding a chair for me with careful courtesy. The Calvados bottle was half empty and I guessed he had half-emptied it himself. He had the polite manner and cautious diction of the very drunk. I recalled the steadiness of the hand which had constructed that elaborate pagoda with increased respect.

I sat down so that he could sit down too.

"Yes, she's silly," he said again like a gramophone record when the needle is stuck in the groove, "very silly, but . . ." He refilled his glass with Calvados, "But . . ."

"Irresistible?" I suggested.

"Irresistible," he agreed sadly. "I forgot to ask you what you're having. *Garçon!*"

I said I'd try the Calvados and the proprietor lumbered slowly over to the zinc counter. Derek eyed the drink he had poured out and squirmed, trying not to touch it until my glass arrived.

"Irresistible," he repeated. "The rub is one has got to resist."

"Are we talking about alcohol?" I said. "Or about Ninette?"

He grinned faintly and shrugged. The proprietor gave me my glass and Derek removed his wallet. I hoped his intention was to settle the bill and go home. Conversation clearly had no future.

He forgot why he had taken out his wallet and dropped it on the table. It fell open. In the place which was meant to hold an identity card or season ticket there was a snapshot. I didn't know whether it was private or whether I was supposed to look at it. He sipped his Calvados in silence. Finally he scowled again and asked:

"Who is Mel Ferrer?"

"A film actor," I said, glad to have found something to talk about.

"That's what I thought. She said I reminded her of him." He sounded resigned. "It all adds up."

"It may add up to you," I began.

"She said I looked like Gregory Peck," he said gloomily.

"I thought you said Mel Ferrer."

"*She,*" he said.

"Oh."

I tried the Calvados. In small quantities it burnt the throat not unpleasantly. In half bottles it doubtless led one to confuse Mel Ferrer with Gregory Peck.

"See what I mean?" he said.

"No," I confessed. "But let it pass."

He gave the wallet a push so that I could no longer ignore the snapshot. I was looking at what seemed to be a photograph of Ninette. It didn't occur to me that she could simply have given it to him today and I exclaimed:

"Don't tell me you knew Ninette before this trip!"

"That would be quite a coincidence, wouldn't it? Mathematically, let's see, about forty-five million times forty-five which is . . ."

I let him work it out over another glass of Calvados while I examined the photograph. It was in the happy-holiday-snap tradition and taken on the crowded beach at Ostend. The girl was wearing a bikini and a comic hat which said: "Souvenir d'Ostende" and waving a streamer which said: "*Embrasse-moi vite!*" She was fair and about nineteen and as ravishingly pretty as Ninette.

But it wasn't Ninette. The resemblance was striking, but

superficial—a resemblance more of type than actual features. There was something artless and naïve about them both, something silly and impulsive and generous, something vulgar and defenceless and—to Derek evidently—irresistible.

"She's lovely," I said. "Who is she?"

"Two thousand and twenty-five billion," he announced, refilling his glass as a reward for having solved the problem. "Quite a co-inch, co-ince . . . Quite. Things like that happen to me all the time." He made an effort. "No, of course I didn't know Ninette before today. She reminds me of someone."

He fumbled in the inner pocket of his jacket where he kept his wallet. Not finding it there he began to rummage through his other pockets in sudden panic. I pushed the wallet across the table to him, but he still didn't see it. He looked foolish, but relieved, when I drew his attention to it.

"Yes, I see why she reminds you of Ninette," I said. "What is her name?"

"Yvonne," he murmured. Then exploded: "Damn it all—they both even have ridiculous, Peg's Paper names!"

He tore the snapshot from the wallet and stared at it angrily. He was holding it upside down.

"She looks prettier the right way up," I said. "Try without the dark glasses."

He removed them mechanically. His eyes blinked and filled with water from the curl of smoke which rose from the cigarette end stuck to his lower lip. He turned the snapshot around, though I doubt if he could see it. He was quite literally blind drunk.

I suggested we walk back to the hotel, but he didn't hear me. The two workmen had abandoned the pin table and left with a "*bon soir, patron,*" and a nod to us. The proprietor had finished the soup tureen and was polishing the zinc counter. I told Derek they wanted to close the place. There was no response.

"Are you," I said, hoping to make contact, "very fond of Yvonne?"

This elicited a grunt. Then he flicked his cigarette lighter and held the flame under the photograph in his fingers. I was again impressed by the steadiness of his hand. He watched the snapshot burn until it was all ash. It must have burned his fingers badly, though he showed no sign of feeling it.

I took the opportunity to slip the Calvados bottle onto a neighbouring table and tried to catch the proprietor's eye. When I looked at Derek again his forehead was resting on the marble table-top. I thought for a moment he had fallen asleep. Then I realised he was quietly sobbing.

I wasn't sure what to do next. The proprietor had returned unhelpfully to *France-Soir*. I found my handbag and called him to the table. I was about to settle the bill when Derek abruptly came to.

"*Madame—pas payer*," he said sternly. "*Certainement* no." He rose with dignity and made a safe crossing to the bar. He tossed a thousand-franc note negligently across the counter and said: "*Voila*, and *guardez* the change."

The proprietor was not behind the bar, but he appreciated the gesture. He thanked monsieur gratefully—grateful less for the tip than because we were going—helped him into his coat and showed us to the door. I heard him lock it behind us and close the shutters.

"Where shall we go now?" Derek asked.

"Home, do you think?"

I took his arm, but he swayed only slightly. The cold night air seemed to brace him. With the unerring instinct of the intoxicated he started out in exactly the opposite direction.

"We might," he said, "have a small drink, just to celebrate."

"There's a bar in the hotel," I said. "And Bobby wants to get away early in the morning."

"Isn't that a pub on the corner? Good old Bobby—he's promised that Ninette and I shall sit in the back seat together, so cosy! D'you know," he added gravely, as though he'd given the matter much serious thought, "I think I *will* have that final nightcap."

Fortunately the pub on the corner turned out to be a fire station and by devious side streets I lured him on in the direction of the square.

"We'll find somewhere on the way," he said confidently. "I keep worrying about that figure of two thousand and twenty-five billion. . . ."

"It's enough to worry anyone," I soothed him.

"Of course we're assuming that everyone in England entered the competition, which is ridic—shilly. Chances that one winner previously knows other winners are only number competitors squared, say ninety thousand times ninety thousand. . . . How much is that?"

I didn't follow this, but it seemed to be safe ground.

"I don't know," I said, hoping the subject would last until we reached the hotel. "You work it out."

"Eighty-one million," he said.

"Amazing."

"But there are six other winners, so you divide by six. Thirteen and a half million chances against, say, you meeting, say, me."

"It doesn't seem fair, does it," I murmured, eyeing the hotel across the square with relief. "You seem to have given the subject of gambling odds much thought. I remember in your interview with Bobby you mentioned being keen on a flutter."

"Me gamble? Never!" He tripped over the kerb but righted himself. "Well, hardly ever. Don't I know that place across the way?"

"It's the Grand Cerf!" I exclaimed gaily. "Where we live."

"Not where I live, Mrs. Brown," he shook his head gently.

"I live in a li'l pagoda scattered amongst sawdust and shigarette ends on the floor of a li'l bistro in— Where are we? Ostend? No, don't tell me—Chartres!"

"Chartres," I agreed. "Will you take my arm please?"

"A pleasure. Did we," he added in a practical voice, "finish that bottle of Calvados?"

"More or less;" I said, steering him across the road. "Do you remember your room number?"

"Seven," he said. "As Marcovitch wrote, I always was a lucky type. Mrs. Brown," he added, reproving me with the sudden astuteness of the very intoxicated, "you have tricked me into coming meekly home with an unquenched thirst. Is that kind?"

The hotel was still open but most of the lights in the public rooms were out. The bar was firmly closed. I asked the sleepy night porter for the key to room number seven and gave it to Derek. He thanked me courteously and put it down on the counter again. My own key was missing; I must have left it upstairs after dinner when I fetched my coat.

"Mrs. Brown and I," Derek said to the porter, "were about to adjourn for a quiet glass and a technical discussion of gambling odds. Perhaps you would care to join us? Or alternatively recommend a *boîte*."

The porter understood little of this and Derek sought to translate it into French. The porter's bewilderment increased. I said good-night and started up the stairs. Derek grew more insistently confidential.

"Gambling," he told the porter, "is a strange business. Now you will be surprised to hear I have gambled only twice in my life—*deux fois*. Once, *mon vieux*, I lost—*perdu*. The second time . . . I won—*gagné*. But—now this is what I want you to understand—there will be no third time. *Pas troisieme fois. Compris?*" His voice rose aggressively. "Get that quite straight, *mon vieux*. Is that ab-so-lute-ly clear?"

I heard the porter assuring him suavely all was perfectly clear and that room number seven found itself on the first floor. By the time I had reached the second floor I could no longer hear Derek's voice. The porter seemed to have the situation under control.

My room was at the end of the corridor where a window overlooked the deserted square. I glanced out and realised why Derek's voice was no longer raised. He was tacking across the road towards the fire station. I hesitated, debating in my conscience whether or not to drag out after him again.

The debate was cut short when I noticed that the door of my room was ajar. There was no light inside, and from the bed came the sound of gentle snoring.

Chapter 7

THE SOUND WAS not unfamiliar, but just in case I was wrong I switched on the lights. Dagobert opened an eye.

"Thirty-five," he murmured with dreamy approval, "twenty-two, ummm . . . thirty-five?"

I retreated a step. I'd had enough for one evening of men vaguely muttering figures.

"Vital statistics," he said. "And there *is* a touch of mystery about you. Where you've been all night, for instance. An indefinable something . . . perhaps if you took off your coat?"

I took it off and hastily locked the door.

"Yes," he nodded critically, "it certainly might be described as beauty."

"This," I said, "is a single room."

"That's what the night porter explained. What time is it?"

"About a quarter past twelve."

"Oh dear," he said in dismay, "no visitors allowed after midnight. Can I help you with the clasp of those pearls?"

I went over and sat on the bed beside him. He succeeded in removing the pearls, so effectively in fact that I heard them rolling around the floor for some time. They were valueless and Dagobert promised to collect them later.

"What time did you say it was?" he asked sleepily.

"I said a quarter past twelve. But that seemed to be four o'clock striking."

"How time flies," he said. "And there were so many things to talk about. Perhaps if we turned on the lights again . . . ?"

"Where," I asked in alarm, "do you live?"

"Nowhere in particular. I left my luggage with the motor-scooter in a garage."

"Have you had anything to eat?"

"I took Albert to tea at the Coq d'Or," he said. "Settling the bill made rather a dent in my budget so I skipped dinner. One eats well and very reasonably in Barcelona, I believe. We get there the day after tomorrow."

"Poor darling!" I whispered impulsively. "And you could have been stuffing yourself on steak and kidney pie. What was it, honestly, that made you come—the rock 'n' roll?"

"No. I resented Mrs. Petherbridge's crack about respectable married women."

"Yes, no love life," I said somnolently. "Who is Albert?"

"I found him just outside Boulogne. His feet hurt."

"Where's he going?"

"He read a book called *Around the World on Eight Pounds,*

but he says he doesn't care—anywhere will do so long as it's cultural."

"Nice for you to have congenial company." I tried to stay awake. "Did I say I heard four striking? I'm terribly afraid it was five. And there was something important. Not *really* important but . . . something about the channel crossing. Oh . . . Did you find out anything about it? I mean where were you?"

"During the channel crossing?" He shuddered. "I was flat on my back—unconscious, I'm glad to say. I came round when the ship stopped standing upright, which was about half an hour after it docked. Did anything else occur?"

"Juan Roig," I said.

"Ah yes. I'd be grateful if you could find out from him something about Hand-Fed Platen Minding. Such as what it is. Also, if there's a *croissant* or a *brioche* at breakfast that's going begging you might slip it into your handbag."

"You don't *know* about Juan Roig?"

"Yes, he was born in Tabarca," he said soothingly, for I must have raised my voice. "Remarkable coincidence."

"Not so remarkable as the fact he jumped into the channel and hasn't been seen since."

I felt Dagobert's arms tighten around me.

"Say that all over again very slowly," he said.

I told him the little I knew. I told him that no one except Bobby realised why Juan Roig was no longer with us.

He asked what impressions I had of the others. I seemed to hold his interest better than I held my own, for by the time I heard seven striking I'd talked myself back to sleep again.

I had a vague and comforting impression of him, fully clad, leaning over me. I thought, though I may have dreamt it, I heard him murmur: "The day breaks not, it is my heart . . . and how would you like to try riding pillion for a while?"

"Lovely," I sighed as I felt his lips on my forehead.

"Lovely," I repeated, but it was only the maid bringing in my breakfast tray.

The tray was set for one and there was no sign of my lodger, even on the maid's face. The pearls were neatly piled in the ashtray. Our leader, the maid told me, was impatient to be off. I drank my coffee in haste and put two spare *croissants* in my handbag.

The boy came for my luggage. In the corridor outside I met Colonel Warrington whose room was opposite my own. He greeted me warmly and with a touch of gallantry which I had not previously experienced.

"Oh, do call me Hugo," he urged when I said good-morning. "And did you enjoy an, er, restful night?"

I said yes thank you, and trusted that he had too. Bobby, I added, seemed to be in a hurry to press on, and I continued to follow the boy with my luggage. The Colonel caught up with me before I reached the ground floor.

"I took a final glance through our rooms, Jane," he explained. "Always do that when travelling. One never knows what one may leave behind. For instance, my dear, this . . . under your bed."

He handed it to me. It was Dagobert's deer-stalker.

Chapter 8

I DISPOSED OF the deer-stalker behind a potted palm. I wasn't sure it was going to be equally simple to dispose of the Colonel who continued at my side, chatting of this and that. I seemed to have acquired a new friend.

"I'll ask Marcovitch to seat us together this morning," he said. "We go through the Loire country and there's a chateau or two I'd like to point out—notably old Lesparre-Perret's place where I used to do a little shooting. The duchess was a delightful creature—years younger than he and naturally she, er . . . well, you know what the *vraie* French aristocracy is like. But charming person. Charming. As a matter of fact, rather your type, my dear."

We found Bobby with Mrs. Penrose and Flossie Martin in the dining room. Flossie had somehow managed to get bacon and eggs for breakfast. Bobby was too distracted by maps and guidebooks to observe this extra, unmentioned in the souvenir programme.

"Mrs. Brown and I were, er, wondering," the Colonel said to him, "if you'd seat us next to each other on . . ."

"The seating arrangements are already fixed." Bobby came to my rescue with unexpected petulance. "That is, if you don't mind, sir. One could, of course . . ."

He left the sentence and his coffee unfinished and flounced

out of the room. I glanced at the others. Flossie continued to eat and Mrs. Penrose raised an eyebrow.

"A nasty little man," she murmured gently.

I saw Bobby's face at the dining-room door. He was trying to draw my attention. With the excuse that I wanted to see about luggage I joined him in the hall. He was on the verge of tears.

"Sorry about that scene," he apologised. "I try so hard to make everyone happy. I don't give a damn where anybody sits. But really this is too much! I'm at the end of my tether, Jane."

"Because the Colonel—"

"No, not the Colonel!" he interrupted impatiently. "Derek Upjohn."

"What's Derek done?"

"That's just it. I don't know. No one knows." He began to bite his manicured nails. "Jane," he cried in despair, "why didn't I listen to your advice yesterday and call the whole bloody thing off? First Juan Roig. Now Derek Upjohn!"

"What!"

He couldn't resist dramatizing it. "The Lucky Seven! Seven . . . then Six." There was a catch in his voice. ". . . now only Five."

He began to wring his hands. He stopped abruptly, struck by a sudden thought. It would perhaps be uncharitable to imagine the thought which struck him was that Derek too was insured for ten thousand pounds.

I said angrily, for he had frightened me badly:

"Before you have a nervous breakdown and scare the wits out of everybody, do please verify your facts."

"We've searched the entire hotel," he wailed. "He didn't even sleep in his room."

"In a way, Bobby, I hate to put you out of your agony," I said, "but take a look across the square. I am now going to have another cup of coffee and you can put it on the expense account!"

Bobby didn't argue the point. He too had just seen Derek Upjohn sloping back towards the hotel. Derek was accompanied by the night porter who had, it appeared, recommended a boîte after all.

I didn't wait to greet him on his untriumphal return to the fold. His moustache was bedraggled, he had lost his coat, his grey flannel suit was crumpled and bore traces of sawdust. He had enough to cope with in any case: Bobby's strident cross-questioning and, more affecting, Ninette, who rose quickly from a chair in the lounge, alternately pale and pink. In her eyes was the rejoicing associated with the return of lost sheep.

In spite of Derek we got off in good time. Toulouse, tonight's objective, was over three hundred and fifty miles away and Bobby, in lieu of the advertised conducted tour, drove up to and once around the cathedral.

Originally an abbey church, he told us briskly, it was built to shelter the relics of Saint Saturnin. The present edifice, begun in 1060, was designed as a gathering place for pilgrims going to Santiago de Compostela and was one of the glories of Romanesque architecture. The five-storey octagonal tower—

"Don't see it," the Colonel said.

"Mr. Marcovitch," Margaret Penrose said, "is of course talking about the church of Saint Sernin in Toulouse which we shall doubtless be rushed past tomorrow."

"I think it's heavenly," Ninette said. "It makes you feel—kind of eternal."

"That's the Last Judgment," Margaret pointed out as we slowed down in front of the south portal. "Perhaps the finest bas-relief of the Middle Ages."

Bobby, piqued by having others take over his role of guide, changed gears and accelerated.

Flossie Martin, who showed not the slightest interest in the cathedral, said she preferred a decent clean skyscraper any day: all that old chipped sculpture was a lot of superstitious, medieval nonsense. I caught her eye as she spoke. She met my glance with perfect aplomb. I had to remind myself that she did not know I'd seen her last night on her knees before the sanctuary lamp.

It was Flossie's turn to sit in front beside Bobby. I, obeying instructions, sat in the back next to Ninette and Derek. Hugo Warrington nodded in approval at what he decided was my discretion. In not arguing about the seating arrangements I was doubtless behaving as the Duchesse de Lesparre-Perret would have behaved in similar circumstances. He took his place with good grace on the folding seat beside Margaret Penrose and desultorily discussed the Loire chateaux which we were approaching. Forewarned by Margaret's authoritative reference to Saint Sernin he avoided architectural dicta and confined himself to anecdotes of the families who inhabited them.

The morning's drive must have been dull for Ninette who sat between Derek and me; both of us had sleep to make up and we frequently dropped off. I was reassured by an occasional glimpse of the motor-scooter; Derek may have been comforted by the travelling rug Ninette had quietly tucked around him.

"Because he hasn't an overcoat," she whispered to me. And later, when it was certain that Derek was sound asleep: "I think he got squiffy last night and went to one of those places."

"He certainly went pub-crawling."

"I should have gone with him," she said. "I wanted to, but he got kind of angry with me, and ordered me off to bed. Men are funny."

This profound reflection carried us through Orleans and halfway to Chateauroux where we were supposed to stop for elevenses. Derek continued peacefully to sleep. Ninette gazed at him with maternal indulgence.

"I think he's sort of scared of me," she said, smiling tolerantly to herself. "Sometimes, when I catch him staring at me, he blushes and looks away, and scowls as though he half-hated me. Or maybe," she added seriously, "he's scared of himself. He's just a crazy, mixed-up kid."

The car jolted gently. Derek's head nodded forward and came to rest against Ninette's shoulder. She resisted the temptation to smooth back the shock of ginger hair which had fallen forward over his pale brow. She wrapped the travelling rug more snugly around his knees. The pressure of her hands roused him and he made an effort to open his eyes. They blinked vaguely at Ninette and he mumbled something which sounded like "Yvonne." He blinked again as though the light hurt his eyes, closed them firmly and with a grunt of disgust squirmed away into his own corner where he promptly fell asleep again.

I felt the gesture was purely symbolic: the angry flick of a fish which is hooked and knows it. Ninette, too, was undisturbed by this show of independence. Her smile remained serene.

"I guess Yvonne is some girl he once thought he was in love with," she said. "Poor Yvonne."

Poor Derek, I thought, noting the confidence with which she referred to Yvonne in the past tense. Had she needed further reassurance I could have told her how Derek had burned Yvonne's photograph last night—and wept like a person at the end of a sentimental chapter in his biography.

"Love can be cruel, can't it," she sighed. "Though probably you don't suffer so much when you get older."

"Love?" said the Colonel, catching the word. "Present generation doesn't know the first thing about it. Eh, Mrs. Penrose?"

Though he addressed the words jocosely to Margaret he glanced round at me with something like a twinkle in his eye. I wasn't sure which generation I was supposed to represent.

Margaret Penrose made a grimace of distaste.

"Love is not a subject on which I am particularly expert," she said.

Flossie looked round from the front seat, interested.

"Say!" she exclaimed suddenly. "I meant to ask you. Who is George anyway—that Bobby was so mysterious about in last week's Chit-Chat?"

"George," said Mrs. Penrose, "was my husband. He died about two months ago. His death had no news value and was not reported in the press, not even in *Home Truth*."

The subject, her tone of voice indicated, could be of no possible interest to anyone. Idle talk about love abruptly ceased. Flossie went pink in the face and muttered: "Sorry." Bobby discovered that it was time for elevenses and drew up in front of a cafe.

As we got out Ninette, with more penetration than I'd realised she had, said to me in an awed whisper:

"Gosh! I could have been wrong about not suffering so much when you get older."

Chapter 9

By lunchtime Derek had recovered. He was about four hours' sleep up on me. A wash and brush-up and the dark glasses restored his appearance. He complained ruefully of a hangover and drank nothing but Vichy water. He and Ninette exchanged much noisy banter and one felt that young love was running smoothly on its somewhat hackneyed course. Flossie thought they were "sweet" and her eyes filled with tears—perhaps at some tender memory, perhaps at the sight of the *crepes suzette.*

Dagobert was not with us, but I was relieved to catch a glimpse of him and Albert in the workmen's cafe across the road. There was a bowl of nourishing potato soup in front of them and checked napkins tucked under their chins.

Hugo Warrington continued to be attentive; he was so attentive that I had some difficulty in slipping the *foie gras* into my handbag. Later, in the confusion of re-seating everyone in the car, I was able to leave a neat paper parcel on the tool-box of the motor-scooter.

The drive that afternoon was long and tiring. By the time we reached the mountainous region between Brive and Cahors our driver was beginning to feel the strain. So were the rest of us. Even the Colonel's gallantry faltered and he broke off occasionally to say: "Steady on," when Bobby took a curve on the wrong side of the road. We were well ahead of schedule, but Bobby seemed to be in a hurry, unless—as I once suggested to him in facetious manner—he was trying to collect the insurance money on the lot of us all at once.

My facetiousness was affected, for it was plain that Bobby was in a bad way. When he ought to have been concentrating on the road his eyes would stray towards the driving mirror, waiting for the inevitable motor-scooter to round the bend behind us. Dagobert, I suspected, had begun to get on his nerves.

Once we lost sight of Dagobert for nearly an hour. Neither of us commented on the fact but we both fell silent. I kept trying not to think of the peculiar wobble which worried Mr. Jenkins. I don't know what Bobby kept trying not to think of. Wearing his man-of-action expression, he gripped the steering wheel and drove faster than ever.

He did a racing skid around a hairpin bend which terrified everybody and reminded Hugo Warrington of an early Monte Carlo rally. The Bentley team had needed a spare driver and he had lent a hand.

"Then why," Flossie urged, "don't you take over from Bobby for a while?"

Bobby accelerated grimly, and at the same time in the corner of the driving mirror the motor-scooter reappeared. Like a man who has given of his best and been unappreciated, Bobby jerked the car to a standstill and resigned his place behind the wheel.

"Anyone who wants to can take over," he said huffily.

The person who took over was, unexpectedly, Mrs. Penrose. Within five minutes we all settled back and breathed more easily. Margaret Penrose handled the Rolls-Royce as though she had driven one all her life.

Towards evening we reached Montauban and knew that we were in the Midi. The quality of the light had changed. Though already fading it was clearer and more golden. Cypress and evergreen oak stood out against a pale blue sky. In the air there were faint new scents—thyme and rosemary. Daylight lingered longer than in the north and it was appreciably milder. We slipped our fur coats off our shoulders. Ninette began to wonder where she had packed her new three-piece rumpus suit.

We all suddenly remembered we were on our way to the Mediterranean. The Colonel, now dozing at my side, stirred and murmured:

"Tabarca! Wonder if that's the place we called at that time —I hate to think how long ago. With the Westminsters, I mean. Don't quite know what Fruity and I were doing aboard, but," he said, feeling this needed clarifying, "it was one of those parties. You won't remember the Westminsters' yacht probably. Before your day, Jane. And before the days of people like this Henry Howard Hutton Junior—whatever that indicates.

That he had a father, presumably. Not that I have a thing against the fellow, far from it. Some of these self-made men, splendid chaps. Fact is I never heard of him before this business about marrying royalty—if you can call the Branzas royalty. Anybody ever met him? Marcovitch? You must have, since he's your boss."

"The editorial policy of *Home Truth* is completely independent," Bobby said with dignity. "I am my own boss."

"Well, your colleague, if you prefer . . . Anyway what sort of fellow is he? How old? What's he do—apart from making millions? Is he a gentleman? Does he drop his aitches? What's he like?"

Bobby seemed distressed by these direct questions.

"More or less what you'd expect," he muttered and began to talk about dinner tonight in Toulouse. Even Flossie was not to be side-tracked by tonight's specialties.

"But what *is* he like?" she prompted.

"I see Henry Howard Hutton Junior vividly," said Ninette. "He's about fifty with iron-grey hair and a harsh rasping voice —used to giving orders and used to being obeyed. He's fought his way up from the gutter with his bare fists and will stop at nothing to attain his ends. Business associates, friends, loved ones will be crushed beneath his ruthless heel if they get in the way of his boundless ambition. He's a tycoon, if you know what I mean."

"No," Derek grinned. "What do you mean?"

"Well, kind of stormy and elemental."

Bobby smiled in a fatherly way to indicate that he could if he wished explain the difference between a tycoon and a typhoon. But he looked as though he would rather discuss something else, such as the scenery. He glanced out at the fertile plain through which we were passing. In spite of himself his eyes strayed towards the dusty road behind us. It offered no distraction. All he saw there was the motor-scooter.

"Then one day," Ninette continued dreamily, "Henry meets a woman, a simple, innocent girl . . ."

"He's already met a woman," Derek said. "The Princess Juana."

"That's right," Ninette said reluctantly. "But I wonder if she is *the* woman for him. You couldn't tell much from that portrait on the cover of *Home Truth*. She looked sort of sophisticated. Henry's the sophisticated one . . . I can't decide whether he's like Victor Mature or Jean Gabin."

"Anyway," Derek laughed, "not like Mel Ferrer."

"No," she said seriously, "more—more earthy. Not the sort who'd run away from Life. . . ."

Flossie laughed too. "And get drunk," she added. "Puts you in your place, Derek! Still it *is* funny no one knows anything about Mr. Hutton."

"Come to think of it," Derek said, "I've never seen a picture of him; pictures of his yacht, of Tabarca, yes. But not of the great tycoon himself."

"Perhaps he has a hideous scar," Ninette shuddered.

"Nor anything else about him," Flossie mused.

"He was born in Quebec," I contributed.

"Lots of people were born in Quebec," she said briefly. "But, as Colonel Warrington said, what's he like?"

"We are," said Margaret Penrose who had seemed to be wholly occupied with driving, "still waiting for Mr. Marcovitch to tell us."

"I never discuss business associates," Bobby said primly.

"You discuss everybody else," Derek said.

Bobby said: "The reason you've never seen his photograph is that H. H. does not permit photographs of himself to be printed. He refuses to give interviews and in the publications he controls he does not allow even his name to appear. We are most privileged to be invited to his wedding."

"How did you wangle it?" I asked.

"It was the Princess Juana's idea. Well, actually, it was my idea but the Princess enthusiastically okayed it and H. H. gracefully gave in. He usually avoids publicity like poison."

"The two things are not unsimilar." Margaret nodded. "One must, I imagine, be very rich indeed to afford privacy."

"Depends on who you are," Bobby said frankly. "If you're marrying a princess—yes, then it comes pretty expensive."

"I'd like to have my picture on the cover of *Home Truth* someday." Ninette pursued her own fantasy.

"At least," Flossie said, "you were recognisable in last week's issue, which is more than I was."

"I meant to apologise about that, Flossie," Bobby said. "We went to press in such a hurry we couldn't take another one. I nearly sacked the photographer."

"You seem to have strayed from the subject of Hutton," the Colonel pointed out. "We still know nothing about the fellow. Thought you prided yourself on knowing everything about everybody, Marcovitch."

"He has his blind spots," Margaret said drily. "I suspect Mr. Marcovitch knows as little about Henry Howard Hutton as the rest of us. Indeed, I very much doubt if he has ever seen him. The octagonal tower on our right," she turned to Bobby kindly, "is, for your information, the tower of Saint Sernin."

Chapter 10

Bobby smiled in a superior way at the notion that he knew no more about H. H. than the rest of us: the absurdity of Margaret's theory was, he said, rather amusing.

He seemed, however, unamused, as we drove to the Grand Hotel des Pyrenees; and he volunteered no further details about his colleague. You could see it cut him to the quick to appear uninformed; he did his best to convey the impression that he could have talked had he cared to. I wondered whether his reticence was professional or whether, after all, Margaret Penrose had guessed the truth.

"She's always getting in dirty cracks," he whispered as I went with him to the desk to make sure our rooms were booked. "What's she got against me, Jane?"

"That's one of the things you should have checked up before you announced the prize-winners," I said.

He was outraged at the suggestion there had been any checking up.

"That isn't the way *Home Truth* does things," he said. "There's such a thing as accepting people at their face value, mutual trust."

The receptionist assured us that all was in order and gave me a telegram. I opened it before I noticed it was addressed to Bobby. It read:

"So far nothing re Margaret P. Trying fresh lead. Saunders."

Saunders, I remembered, was *Home Truth*'s legal representative. I handed the telegram to Bobby without comment.

"What," I changed the subject, "do you know about Flossie?"

"Flossie?" he echoed. "Has she . . . *is* there anything to know about her that wasn't in last week's Chit-Chat?"

He crushed the telegram into his pocket and stared at me severely.

"Really, Jane, if we're going to indulge in this kind of petty talk behind each other's backs, to create this atmosphere of hints and innuendoes, we shall be a most unhappy family." He lowered his voice. "Er, what have *you* found out about her?"

"Would she be from Quebec?"

Bobby shrugged. He had, he implied, other more pressing things on his mind. The rest of the party was straggling into the lobby about to descend on him, demanding room numbers. He kept a wary eye on porters bringing in our luggage and at the same time watched Margaret Penrose, through the entrance doors, backing the Rolls-Royce into a parking space. Flossie spotted us and pushed eagerly forward.

Bobby winced as though something had bitten him. I saw what his trouble was. Margaret had almost backed the Rolls-Royce into the motor-scooter which had just drawn up behind it.

"If you want to be useful," he muttered, "you might try to find out who that man is."

"I know," I said.

"Yes?"

"He's the one who's been following us ever since Boulogne," I said.

"I've seen him somewhere before that." He gave me a thoughtful look and wandered towards the door. Before he reached it Dagobert had driven on. Flossie joined me at the desk.

"Wasn't Bobby here?" she said. "I wanted to see him about something—about my room."

I told her her room number was twenty-five, next to mine, and the clerk handed us our keys. He also handed me another telegram under the impression I was Bobby's secretary. The second telegram was also addressed to Bobby. Flossie eyed it, hoping I would open it. When I didn't, she said:

"I'll give it to him. It's probably something to do with reservations." She took it from me and tucked it into her handbag. "I see they've already started dinner. Smells good. Are you going to change?"

In the lift I said to her: "I wonder what the telegram says."

"What telegram? Oh! I'd forgotten all about it. I'll give it to him at dinner. We're having *cassoulet au confit d'oie*."

I said I'd always wondered how you pronounced it and she said quickly: "Probably a lot of stuff messed up in a casserole."

"The telegram," I said, "wasn't even stuck down."

"Oh, wasn't it? Do you—do you think we ought to look?"

"No, but I'm curious too."

She flushed, then grinned. "It can't be very important, can it?"

We had reached our rooms. Porters had opened our doors and were carrying in our bags. I remained with Flossie and with the still-unopened telegram. She had taken it from her handbag and was toying with the unstuck edges.

"We can gum it down afterwards," she said. "Okay. We're in this together."

She tried to smile as she opened it, but she had gone rather white. She read it without comprehension. Like the message reporting no progress in the investigation of Margaret Penrose it was signed Saunders. Saunders was plainly a busy man.

This time his enquiries did not concern any of the party, at least not any of the surviving members of the party. He reported:

"Body recovered near Boulogne yesterday. Result of this afternoon's inquest highly satisfactory: death by misadventure."

Flossie looked at me blankly. "B-body?"

"Juan Roig," I said.

She sat down cautiously on the edge of her bed. It creaked under her weight.

"I don't understand. He died? That—that's why he didn't come?"

"It seems he fell overboard during the crossing. Bobby thought it would upset us if we knew."

"What," she asked in a small voice, "what can it possibly mean—result of inquest *highly satisfactory?"*

It was the first question I asked Bobby when I gave the telegram to him. Flossie had decided to let me deliver it, which permitted me to make a copy of it first.

"What," I said to Bobby over a brandy and soda at the bar, "is so highly satisfactory about it?"

Bobby ran an exasperated hand through his curls. "Jeeze!" His voice rose in a controlled whine. "Use your head—of course it's satisfactory! Whatcha want? A verdict of suicide, so the poor beggar couldn't collect the insurance money? What did you expect?"

I finished my brandy and soda, feeling foolish. I hardly cared to explain that the verdict I'd not exactly expected—but half-dreaded—was a verdict of murder.

"Did Flossie see the telegram?" he asked.

I explained it had been unsealed and we'd both seen it.

"There's no such thing as privacy these days," he grumbled, "what with people snooping and checking up on each other. How did she take it? Maybe I'd better go up and hold her hand."

"She'll be down in a minute for the *cassoulet au confit d'oie."*

He shook his head. "She just telephoned the desk to say all she wants for dinner is a cup of weak tea and a dry biscuit on a tray. She says this afternoon's drive upset her. People are so self-centred. What's she think it's done to me?"

"Oh, the man on the motor-scooter," I smiled. "Have you found out yet why he's following us?"

"There's nothing to be amused at, Jane," he said reproachfully. "No. No," he added more briskly, "now you mention it, I haven't."

A few minutes later on our way to the dining room we saw Bobby at the desk. He was writing out a telegram. He covered it ostentatiously as I went past, only permitting me to see that it was addressed to Saunders.

"What are we investigating now?" I asked him. "Flossie's loss of appetite?"

For the first time that evening Bobby permitted himself a slight smile. Then, giving way to an irresistible impulse, he let me catch a further glimpse of what he had written. He had asked Saunders for fuller details about me and Dagobert.

Chapter 11

DINNER AGAIN WAS excellent, but after the Grand Cerf in Chartres last night and an almost equally recherche luncheon this afternoon the company had become more critical. All in all, the Colonel said, nothing was quite like a new-laid English egg with a rasher of crisp bacon, washed down by half a pint of honest draught bitter. Ninette put in a word for Walls' ice cream.

Without Flossie to mop up everything in sight, I was able, with the connivance of a sympathetic waiter, to smuggle up to my room afterwards a variety of cold hams and exotic sausages, a loaf of bread, Roquefort and a basket of peaches.

Dagobert, however, was not there. I left the key hopefully in the door and started downstairs again. I had not seen the Colonel lurking in the corridor.

"In Edwardian days," he told me, "one used to leave a rose in the keyhole—a delicate invitation. You are looking radiant tonight. Shall we join the others, dear lady, or have you, perhaps, plans of your own?"

"I thought of a brisk walk," I said.

"Splendid," he said. "Permit me to offer you my arm."

I thanked him but said I was still able to walk unaided. We found Derek and Ninette below also preparing to try the night life of Toulouse. Derek seemed relieved when I asked if we could join them. Ninette gave me a conspiratorial smile; men, it reiterated, were funny—as we had earlier decided. In her strapless cotton frock she looked as appetising as the peaches I had left upstairs for Dagobert.

"The Colonel," she said, "is looking very dis-tang-gee tonight. There's something about mature men, isn't there? Something, well, kind of distang-gee?"

"There is something about all men," I said.

She began to giggle, but thought it over. "Yes, I suppose there is," she sighed.

Derek fell back a pace and walked beside me. "How besotted can a man become?" he said with suppressed irritation. "She's been pulling my leg openly all the evening about Yvonne—and instead of strangling her I've taken it with a fatuous grin! I didn't come on this trip to make a fool of myself.

Incidentally, I remember last night in Chartres in detail, even to the melodramatic way in which I burned that snapshot. Sorry—and thanks. You were very patient. Drink is supposed to make you forget. Unfortunately it doesn't. I could, of course, try again," he concluded more lightly.

But when we stopped at a cafe where an orchestra was playing all he ordered was a small glass of beer. When we left an hour later his glass was still untouched.

Hugo, meanwhile, was plying Ninette and me with green Chartreuse. He was, as Ninette had said, looking very distinguished tonight. He had put on a yellow suede waistcoat and wore a silk stock, fixed with a small pearl horseshoe pin. His grey moustache was newly clipped and scented with eau-de-cologne.

He complimented me on my frock: few women nowadays had the figure and carriage to lend such elegance to simplicity. He was, he murmured, doubly fortunate in having won this absurd competition of Marcovitch's. The extravagant odds, he said with a deprecatory smile, were not so much against being one of the Lucky Seven as against finding a person of one's own sort among the winners. Frankly, he had been worried. The sight of me had agreeably altered the whole aspect of the fortnight.

Should we, he suggested, continue our stroll and leave these two pleasant young persons to amuse each other in their own language?

"Mrs. Brown," he explained to the others, "feels a little tired and begs you to excuse her."

"I'll walk back to the hotel with her," Derek volunteered.

"Yes, do," Ninette urged. "The Colonel and I will get tiddley together, won't we . . . Hugo?"

Hugo smiled benevolently, but he was already on his feet, holding my coat. We left them in a corner of the cafe listening to the orchestra play "Oh My Papa." Ninette had edged closer to Derek and was regarding him with half-closed eyes and half-parted lips. Derek watched her gently heaving bosom in a state of stupor. When he recovered from the spell he would discover that Colonel Warrington had left him to pay for all the drinks.

I explained to Hugo that I actually was a little tired; he at once offered to call a taxi.

"It's only a hundred yards," I said. "I think I can manage it."

Hugo Warrington was, of course, a bore—though no man who constantly flatters you is altogether a bore. Time had passed more quickly than I had realised. It was about eleven when we got back to the hotel.

Hugo left me tactfully at the door of the lift. He proposed, he said, as he bent lightly over my hand, to smoke a final cigarette. He wished me good-night and added for the benefit of the lift-boy: "A *demain*, dear lady."

I locked and bolted my door.

"I saw the rose in your keyhole," Dagobert said, "and on the offchance dropped in."

"Oh, you were lurking in the corridor too!"

"Yes," he said. "You look, if one may say so, radiant tonight, dear lady."

I glanced at him, puzzled. He himself was looking dishevelled and rather grim.

"Dagobert," I exclaimed, "you're not—yes, you are—you're jealous!"

The thought was new to him and he considered it impartially. "Is that what it is?" he said, astonished. "I believe you're right. Most unpleasant. It spoils the appetite."

He regarded the food I had brought up after dinner with new interest. It had not been touched.

"All for me?" he said.

"All for you . . . And," I added, when I had disentangled myself, "for Albert, of course. How is he?"

"Complaining bitterly of the 'liver paste' you left us after lunch. That's why we fell so far behind. Albert was sick."

We discussed matters which have no bearing on the story and may be omitted. I was just working around to suggesting that I might change places with Albert when there was a gentle tap on my door. I ignored it, hoping Dagobert hadn't heard. It was repeated.

"Oh dear!" I said. "The Colonel!"

"Humph!" said Dagobert.

"What shall I do?"

The rapping continued.

"I'll do it," Dagobert said, striding to the door.

I got there before him. The raps had quickened. There was a note of insistence in the sound which could no longer be ignored. It was well after midnight and the whole hotel would be roused.

"Into the bathroom," I whispered. "I'll get rid of whoever it is."

I unbolted the door as Dagobert reached the bathroom. I opened it an inch or two, prepared to bar the intruder's entrance, physically if necessary.

But the appearance of my visitor was such that I fell back without a word. Flossie Martin was in her dressing gown. Her feet were bare and her hair net was askew. She looked behind her down the dimly lit corridor as though she could discern there creatures, invisible to me, perhaps those writhing figures from the Last Judgment which had pursued her from the south portal of Chartres.

I said: "Come in," but she was already in. She leaned back against the door, panting.

"Somebody," she gasped, "I think somebody is trying to kill me!"

Chapter 12

I LOCKED AND BOLTED the door again, and said:

"What are you talking about?"

She drew a distraught hand across her forehead. It was still shining with nourishing cream. Her soft, plump features twitched and she fought for breath as though unseen hands were strangling her. Her eyes blinked, surprised by the light and apparently by seeing me there. I don't think she knew herself what she was talking about.

"What," I prompted, "makes you think anything so—so unlikely?"

"I was fast asleep," she stammered. "I mean I'd finally gotten to sleep—I took some barbitone, in case—and . . . do you mind if I sit down?"

"Of course not."

She slumped down, breathing heavily. The barbitone may have accounted for the dilation of her pale yellow pupils. She was still dazed.

"About five minutes ago," she said. "I've been lying there in the dark ever since, trying . . . Then I remembered you next door. Can I stay here? The bed's pretty wide—or I can just sit in this chair."

"What happened about five minutes ago?"

"I don't know. I was dreaming about . . . well, the house

was on fire and Pete—he's my little boy—was locked in his room and, and all at once I realised *I* had set the house on fire *myself*, and . . ." She shook herself, aware that she was wandering. "Then suddenly there was this tap on the door . . ."

She made it sound like the tap of doom. I asked:

"Is that all?"

She went white in the face and murmured: "Water."

I went into the bathroom to fetch a tumbler. Dagobert had it ready and handed it to me.

"The tap on the door about five minutes ago was probably me," he whispered. "I had the wrong room number."

"Who's there?" Flossie cried out, and I reappeared swiftly with the water.

"So you thought you heard a knock on the door," I said. "Then what?"

"Then . . . nothing."

"So you immediately assumed someone was trying to kill you." I nodded.

She managed a sickly smile. "It does sound kind of crazy."

I gave her the glass of water, though I wondered if it would not be more effective if poured over her head.

"Yes," I agreed, "fairly crazy."

"I lay there in the dark, thinking," she said. "Thinking about . . . Juan Roig."

This time I made no comment. I'd done a little thinking about Juan Roig myself.

"Why," I said finally, "didn't you get up and lock your door?"

"I did that hours ago," she said. "The tap wasn't repeated but a little later—just now, a moment before I came in here—I heard them again in my bathroom. The bathroom is shared with the room next door, not this one, the one on the other side—I don't know who's in it."

I did. It was occupied by Margaret Penrose, but I didn't say so. I said:

"Then it's quite logical to expect someone to use it."

"I suppose so," she said doubtfully. "I wasn't thinking very logically. But this I do know. There was someone sneaking along the corridor behind me when I knocked on your door. He slipped back into the shadows when I looked round, but I *know* he was spying on me."

"He? You saw who it was?"

"I can't be sure," she said. "But . . . but it looked like Colonel Warrington, which doesn't make much sense, does it? Nothing makes much sense. It's all so vague. I wish I could explain. I felt suddenly . . . trapped. Oh, Jane, please let me stay here with you."

I was beginning to feel a little trapped myself, though not, presumably, as trapped as Dagobert was. Flossie lowered her voice.

"It didn't start tonight. It began yesterday after Boulogne—that motor-scooter following us. Then last night in Chartres. I, as a matter of fact, well, I went for a walk by myself after dinner. Someone shadowed me."

"Shadowed you? Do you mean followed you into the cathedral?"

She looked at me with a glimmer of suspicion which at least indicated returning intelligence.

"W-what makes you think I went into the cathedral?"

"Because I went in after you."

"Oh."

She studied her fingernails. The varnish was peeling off at the edges. She began to toy with a peach. She bit into it, found the flavour to her liking and absent-mindedly finished it.

"The person you imagined to be shadowing you, Flossie, was simply me," I said. "I'd strolled up to the cathedral too and finding a door open walked in. Five minutes ago when you were asleep someone knocked by accident on your door. This naturally startled you. Shortly afterwards Margaret Penrose probably went into the bathroom you share with her. I don't quite know why Colonel Warrington should be roaming this corridor, since his room is on the floor above, but there is doubtless a simple explanation. I don't see why these four perfectly innocent and unconnected occurrences should make you jump to the fantastic conclusion that someone was trying to kill you."

"No, I don't either," she said, fortified either by my words or by the peach. She began to nibble at a slice of ham. "Sometimes I get terribly worked up, in one of my states, as Jim calls them. Jim's my old man."

"I remember his photograph in last week's *Home Truth*."

This remark seemed to be a mistake, for again she began to tremble. She crammed the rest of the ham into her mouth and said with some difficulty:

"Yes, that picture—that's something else I thought about. Jane! Why wasn't *I* in it?"

"Bobby explained that this afternoon. There wasn't time to take another one."

"They took about five," she said. She made a feeble effort to smile. "Maybe Bobby didn't want to spoil the look of the page."

There was a copy of last week's *Home Truth* on the table. Bobby had made sure we were all lavishly provided with copies. Flossie leafed through the pages until she came to the one devoted to herself. Her smile became warmer as she contemplated Jim and the two children.

They made a pleasant family group on the verandah of their semi-detached suburban villa, welcoming Bobby in his role of fairy godfather. It was a good photograph of them all except Flossie. She was in it—just. But her face was in shadow and quite unrecognisable.

Jim, who had been mowing the lawn, was in braces. In his arms he held Doreen, an eighteen-month-old baby whose resemblance to him was striking. Pete, the older child, was about eight. He had freckles and wore a Davy Crockett hat. He was aiming a space-gun at Bobby Marcovitch who was trying not to look nervous.

"Jim's so good to them," she said. "To both of them. No favouritism. And to me, too. Maybe I *am* one of the seven luckiest people in England after all. Like it says."

She began on the Roquefort. She ate it mechanically as she continued to study the picture.

"They'll be living out of tins," she said. "I had on that awful apron. You can see *it* clearly enough. Not that I mind not having my face in the limelight—a great improvement, I daresay. The only thing is—" She dropped *Home Truth* suddenly and went rigid. "What was that?" she started. "Somebody in *your* bathroom!"

"Also shared with the room next door," I improvised. "You were saying, 'the only thing is . . .' "

She shook her head vaguely. "You know the crazy kind of things you think of in the middle of the night. Not worth repeating. I think something I ate at lunch upset me—and then that telegram." She grimaced. "Highly satisfactory!"

"There's a simple explanation of that too," I told her. "It means that Juan Roig's family will get the insurance money without complications."

She wasn't listening. Her eyes were fixed on the bathroom door which was an inch or two ajar. She fingered the sausages distractedly, taking a bite out of each in turn until she came upon a rich red salami which reeked of garlic. She swallowed it avidly. I went on to explain:

"You see, we are all insured by *Home*—"

"There *is* someone in that bathroom," she whispered.

It was beginning to get on my nerves too. I went noisily to

the bathroom door and jerked it open.

"No one here," I said gaily and then, slightly shaken, I saw that there wasn't anybody there.

"I could have sworn . . ." Flossie breathed at my shoulder. "I must still be half asleep. Maybe a cold shower . . ."

I changed the subject hastily. Beneath the plastic shower curtains I had caught a glimpse of Dagobert's boots. I said:

"You speak French very well, don't you, Flossie?"

"No-no," she said, no longer in need of a shower to wake her up. "Why on earth should I?"

"I thought many French Canadians spoke French. Aren't you French Canadian?"

"How did you know?" she exclaimed, genuinely surprised. "Oh, of course. Bobby told you!"

I made noncommittal sounds and closed the bathroom door. Flossie seemed to be glad to get back to the sausages.

"It was silly anyway, if you ask me," she said. "Bobby said there had to be one typical suburban housewife among the Lucky Seven—and I was elected. I think he'd already written me up for *Home Truth* before he interviewed me! I wasn't to let anyone know I spoke French—because your typical suburban housewife doesn't speak French. *Home Truth* doesn't circulate in Canada—so I wasn't to say I came from Quebec. I'm supposed to conform exactly to the character Bobby made up for me. That was part of the bargain. I shouldn't tell you all this. You won't pass it on to the others, will you? You know how Bobby likes to think he's the only one who has inside information."

"Did you tell him you were French Canadian?" I asked. "Or did he know it already? I mean before he first interviewed you."

"He already seemed to know it," she said pensively. "Say, maybe he does have . . . well, some information about people. What was dinner like? I'm starved. Why don't you eat something?"

I shook my head, not pointing out that there was almost nothing left to eat. I recovered the copy of *Home Truth* she had dropped on the floor and opened it again at the photograph of the Martin family group.

"As the Colonel said in the car this afternoon apropos of Henry Howard Hutton," I said, "we seem to have strayed from the subject. Which was—what is it about this picture which so disturbs you?"

This time instead of going pale she went pink in the face. "Like I said," she stammered, "it was only one of those crazy ideas you get in the middle of the night."

"What idea, Flossie?"

"You know—no picture of me. I began to lie there in bed asking why, why? Because, you remember, there was *no picture of Juan Roig either*."

"What has that got to do with anything?" I asked sharply.

"Nothing," she said, imperturbably munching another peach. "Nothing, only . . . I guess it's too late to send down for more butter. Only lying there in the dark it seemed kind of significant. You know how you begin putting two and two together and getting five."

She took a thoughtful bite out of the last peach. With the end of the food in sight I wondered if I might tactfully raise the subject of her going back to bed. She said:

"I can't tell you how much I appreciate your letting me stay here. I don't know what time it is, but it shouldn't be long now. This chair's quite comfortable. Do you mind the light?" She wrapped the fluffy dressing gown tight around her as though settling down for the rest of the night. But there was still something on her mind. Finally she said:

"Jane . . . that first morning on the way to Dover. I thought I heard Juan Roig telling you how surprised he was at winning the competition."

"We all were, I imagine."

"He said he didn't even remember entering for it. He thought it was for an electric dish-washer."

"Did he?" I shrugged. "People go in for so many competitions they forget which is which."

"I don't," she said shortly.

"No?"

"Because I've never entered for a competition in my life."

"You mean until this one."

She shook her head hesitantly. At last she said: "I didn't enter for it. When Bobby called at the house with the orchids and the fur coat and the Rolls-Royce it was the first time I'd ever heard of the competition—or, for that matter, of *Home Truth*."

Chapter 13

FLOSSIE MARTIN PASSED the night more comfortably than I: she occupied at least two-thirds of my bed. When towards dawn Dagobert, complaining that the shower leaked, finally crept away she was sleeping peacefully. She had pulled most of the bedclothes over her head and was a lump of contented oblivion. The confession had done her good.

At first Flossie had, she told me, been stunned to learn she had won a competition she'd never heard of. Bobby explained how the confusion had occurred. The staff of *Home Truth* were forbidden to go in for their own competitions, but sometimes they did so nevertheless. They would take a name and address from the telephone directory or a mailing list and, if they won, would come to an arrangement with the person whose name they had borrowed.

This, Bobby said, was what had happened in the present instance. One of *Home Truth*'s typists had filled in Flossie Martin's name and address on the entry form. The form was among the seven winners. The typist intended to call on Flossie and propose they split the profits—Flossie going on the trip for a modest payment to be made to the typist. Fortunately Bobby discovered this in time. Unfortunately Flossie's name had meanwhile been publicly announced.

Bobby begged her to help him out of an embarrassing situation. If she said nothing about not having entered the competition she would be regarded as a legitimate winner. Bobby would be saved a headache. Flossie would reap the reward with no strings attached.

She refused at first, but the thing seemed like a gift from heaven. She needed the holiday and Jim urged her to accept it. Bobby was kindness itself and had even offered to make room in the car for her son Pete since she was so reluctant to leave him. The publicity value of taking a child along would, he said, be worth the extra expense. Jim, however, had put his foot down on that idea.

"He adores Pete," she said, finally switching off the light. "Bless him."

Remembering the young barbarian with the space-gun in the photograph I, too, inwardly blessed Jim.

"Did you meet him in Quebec?" I asked.

"Yes. He'd just emigrated," she said dreamily. "It was after the Suez crisis. Jim was very lonely. We were both very lonely. I worked in the cafeteria where he used to eat. It was pretty hard making ends meet what with, well, one thing and another.

But what really made me marry Jim was his unfailing kindness and understanding and tolerance. I wasn't so used to that. He came back to England mainly because he guessed that was what I wanted. I've tried to make a decent home for him. . . . I wish I was there now."

Her voice trailed away. I wondered if she was asleep or merely feeling homesick for Jim and the two children in the semi-detached villa in Lathomstowe. She lay so still that I put a cautious foot on the floor at my side of the bed. She sat up instantly.

"He's in this room!" she rasped.

"Who is?" I said, as Dagobert rapidly retreated into the bathroom again. "Who do you mean, Flossie?"

The question did not seem to penetrate. I felt her body quivering in the darkness. "I knew he'd come back . . . someday," she whimpered. "Oh, Jim . . ."

And she buried her face in the pillow. I softly repeated the question. Either she didn't hear or refused to answer it.

Flossie was, as I have said, peacefully asleep towards dawn when Dagobert made his escape. He rescued an uneaten roll and a peach with only one bite out of it, and I followed him out into the corridor. A night in the shower had not refreshed him.

I gave him the copy I had made of Saunders' telegram. He showed a flicker of interest when he read the phrase "result highly satisfactory" but looked discouraged when I told him how Bobby had explained it away. He had never put it into so many words but I knew Dagobert well enough to guess he was working on the assumption that Juan Roig was murdered.

He changed the subject. "How old would you say Flossie's son Pete is?"

"About eight."

"She met Jim after the Suez crisis," he nodded. "A

couple of years ago. Generous of Bobby to offer to bring the boy along. For that matter I wonder why he's going to Tabarca himself."

"He doesn't," I admitted, "seem to be enjoying the holiday. Margaret Penrose is getting on his nerves. So are you."

I told him that Bobby had wired to Saunders and asked him to telegraph further details about ourselves urgently to the Ritz-Carlton in Barcelona.

This, for some reason, restored Dagobert's humour and he crept down the corridor, promising to see me in Barcelona. I went back to bed where I got in my usual half an hour's sleep before the maid knocked at the door with breakfast.

She had just placed the tray beside the bed when the door burst unceremoniously open. It was Bobby. His curly hair was unbrushed and his blue eyes were wild. He breathed as though he had raced up the stairs three at a time.

"Now what?" I asked, in no mood for further drama, especially from Bobby.

"Now what!" he echoed in despair. "Now what indeed! This time perhaps you'll believe me when I say it's *too* much! Frankly, Jane, I've had it. She's . . . oh God! She's . . ."

"She's what?" I snapped at him. "Who is?"

"She's gone. Vanished. This time—Flossie!"

I sank back on my pillow, unable to do more than gesture feebly towards the bathroom door. It opened at that moment and Flossie, in her pink dressing gown, stepped back into the room. She gave a little hysterical scream at the sight of a man in the bedroom—or it may have been Bobby who gave the hysterical scream.

They both began to giggle and chatter.

I pulled the bedclothes over my head.

Chapter 14

Bobby's account of that day, the twenty-first of October, appeared in the next issue of *Home Truth*. It speaks of an early morning tour of the handsome southern capital of Toulouse with its wide, tree-lined avenues and quaint medieval streets, its rose-brick buildings and dreaming spires.

Refreshed by this, he goes on, the party set forth in glorious balmy weather for Carcassonne with its high walls, dizzy towers and frowning battlements. Romantic Carcassonne—peerless evocation of the age of chivalry, unsullied by the commercial hand of modern man, unspoiled and untouched. (Untouched, except by Viollet le Duc's elaborate Victorian restoration—though this is quoted from Margaret Penrose, not Bobby.)

Then on through teeming vineyards to Perpignan and the blue Mediterranean! Our hearts, Bobby wrote, quickened with the thought that across that shimmering expanse lay the tiny dream-island of Tabarca.

But first there was the thrill of sunny Spain—the click of castanets, dark-eyed Senoritas, the swirl of multi-coloured skirts, perhaps a glimpse of a *bravo toro* and a slim *torero* in his glittering "suit of lights."

Impatiently our laughing group reached Barcelona, the thriving colourful seaport where the old and the new blend and where—more thrilling still—a white yacht, a royal yacht, Henry Howard Hutton's own yacht, is moored, waiting to waft us at dawn across the wine-dark sea.

And speaking of wine, what a night awaits us here in Barcelona! *Barcelona de noche!* None of us will ever forget it! (One of us did forget it, but by and large Bobby did not exaggerate.)

And how were we all? How was our morale? That's what readers of *Home Truth* would be dying to know.

The Colonel, widely travelled, full of anecdotes, immensely entertaining, was in fine fettle. He lent distinction to our little party and made us proud of the G.B. plate on the back of the Rolls.

Margaret Penrose, too, was in her element. A woman of broad culture, she was invaluable in pointing out architectural subtleties, telling us the names of the rare wild flowers, and lending a skilled hand to the driver.

Jane Brown was her own poised self, calm in crisis, always helpful, a firm favourite with one and all.

Flossie Martin was in great form, relaxed and already looking happier, prettier for her rest from arduous domestic duties. She sent a special message of love to Jim and the two kiddies.

Derek and Ninette? It had been a slip of Bobby's pen—so often indiscreet!—to couple their names. *Milles pardons. Mais oui,* it could be safely whispered that Derek and Ninette were *loving* every moment of it!

Finally Bobby himself. (No mention of Juan Roig.) Bobby, your Bobby, was having the time of his young life. Not a care in the world. All sheer fun. Indeed he sometimes thought he was the luckiest of all the Lucky Seven to be travelling with such wholly delightful companions. If only every reader of *Home Truth* could be with us Bobby's happiness would be complete!

Next year—and this was a promise—there would be another Heavenly Fortnight, so Keep Your Subscriptions up to date and Don't Miss next week's grand issue which would contain, as well as your usual favourite features, special articles on: "Call Girls, the Revolting Facts," "What Belgravia Demands from a Masseur," and "Baby-Sitters: Some Disgusting Revelations."

Meanwhile, from the shores of the sparkling Mediterranean, from old Barcelona, hail and a reluctant farewell. From the pavement cafe in the Rambla where our little party has gathered comes the gay clink of glasses. It is the hour of the aperitif, the *aperitivo* as we call it here in España. It is as mild as midsummer, music and romance are in the air, our hearts beat high and there is laughter in our eyes . . . Bobby bids you *Adios.*

Bobby wrote all this long before we reached Barcelona; but the report was not in every detail inaccurate. For instance it was as mild as midsummer.

Ninette had changed into her 'Gee-Gee' (Glamour Gown) which caused excitement even among the strollers along the Rambla who since the tourist invasion are accustomed to most things. Dagobert and Albert, on the other side of the road, stopped and gaped. Impelled by the crowds behind them they shuffled forward but, hands in pockets, sneaked past again shortly afterwards. It was the hour of the *paseo* when Barcelona mills to and fro under the plane trees in the Rambla to work up an appetite for the vast meal eaten at about ten o'clock, at least by those who can afford it.

It was so warm that even Margaret Penrose had put on a printed paisley afternoon dress and carried her cardigan over her arm. Flossie was shining with perspiration.

I was as poised as it is possible to be on a chair placed on the edge of the kerb, brushed by passing trams, jostled by lottery-ticket sellers and hissed at by itinerant salesmen of "genuine" stolen diamonds.

There had been no crisis as yet to be calm in; and I rather doubted if I was a firm favourite with one and all. Bobby himself treated me with distant courtesy, tinged with disappointment, as though an old friend had let him down. What he had been trying to find out all day was, of course, just how much Flossie had told me. I had been evasive.

He approached our table in a flurry of busyness: so much to arrange, he explained, but we were not to despair: he'd be with us shortly. He observed that the Colonel and Derek were missing.

"Girls!" he reproached us coyly. "Surely not all alone? This will never do."

The four of us regarded our modest glasses of vermouth self-consciously. Derek had strayed off by himself; the Colonel had gone to root out his tropical kit. Bobby, distressed by their neglect of us, paused for a second beside me.

"Remember the telegram I sent last night from Toulouse?" he whispered. "Saunders has just answered. Interested?"

I said I was consumed with curiosity. His cheeks dimpled and his little blue eyes danced with boyish malice.

"Yes, I thought you might be. We'll have a little chat about it—later."

Delighted with himself, he bustled away.

"What's Bobby so pleased about?" Flossie asked.

"He's picked up more inside information," I said.

She avoided my eyes and muttered something about ten o'clock being a crazy hour to have dinner.

I had not been such a firm favourite today with Flossie either. She regretted having said so much last night, and had begged me several times not to repeat—especially to Bobby—what she had told me. "To have poured out the whole story of my life like that!" she had murmured in dismay. "What must you think?"

What I thought was that she had not poured out quite the whole story.

"That man over there!" Ninette said suddenly. "He's leering at me."

"Which one?" I asked. "I don't see anyone exactly averting his eyes."

"The tall one by the flower stall," she said. "As a matter of fact he looks rather nice, handsome in a kind of hungry, unsatisfied way. D'you know, I've seen him somewhere . . ."

She had seen him through the dining-room windows at the Grand Cerf in Chartres, wearing the same air of esurience. She readjusted the low neckline of her Gee-Gee and said in a shocked tone:

"I think it's awful the way men are always staring at girls!"

"But don't you dress in that interesting manner," Margaret Penrose inquired, "deliberately so they shall?"

Ninette blushed, began to protest, then grinned. "I suppose I do at that. . . . I wonder what's happened to Derek?" She lost interest in her drink and in Dagobert. "He's in one of his independent moods again. I just learned today that this girl Yvonne he was once so keen on . . . well, she's dead. I'd been teasing him about her. Not so bright." She bit her lower lip. "If dinner's going to be long I think I'll go for a walk."

I offered to go with her, but she shook her head and said: "Thanks, you needn't bother." We watched her cross to the centre of the Rambla on her high heels, her shapely bottom waggling beneath her tight skirt.

"I suppose she *is* quite safe," Margaret said.

"I'll back our Ninette to keep the Spanish wolves at bay," said Flossie patriotically.

"I wasn't," Margaret mused, "thinking entirely of Spaniards."

A waiter appeared to say that Senor Marcovitch had left instructions that we were entitled to one more drink if we wished.

"I'm beginning almost to like Bobby," Margaret said unexpectedly. "He's so consistently vulgar."

Flossie, whose attention had wandered, turned to her abruptly and demanded: "Who *were* you thinking of? What other danger could Ninette be in? Why isn't she safe? What possible danger could she—or anyone else—be in?"

We looked at Flossie in alarm. Her face was congested and her patterned rayon dress was soaked with sweat.

"I didn't mean to sound enigmatic," Margaret said hastily. "I merely meant there are wolves and wolves—and some of them wear normal English clothing."

She glanced at me quizzically. We had both just caught a glimpse of Ninette beside the flower stall where shortly before Dagobert had tarried, allegedly leering at her. Ninette had pause to adjust a stocking. Albert was nudging Dagobert who pretended to buy a newspaper at the kiosk next door. It was kind of Margaret to refer to his cycling breeches and striped polo-sweater as normal English clothing.

"I see what you mean," I nodded.

Behind the rimless glasses Margaret Penrose's grey eyes were amused. They were plainly more observant than I'd supposed.

"I sleep badly," she said, "and sometimes wander about hotel corridors. . . . Flossie, my dear, shall we take advantage of Bobby's generous offer and accept a second drink? I shall have gin this time."

Flossie said anything suited her; but before the cocktails arrived she had gone inside to powder her nose.

"She's very highly strung," Margaret frowned. "I hope she's had no bad news from home."

There had been letters for the party when we arrived, two for Flossie, both of which she had insisted on reading aloud to me. Jim said all was okay, they were missing her and the sink was stopped up. Pete reported that Pop was a smashing cook and they'd had tinned sardines and tinned salmon and tinned herrings and had made fudge only it hadn't got very hard and they'd eaten it with spoons and Doreen was sick on the carpet in the lounge.

"Have you noticed," Margaret asked, "how some people, when nervous, eat to excess? Popularly they're supposed to drown their worries in drink, but not infrequently they stupefy themselves with food instead. . . . Poor George grew immensely fat towards the end."

"And he was highly strung?" I said, for lack of anything better to say.

"He became highly strung." She rarely smoked, but when I offered her a cigarette she accepted it. "He had something to be highly strung about," she said as I lighted it for her. "Financial worries among other things. He left me poor and that distressed him too, I'm afraid. We had been very comfortably off."

"I thought you seemed familiar with the Rolls-Royce."

"It was an old Daimler actually," she smiled. "It went a couple of years ago, shortly after the horses and just before we moved from the Rectory to a cottage nearby—so much more convenient for the church, we said. The villagers said it was George's frequent trips to London—which was, of course, not untrue. I also wondered what George did in London. It was during these bouts of wondering that I developed my taste for gin, most unbecoming in a clergyman's wife."

She sipped modestly from the glass in front of her and, catching my eye, smiled.

"I've quite recovered since," she assured me. "You won't, I promise, have another hysterical female on your hands! Just a very talkative one. Do you mind?"

"Of course not."

"I developed a taste for gin," she reflected, "while George developed a passion for cakes and Cornish cream, soft-centred chocolates and baked jam roll—not the ingredients of high tragedy one would imagine! Low tragedy would perhaps be a better description. Poor George! He was a little ridiculous even in death."

She put her cocktail glass, almost untouched, back on the table and studied her plain wedding ring. The smoke from her cigarette stung her eyes. The ring had worn thin with the years, as her neck and shoulders had done.

"And yet I . . . or did I love him? Yes, I think so, in a maternal sort of way. I had no *other* children—thank heavens. If only he'd told me—in any case I'd half-guessed years previously—well, we could have gone abroad or something. Forgiving comes hard to me, but I could have tried. . . ." She stubbed out the cigarette. "Tell me, Jane, does everyone burden you like this with tedious details of her private life? You're a very good listener."

"Did George commit suicide?" I asked.

"Yes, he shot himself."

I found I had finished my gin and french and wondered if Flossie was going to return for hers. I took a chance and decided she wasn't. I needed the extra drink in order to frame the next question which Dagobert, during our hasty conference last night, had asked me to put. It sounded mild compared with what had already been said.

"How, Mrs. Penrose," I asked, "did you happen to go in for a competition in a magazine like *Home Truth*?"

She had been watching the *paseo* and didn't register the question for a moment. I repeated it lightly, as though making conversation. She looked at me indifferently and said: "I didn't, of course."

"You didn't!" I exclaimed stupidly. "You *must* have."

She shook her head. I finished Flossie's cocktail. Margaret's answer had been an echo—and an ominous one—of what Flossie had told me last night. I tried to think what it implied.

Neither of them, then, had entered the competition. It was

remotely conceivable that a typist had used Flossie's name on an entry form, as Bobby had glibly explained. But the odds against two such false entries winning would reach those astronomical figures Derek had quoted the other night in Chartres.

The conclusion was inescapable: the results had been tampered with. In other words, some at least of the so-called Lucky Seven had been hand-picked. Flossie and Margaret Penrose anyway. *Juan Roig?*

But why? And by whom? And what about the rest of us? Me, for instance. I, at least, had sent in an entry form, or Dagobert had sent in one for me.

But why should *anyone* be hand-picked? And hand-picked for what purpose?

My mind spun with queries. I hoped Margaret did not observe my confusion. I must have looked far from calm in a crisis.

I was waiting for the too-familiar story of the borrowed name and address filled in by someone on the staff of *Home Truth,* of Bobby begging her to help him out of an embarrassing situation, when Margaret spoke again. The pause in our conversation had been brief, though to me it had seemed very long.

"No, of course I didn't enter the competition," she repeated, looking at me in a puzzled way. "George did. He filled in my name. My maiden name, incidentally, and the address of my Nanny in Reading whom he knew I proposed to visit. It must have been one of the last things he did before he killed himself. George had his own peculiar sense of humour. That's why the first thing I said when Mr. Marcovitch called to tell me I'd won was, 'How amused George would have been.'"

I began to breathe more normally. Margaret Penrose, in fact, had won her place among the Lucky Seven much as I had done.

"Somehow I didn't think," I said with relief, "that *Home*

Truth was quite your weekly reading matter. Nor for that matter," I said as an afterthought, "your husband's."

"George was an assiduous reader of *Home Truth*. It always came on the same day as the *Church of England Times*, though in a plain wrapper." The social smile became a little fixed. "George used to retire with it into his study. Afterwards he would put it carefully on the fire. He would stir it gently with the poker," she pursued as though relishing these ritual details, "jab it until it burst into flames, and then watch it slowly, slowly *burn*."

Later, when I repeated this conversation to Dagobert, I tried to convey the curious quality of her voice when she pronounced the word "burn." She said it with a kind of rich satisfaction, as though in her mind's eye she could see something—or someone—loathsome roasting in hell. Forgiving, I remembered her saying, came hard to her.

Chapter 15

SINCE OUR ARRIVAL in Barcelona several hours previous to this talk with Margaret, Bobby had been almost as busy as he pretended to be. Our souvenir programme spoke of the Ritz-Carlton, dinner at Caracoles (*ristorante muy tipico*) and afterwards *Barcelona de Noche* with glimpses of the swirling skirts, castanets, etc. Next morning we were to embark on the royal yacht.

Somewhat to Bobby's surprise the yacht was actually there waiting for us when we reached Barcelona. It was the white steam yacht we had all seen pictures of and it flew the royal pennant of Tabarca, a golden sardine on a field of azure fishing net. It had recently been renamed the Princess Juana. Neither the Princess nor Henry Howard Hutton was aboard, but the captain had orders to put himself at the disposition of the party.

Now *Home Truth*'s responsibility for our entertainment ended as soon as we boarded the yacht—that is, once off the mainland we were the guests of Tabarca. Bobby at once grasped the possibility of saving the price of seven rooms at the Ritz-Carlton and, protesting slightly, we were installed in cabins on the moored yacht. The Ritz-Carlton, possibly, protested more vigorously; and calming the manager down with promises of future patronage and threats of bad publicity was one of the jobs which had occupied Bobby.

He also tried to avoid dinner at Caracoles. But Flossie had found out from the chief steward that only breakfast tomorrow was planned for, and we all mutinied.

"Of course, if dining on a millionaire's yacht isn't good enough for you," Bobby said, "have it your own way. I was only thinking what a thrill it would be for us all."

"Tied up to a filthy dock," Flossie said, "eating out of tins?"

The Colonel thought the bunk in his cabin looked rather short for him; since his cruising days with the Westminsters, yachts, he implied, had deteriorated.

"I'll lodge a complaint with Her Highness," Bobby promised. He was still nettled by our refusal to let the steward "toss up something in the galley."

Bobby's own quarters left nothing to be desired. He had appropriated the owner's suite with its gold and blue, air-conditioned drawing room, the bathroom tiled with heraldic sardines, and the royal bedchamber fitted with a small Louis

Quinze soda-fountain and built-in television set which threw an image on the ceiling above the oval bed.

Margaret and I caught him studying the elaborately embroidered bedspread. H. H. H.'s, picked out in gold thread, were cunningly intertwined with the royal arms of the Branzas. He was, I imagine, trying to visualise how the initials B. M. would look thus treated.

We watched him sit tentatively on the edge of the bed and give a quick little bounce. The action seemed to please him.

"Someday, you know," Margaret said to me in a tone clearly intended to be overheard by Bobby, "Mr. Marcovitch is going to venture out of his depth. Which would be a pity."

She went on to her cabin for her cardigan and Bobby appealed to me. He had gone a little pasty in the face.

"That woman's beginning to give me the creeps," he winced. "What's wrong with her? Did she want the royal suite herself? I only took it out of pure tact, so that no one could claim there was any favouritism. The skipper suggested it, more or less. Anyway *Home Truth* helped to pay for it. Oh, incidentally, I'm sorry I had to double you up with Ninette. The skipper tells me some of the cabins are still being redecorated. We could, of course, have put you with Flossie but . . . well, I daresay you've already found out all there is to know about Flossie."

He paused inquiringly.

"When was she married?" I asked.

He looked at me with his candid blue eyes. He had not been caught off balance.

"Her oldest child Pete is eight," he said ingenuously. "So . . . I make it at least eight years ago. What do you estimate?"

"Jim," I said, "emigrated to Canada during the Suez crisis. As though you didn't know."

He grinned. "Was that eight years ago? How the years roll by! Er, Jane, just a point to chew over— I suppose you wouldn't consider working for *Home Truth*? When we get home I may be in the position to offer you something fairly good. I'm quite serious."

"I think Margaret Penrose was quite serious too," I said, refusing to be side-tracked, "when she spoke just now of getting out of your depth. Bobby, why *did* you bring Flossie along on this trip?"

"Surely she explained all that?" He was still smiling, but he watched me warily. "Flossie didn't, er, suggest there were any strings attached? Because I assured her there aren't."

The others, impatient to go ashore again, joined us; and this unsatisfactory scrap of conversation was the last I had with Bobby until he met me a couple of hours later at the cafe in the Rambla to tell me that Saunders' report on Dagobert had been received.

Meanwhile, herding us together, he prepared in a perfunctory manner to fulfil the afternoon and evening entertainment programme as outlined in our souvenir programme. He drove us past the Gothic cathedral, out to the Sagrada Familia and around the bullring.

Then he dumped us at the cafe in the Rambla. This was when Derek, who was still on the waggon, wandered off by himself and the Colonel decided to return to the yacht to root out his tropical kit. Bobby gave his instructions to the waiter that we were to be supplied with two drinks each and hurried off. In spite of his reassurances, we all had the neglected feeling that the welfare of the Lucky Seven was not Bobby's sole preoccupation.

He was not his usual sunny self even when we sat down to dinner at Caracoles that evening. He fidgeted while waiting for the first course and doodled with one of his self-propelling pencils on the edge of the bill of fare. I wondered if the prices bothered him—for Bobby was alternately mean and lavish; but when I glanced at the pencil marks he had made I saw they were a series of interlaced H. H. H.'s.

"Interesting to see what he's like," I murmured as Bobby broke the point of his pencil.

Caracoles specialises in shellfish and atmosphere. It is in one of the narrowest, most crowded streets in the old part of Barcelona and outside—maddening the hungry passer-by—there is a charcoal grill before which chickens sizzle and brown as they turn on spits. It is, as our programme told us, "a little corner of real Spain, where authentic Spanish food is served at its best, a discovery to write home about."

It was, in brief, *muy tipico:* there wasn't a Spaniard in it.

There is nothing like mealtimes to re-establish group solidarity, and all seven of us were present. Actually we were nine, if you could include Dagobert and Albert who were gazing at the charcoal grill outside.

The first course was called *Zarzuela* and consisted of grilled shrimps, prawns, langouste, mussels, clams and other unidentified fruits of the sea. It cheered up Bobby considerably. It cheered me up too. My recent sense of oppression was plainly the result of being kept waiting until ten o'clock for dinner.

Flossie ate with her usual greed and speed, only betraying a return of nervousness once when she paused over a ring of octopus to reflect that you got ptomaine poisoning from shellfish. As though to set her mind at rest on this point she pitched with renewed enthusiasm into the chicken which followed.

"You'd think," Hugo Warrington said in my ear, "it was her last meal on earth."

"Bobby, too—" Margaret Penrose caught my eye—"seems to have developed a more than healthy appetite—though he may of course only be making sure he gets his money's worth."

Though to his face Margaret still addressed our host as Mr. Marcovitch she sometimes referred to him as Bobby, less, one felt, with familiarity than with contempt.

"When," she asked him, "do we reach Tabarca, Mr. Marcovitch?"

"About midday tomorrow, the skipper says. Princess Juana is going to meet us herself."

"And Mr. Hutton surely?"

"That's right," Bobby agreed with his mouth full. He swallowed the wrong way and prevented himself from choking by gulping down a glass of wine. I asked:

"When does the ordinary service to Tabarca arrive?"

"Ordinary service?"

"How do people who haven't yachts go to Tabarca?"

"They don't. There aren't any regular sailings. Tramp steamers occasionally call, once every few months."

"Oh," I said. It was the first time I had wondered how Dagobert was going to get there.

"What about the other wedding guests?" Derek said. "The press, et cetera?"

"There won't be any. Now I think of it *I'll* be the only member of the press." Bobby's professional satisfaction was momentary. "The skipper said H. H. put his foot down—everything quiet and dignified. Only the islanders and a few family friends who are already there. No wonder they call him Enrico El Loco."

"Rummy sort of way to get married," the Colonel agreed.

"Yeah . . . if he's going to be," Bobby murmured thoughtfully.

"He sounds mysterious and rather romantic," Ninette said. "Perhaps there's a great tragedy in his life and—" She flushed, remembering Yvonne's death, and bit her lip. "What sweet are we all having?"

She turned brightly to Derek as though to consult his opinion. Derek was, as a matter of fact, pretending to study the bill of fare.

"Oh, you're trying to read it upside-down," she blundered on. "I think I'll have *that*. What about you?"

She jabbed a nervous forefinger at a random item among the *postres*. A hovering waiter congratulated her on her choice. It was, he explained, something the chef had created in honour of *another* very beautiful lady who had once dined here—the famous film star, Miss de Carlo.

Poor Ninette had singularly bad luck that evening. She did her best to face the flaming pancakes the waiter brought her. They were called "*Crepes Yvonne.*"

Even Derek was a little sorry for her. He laughed out loud and said he would have them too. But, with a look of controlled eagerness which I recognised, he accepted the brandy which came with the coffee and to Bobby's chagrin had the waiter twice refill his glass.

The yacht, Bobby reminded us, sailed in the morning at five o'clock sharp, so doubtless we would prefer to go on board at once and leave *Barcelona de noche* until next week when we returned. Everyone said certainly not; the programme definitely promised us a night out in Barcelona, seven bars and night clubs, and we were going to visit every one of them. The spirit of mutiny was still strong. Bobby sighed and threw in his hand.

"Sometimes," he told me sadly as we regained the street, "I think I'll be glad to see the end of this bunch. Margaret, at her age, wanting to see 'night life'!" he said with disapproval. "Margaret and her George, whom I was so decent about. George and Margaret," he said in an altered tone of voice. He stopped dead in his tracks. "George and Margaret," he said again.

"Ring a bell?" I asked, watching Dagobert and Albert bolt up a nearby alley.

"Yeah," he muttered. And recovering his aplomb: "There was once a famous play by that name. Surely you remember it,

Jane. I wonder if there's a telegraph office open around here?"

"A fresh lead for Saunders?"

He ignored the question. "I'll meet you later, with the others at El Toro as arranged in our programme. It's just across the Rambla. Anybody will tell you." He broke off in exasperation. "Now what?"

It was Flossie a few yards ahead of us. She was holding on to a lamp post, fighting for breath. In the blue and green neon lighting of the bar beside us her face was ghastly.

The others, gathered round in consternation, were all talking at once. "Something she ate—seafood, always fatal—looks like ptomaine poison."

I don't know what ptomaine poisoning looks like, but I knew what Flossie looked like. I'd seen the same expression on her face before—last night in Toulouse when she burst into my room saying somebody was trying to kill her.

Chapter 16

LIKE LAST NIGHT the attack was brief. Flossie recovered almost at once and apologised for behaving stupidly. Yes, perhaps she had eaten something which disagreed with her. Yes, that must be it. There was no other explanation. She would be all right in a minute. If no one minded she would miss tonight's party and return to the yacht. Perhaps Bobby would drive her back.

Bobby, with suppressed irritation, explained that the Rolls-

Royce had already been put in a garage until the return trip.

"Well, I don't mind walking. It isn't far."

Derek had already stopped a taxi.

"I'll go back with her," I said.

"Thank you, Jane. But Bobby won't mind taking me."

Bobby, however, did mind. He was extremely sorry if Flossie didn't feel up to coming along with us. Unfortunately he had the rest of the group to consider. Besides, the taxi was quite capable of finding the yacht, unless of course Flossie really felt ill, in which case, well naturally . . .

Derek and I cut short Bobby's dithering by bundling Flossie into the taxi. Derek offered to come along too; but I shook my head and promised to rejoin the party at El Toro shortly. Flossie made a final, halfhearted appeal to Bobby, but when the taxi jerked forward she sank back on the seat as though relieved he hadn't come along. She reminded me of someone who has postponed a visit to the dentist.

"I'm being a lot of trouble to you lately," she said. "Of course Bobby's quite right. There is no reason why I shouldn't go back to the yacht by myself. I'm perfectly all right. It was just a turn."

"Like last night," I said.

"Yes," she said. "The same feeling, the feeling of being caught up with, closed in on . . . trapped."

"By whom?"

She shook her head. "I—I really don't know. I get sort of spots before my eyes and imagine things."

"Last night," I said, "you imagined *he* was in the room."

"Yes," she said quickly. "Jim says it's because I eat too fast. Indigestion . . . Is he, Bobby I mean, furious with me, do you think?"

"It doesn't matter if he is."

"No, I suppose it doesn't," she said doubtfully. "There's

nothing he can do about it. After all, Bobby and I are in this thing together."

"What thing?"

"Pretending I won the competition, of course," she said. "What else could there be?"

"That," I said, "is what I was wondering."

She said nothing for a long time. I had the feeling she was actually as puzzled as I was myself. At last she said:

"I wish I hadn't been bullied into this trip."

"Bullied?"

"You know what Bobby's like when he's crossed," she said. "Hysterical one minute, persuasive the next. At first when I said I wouldn't come to Tabarca he hinted sort of nastily at the power of the press. He said this typist at his office—the one who filled in my name—had once lived in Quebec and may have known me. I said: 'So what?' He said something about the world being a small place and tactfully talked about something else, detergents, I think. Then he asked my son Pete if he'd like to come along with Mummy. 'I'm sure,' he said, '*you* can make Mummy change her mind about coming on this lovely holiday.' And he smiled suddenly at me with those innocent blue eyes of his, knowing I'd have to agree."

"Bullied!" I repeated. "You mean blackmailed."

She hesitated, then slowly nodded. "You know about Pete," she said. "I see. Yes, I gave it away last night, didn't I?—that about not meeting Jim until a couple of years ago. All right. Jim is not Pete's father. You know that. I guess Bobby does too, though he's never exactly said as much. So what? When Jim used to come to that cafeteria where I worked and I realised we were falling in love I told him I had a child but no husband. Jim just laughed at me. Jim's like that. I wasn't the first girl that happened to, he said. Nor the last. What was I getting hot and bothered about? He admired me, he said, for being honest about it. He admired the way I worked to make sure Pete got everything he needed . . . and he asked, humbly, if he could help. Would I please 'do him the honour'—Jim talks like that sometimes—to marry him? I said no at first. For a long time I said no. Finally I said yes."

She sounded tired, as though resurrecting the old debate still exhausted her. I said gently:

"I'd have said yes in the beginning."

"Yes, anybody with any sense would."

"Surely you've never regretted the decision?"

"No. Never."

The taxi nosed round the statue of Columbus and in towards the docks. It was quieter in this part of town and we heard the lap of waves beyond the breakwater. In the distance a clock struck twelve. Against the skyline we saw the slim tower of the ancient church of Santa Maria del Mar. Flossie looked at it, then quickly looked down at her clasped hands. Churches by night, I remembered, had a curious effect upon her. Nevertheless I was startled when I saw she was noiselessly crying. I was impatient to get back to El Toro because I hoped that Dagobert, who also had a copy of our souvenir programme, would be there; but I felt more than ever reluctant to leave Flossie.

"You wouldn't, I suppose, care to change your mind and join the party?" I said. "I mean, unless you're still feeling off colour."

"I'm all right," she said. "A slight headache. I'll lie down and read for a while. Bobby will be back eventually."

The taxi stopped at the dock gates while we showed our passes to the sentry on duty. We drew up beside the gangway to the yacht where one of the crew stood smartly to attention.

"To you and to Jim," Flossie said, "living in sin probably sounds old-fashioned, kind of dated."

"Particularly when it happened eight years ago," I soothed

her. "As Jim would say, nothing to get hot and bothered about."

She sighed with envy rather than irony. "It must be nice not to know what mortal sin is."

This was beyond me and I said nothing. She said:

"I know, because I committed it."

I murmured something vague about having regretted it and made a fresh start. She shook her head and got out of the taxi.

"I lived in mortal sin," she said flatly. "And I still do. What's more, I intend to go right on in the same way."

Chapter 17

El Toro, our souvenir programme explains, means the Fighting Bull. "Here *toreros* come to spend a leisure hour after the perils of the *corrida,* idly watching pretty, dark-eyed *gitanas* swirl to the pluck of guitars and the click of castanets. We too shall share a glass of Manzanilla with them in this *muy tipico* spot tucked away in Barcelona's strange underworld—the Barrio Chino—which *Home Truth* has discovered for our especial entertainment."

I found El Toro easily by the red neon outline of a bull's head over the door and the *muy tipico* red plaques advertising Coca-Cola. I arrived after midnight when the place was beginning to liven up. In fact as I reached the door someone, violently impelled from within, hurtled across the road and landed with a thud in the gutter opposite.

He sat up promptly, clapped his hands a couple of times and shouted: "*Olé!*" His eyes blinked, widened and focused on me. He touched his cap politely.

"*Olé!*" he repeated and, exhausted by the effort, dropped off to sleep.

It was Albert.

Bobby was fussing in the doorway.

"Oh, there you are!" he said. "We were just going." He saw Albert and averted his eyes, pained at the sight of a fellow-countryman in such a state. "Unfortunately some people do not behave like gentlemen, and can't hold the drinks they cadge. Ninette encouraged him in order to annoy Derek. I don't know what's the matter with everyone tonight. In a most rebellious mood. And another thing!" he said. "There's a man inside who says his name is Brown."

"Any relation to the one we keep seeing in the driving mirror?"

He looked at me with his hurt expression. "I don't think it was very kind of you, Jane," he said. "After I've taken you so fully into my confidence. Of course I knew all the time it was Dagobert. Naturally. What puzzled me was why he was following us."

"Oh, you've had the report from Saunders. I'd forgotten."

"Yes," he said with satisfaction. "Very interesting."

"Anything about Margaret Penrose in it?"

The faint smile vanished. "If that's her name . . ."

"Were you," I asked, "the 'jury' who picked out the Lucky Seven?"

"Yes." He sounded bitter. "Sometimes I think I could have done better."

"The rest of us *were* winners, I suppose? I mean, none of the other results were cooked?"

"Don't suggest things like that!" he said. "I've enough on

my mind as it is." He curbed his impatience to join the others. "So, Flossie—er—explained that extraordinary confusion over her entry form. Most unfortunate."

"At least most extraordinary," I said.

"You don't sound convinced."

"I'm not, very."

"So long as dear Flossie is happy . . ."

"She isn't," I told him. "In fact she's waiting up to have a word with you."

"Is she?" he said. "Is she indeed? What about?"

"About calling off the trip to Tabarca."

"What? I hope I won't have to . . . But why, Jane, *why*?"

"Is she beginning to guess the real reason you brought her along?"

"I don't know why people are always so mistrustful," he complained. "Sometimes even you."

"Yes," I agreed.

This saddened him. "As you know," he said, "I've always thought of you not as a mere prize-winner but as a friend." He gave me his shy, hesitant smile. "Speaking as your friend then —just a suggestion—would it not perhaps be wiser if you left these little problems to Bobby?"

Glancing into his earnest blue eyes it struck me suddenly that the advice was worth listening to. Bobby, in his earnest mood, sent shivers down my spine.

Our programme spoke of "a glass" of Manzanilla at El Toro and I realised why Bobby was in a hurry to get back to the party. He was too late; during his absence they had ordered more drinks.

Waiters were recklessly uncorking bottles. Ours was the only table with paying customers, and dark-eyed *gitanas*, kept at bay while Bobby had been present, clustered eagerly around. *Toreros* were closing in with empty glasses. Among them I recognised Dagobert.

Bobby raised his voice to attract attention. "Come along, everybody! We're behind schedule. You might try to help me, Jane, and not just stand there grinning. Come now, we've had a lovely time and we must go."

No one, except Margaret, paid any attention to him. "Do relax and enjoy yourself, Mr. Marcovitch," she said. "Since . . ." She smiled at him gently. "Since . . . well, who knows what tomorrow may bring?"

The Colonel raised his glass to Bobby. The *toreros* courteously followed suit. "You mean," he chuckled, "since Marcovitch is paying for the party, eh?"

Dagobert, maddened with flamenco music and Manzanilla said:

"No. I am."

"Trying to ingratiate himself," Bobby muttered, but he accepted a glass of wine, mollified though puzzled by Dagobert's offer to pay.

The Colonel, explaining that he used to strum a bit on the banjo in India, had borrowed a guitar and was picking out a tune which we eventually identified as "Clementine." Derek returned to the brandy he had obtained when Bobby wasn't there. Ninette pretended to ignore him.

She threw her arms around Dagobert and made him dance with her. The staff of El Toro resented this amateur intrusion, but consoled themselves with our Manzanilla. Dagobert looked at me sheepishly.

"Isn't he sweet!" Ninette cried. "I found him this afternoon in the Rambla. He's promised to come to Tabarca with us."

"*Olé!*" said Derek with a trace of sarcasm.

"How does he propose to get there?" Bobby said. "Swim?"

"And Albert!" Ninette remembered. "Where's Albert? I love Albert too. I love everybody tonight. Even Bobby."

Bobby thanked her sourly and said that Albert was outside in the gutter where he belonged.

"Where we all belong," Derek muttered darkly.

The party seemed to have thawed out. I found a glass and tried to catch up.

Ninette and Dagobert returned to the table exhausted—at least Dagobert was exhausted—and the guitarist rescued his guitar from the Colonel, together with the Colonel's packet of Players.

One of the *gitanas* danced while the *toreros* refilled their glasses, pausing occasionally to punctuate her performance with dutiful *Olés*. Dagobert continued to ingratiate himself. Derek took refuge behind his dark glasses.

Bobby snatched away a newly opened Manzanilla bottle before the *gitanas* got at it and retired sulkily to a deserted corner of the room. I wandered over to comfort him.

He wouldn't speak to me at first. Apparently I had let him down by not co-operating in the matter of making everyone leave. He continued to study the telegram he had taken from his pocket. It ran to two pages. The Colonel had wandered over after me.

"Sorry to butt in," he said. "But who is he?"

"His name," said Bobby, "is Dagobert Brown. Fourth son of Sir Clovis Brown. Published a book on Adam de la Halle, a thirteenth-century *trouvere*—whatever that is. Has dabbled, unsuccessfully, in private detection. No visible means of support. No fixed address. Oh, and he's married to Jane."

"Lucky fellow," Hugo said. "The womenfolk seem keen on his coming to Tabarca with us. I used to know a Clovis Brown. Made his own mead."

"Bobby," I improvised, "wants Dagobert to come with us."

"Why not?" the Colonel said. "Does he play bridge? He can take that chap—what's his name?—Juan Roig's place."

Bobby concentrated on the second page of the telegram.

"Thus bringing up our number to seven again," I encouraged.

Derek Upjohn had joined us. He felt for the edge of the table to steady himself. "Seven again," he nodded. "At least for the moment."

"What do you mean by that?" Bobby snapped.

"I may drop out myself," Derek said.

Ninette had followed him. "Don't be silly." She gave his hand a reassuring squeeze. "If you go back to London so will I."

Margaret and Dagobert, feeling deserted, came over to us, pursued by waiters and *gitanas*. A blue-chinned torero, who had once swept sand in a bullring and now owned El Toro, reported that we were out of drinks again, and besides this was a new table.

Fresh bottles were produced. The same *gitana* danced again. Her companions clicked perfunctory castanets while the *toreros* drank our health with polite but dwindling enthusiasm. We were still the only foreigners present and the repeat performance lacked spontaneity.

Hugo Warrington cupped a match to my cigarette. He was concerned about Ninette's renewed flirtation with Dagobert. I too thought she was overdoing it.

"Very civilised of you, my dear," he murmured, "to ignore the situation. Pity our friend Upjohn is not equally broadminded. I heard him ask one of the waiters about trains back to London. Amazing what sensible young men will do in the heat of passion . . . Incidentally, your husband reminds me strikingly of Lesparre-Perret. The young one, I mean. You remember—he ran off with that nude danseuse, now what was she called? La . . ."

It was another of tonight's unfinished conversations. At that moment there was a sudden stamping of feet. The *torero* emitted a warlike whoop. His companions downed drinks and rallied fiercely around. Our *gitana* guests scampered away as though the place were on fire.

A fresh group of tourists had come in.

Spurred by new blood, everyone burst into a wild flamenco ensemble. In the subsequent stampede, thunderous clapping of hands, flurry of petticoats and rasping of guitars, conversation took place in inaudible shouts.

The act was reaching its climax when Albert reappeared. The collar of his white shirt was neatly folded outside the collar of his blue flannel blazer and the mud had been brushed off his nylon trousers.

Albert caught the spirit of the dance at once and stalked the prettiest of the *gitanas* with an expression of passionate disdain. He snapped his fingers at her and stamped violently on her feet with his tennis shoes. He shouted '*Olé,*' whirled dizzily and landed with a discordant crash in the lap of a guitarist.

The Anglo-Saxon contingent applauded enthusiastically, and the management of El Toro threw him out again.

Dagobert and I picked him up from the street where formal introductions took place. Albert said he was pleased to meet me, Dagobert had often spoken of me. He had also read that piece in *Home Truth*, very beautifully written: "that about being the sort of woman who gets her own way and not liking to leave Dagobert even for two short weeks." He sighed and concluded obscurely:

"Mother was just the same."

"A woman of great character," Dagobert said.

"That's right," Albert said glumly. "Whatsay we go in and bust up the place?"

He stuck out what there was of his chin. Like his mouth it was small and engagingly rabbit-like. He had big ears and, though he couldn't have been more than thirty, his sandy hair was thinning on top.

"I'd like to take a swing at the one calls hisself Bobby. How," he asked Dagobert, "did you make out with Ninette?"

"Not badly," I said.

"She wants us to come to Tabarca," Dagobert said. "You especially."

"I bet," Albert said, unconvinced. "Do we go? Personally I don't mind. Makes a change from the scooter." His undistinguished though not unpleasant features were resigned, as though he were accustomed to having such decisions made for him. "Tasty little number, that Ninette, now you mention it," he reflected, brightening. "I say! Why not get hold of her and make a night of it?" He remembered me. "You too," he added kindly.

"Albert hasn't made a night of it since last night," Dagobert said. "That's why we were late reaching Barcelona this afternoon; at first the police in Toulouse hated to let him go. Still, it saves hotel bills."

"He's always passing remarks like that," Albert said. "I tell him a chap wants to see a bit of life. Eat, drink and be merry, I tell him, for as they say tomorrow you—"

"Do stop talking rubbish!" Bobby Marcovitch interrupted. He had come out in search of Dagobert whom he suspected of trying to escape without settling the bill. "You're making a perfect spectacle of yourselves out here nattering in the—"

"For as they say," Albert repeated imperturbably, "tomorrow you die." He fixed Bobby with myopic eyes. "You, too," he said. He thought it over and said: "You, especially."

At that moment the owner of El Toro clapped Bobby on the shoulder. He, in his turn, suspected Bobby of trying to escape without settling the bill. Bobby squealed hysterically, but did not lose his head to the extent of forgetting to wave the bill on to Dagobert.

The rest of the party emerged. Our group was immediately swelled by three bootblacks, a passing Swedish couple, a man from Jersey City who had attached himself to Ninette and was telling her about the wholesale-button trade, and half a dozen aggressive children. All had definite ideas about where to go next. Actually it was laid down in our programme that the next stop was El Rincon—another *Home Truth* discovery where arrangements had been made months ago through a tourist agency—but Bobby threw up his hands in helpless inadequacy.

In the general confusion Dagobert borrowed a couple of thousand pesetas from me to pay off the owner of El Toro. Bobby at once led the way to El Rincon. We straggled after him, guided by the children, an interpreter who spoke fluent Arabic and two blind lottery-ticket sellers. Albert wanted to bring the pretty *gitana* along too, but Ninette dissuaded him. He took her firmness as though it merely illustrated a universal law.

"You know something," he said to me with wonder. "*All* women remind me a bit of Mother."

Albert's mother, Dagobert told me, had recently died, and in certain stages of intoxication—unfortunately brief—Albert still felt her restraining hand.

Dagobert and I fell in beside Bobby as we wandered through the narrow alleys of the Barrio Chino.

"About tomorrow . . ." Dagobert began.

Bobby winced at the word.

"I know how you feel," Dagobert sympathised. "As Mrs. Penrose said, you never know what it will bring, do you?"

"Margaret," I explained, "is looking forward to Bobby's meeting H. H."

"Yes, so am I."

Bobby still said nothing. Dagobert, attempting to keep the conversation alive, reflected:

"There's no doubt about it, it *is* better to travel hopefully than to arrive. Still," he pointed out, "you haven't arrived yet, have you?"

"I don't care for that remark," Bobby said.

"It was meant to make you feel uneasy," Dagobert admitted.

"In a way I wish I could do something for you."

"You can. Go away. Why have you been following me anyway?"

"Strictly speaking, I was following Jane."

"Yes, we noticed!" Bobby said, stung into sarcasm. "Flirting with an innocent child like Ninette! Flattering a poor old thing like Margaret Penrose. Splashing your money around!"

"It's part of his work," I said. "He dabbles unsuccessfully in detection, remember?"

"What's he detecting?"

"Things like Juan Roig's death?" Dagobert suggested, and when this made no impression: "I also want to meet Flossie."

"What for?" Bobby asked. "Oh, I suppose Jane has . . ."

"And, naturally, H. H.," Dagobert said.

Bobby looked impatient, as though we were wasting his time, but he did not quicken his step. Finally he murmured:

"I don't see the connection."

"There *is* a connection," Dagobert assured him. "I'll let you know when I work it out."

Bobby's smile was earnest—the same earnest smile which had made my hair rise earlier in the evening when he advised me to leave such little problems to Bobby. He said softly:

"I shouldn't try to work it out."

"Oh . . . is that what Juan Roig did?" Dagobert asked with interest.

Bobby stopped to light a cigarette. His hands were steady, but he had difficulty with his lighter.

"I don't know what you're talking about."

"About Juan Roig," Dagobert said patiently. "I've been wondering what reason you could have had for pushing him into the channel."

"You can get into trouble for saying things like that."

"Did you push him into the channel?"

Bobby abandoned his cigarette-lighter. He was making gurgling sounds like a hot-water system when the boiler is about to burst.

"I think he means no," I interpreted.

"Probably," Dagobert nodded, examining him more critically. "He doesn't look like a murderer. He looks more like the kind that gets murdered. . . . Unless he killed Juan Roig in self-defence."

Bobby let off a little pressure in a controlled hiss.

"Say that again in front of witnesses."

"You didn't kill him in self-defence?" Dagobert said. "Then we'll have to think of something else. Awkward that Margaret Penrose saw you go up on deck with him during the channel crossing. If I were you I shouldn't go up on deck with anyone during tomorrow's crossing. . . . Ah, this looks like El Rincon."

I recognised the Coca-Cola plaques and heard the familiar sound of castanets. The bootblacks, who were not allowed inside El Rincon, were arguing the merits of the Milk Bar across the road which, they insisted, was even more *muy tipico.* Albert, *olé*-ing happily, led the way in.

Bobby held back in spite of his desire to get there first and do the ordering himself. He gazed at the narrow door like a claustrophobic who dreads enclosed spaces. He was breathing asthmatically.

"If," he said, "you think I'm frightened . . ."

Dagobert continued to study him dispassionately. "Yes, in your shoes, I should be too," he said. "It's one thing to blackmail simple people like Flossie Martin, but quite another to tackle men like Henry Howard Hutton."

Chapter 18

A BAR OR TWO later Bobby said to us: "But I have no intention of, er, bringing pressure to bear on Henry Howard Hutton."

"Then there's nothing to worry about, is there," Dagobert said. "Let me buy you a drink."

"No," said Bobby surprisingly, "let me buy *you* a drink. Champagne, Jane?"

The barman brought us a bottle of the sweet sparkling wine that Bobby called champagne. We had left the rest of the party to pursue the official schedule in a night club next door.

"Nothing at all to worry about," Bobby said, eyeing himself from various pleasant angles in the mirrors which surrounded our table. "I shall certainly not tackle Henry Howard Hutton. You will."

"I will?"

"You are now one of the Lucky Seven. You have taken Juan Roig's place."

I waited for an explanation of this startling change in Bobby's policy. Dagobert too was puzzled.

"Am I," he asked doubtfully, "blackmailing you? Or are you blackmailing me?"

"A word which is absolutely taboo in *Home Truth* circles," Bobby said with distaste. "Er, the latter."

He finished piercing a large Havana cigar with a toothpick. A *Guardia Civil* paused in the door. Bobby waited until the policeman had walked on again and said:

"Don't be nervous, dear boy. Very unlikely they will have circulated your description. Does Jane know about it?"

"Only in broad outline," Dagobert said. "About what?"

"I like to think of us more as colleagues," Bobby divagated maddeningly. "As unsalaried workers for *Home Truth*. We might arrange a small expense account later. I want us to be happy together." He toyed with the telegram he had been studying in El Toro. By now it was dog-eared. "Perhaps you'd be more at ease if I destroyed this."

He put a match to it and with the flame lighted his cigar. He knew its contents by heart, of course, but the gesture seemed conciliatory.

"It's from Saunders," I told Dagobert, "and it's about how you wrote a book on Adam de la Halle."

"It gets more interesting from there on."

"I thought it might."

"It touches on your recent employment with the firm of Jenkins and Sons of the Great North Road. You were to test a motor-scooter they are about to put into production. Need I go on?"

"Yes, go on for a while," Dagobert said.

"I had hoped to spare Jane," he said, "but since we're all pulling together . . . Now, Jane will tell you that Bobby never beats about the bush, but comes straight to the point. Yes, I will be frank with you. The thought of talking to H. H. did disturb me. In fact it scared the pants off me. I always prefer to have these preliminary chats through a third party. My own —call it unconventional if you like—er—business technique. It saves such wear and tear on the nerves. I can't tell you, dear boy, what a load you've taken off my mind. And you will like working for *Home Truth*. You'll find the job fascinating, never monotonous, interesting people, full of—"

"That point you always come straight to," I prompted.

"Ah yes," he said genially. "Dagobert has been very naughty. In order to leave England hurriedly he 'borrowed' the motor-scooter he was meant to test. Mr. Jenkins is furious and has gone to the authorities. There is an extradition order out against poor Dagobert because, it seems, he also borrowed his travelling expenses from the firm's safe—several thousand pounds in notes and negotiable securities!"

"You're making this up, of course," I said. "I mean Saunders—"

I caught sight of Dagobert's face in one of the mirrors. It was without expression, but it silenced me. Bobby said shortly:

"I do not pay Saunders to make things up."

"Do you pay him? Or is he—like me—an unsalaried worker?"

"He is reliable," Bobby said, "like everyone else who works for me, because he has to be."

Dagobert refilled Bobby's glass.

"About this fascinating work . . ."

"I hoped we shouldn't have to belabour the point," Bobby said. "In *Home Truth* we try to avoid crudity."

"Yes, I've read the magazine."

Bobby settled back with his cigar. Like all creative artists he enjoyed talking shop. "We have a smallish circulation and our profits, at least on paper, are modest. Our undeclared earnings are more satisfactory. Unhappily some of our best stories remain unpublished. I keep them locked up in my own safe."

He sighed, saddened by the waste of so much good material. Dagobert asked:

"What do we do about libel?"

"It's quite simple," Bobby said. "We publish no libel."

"Last week's article about the nursing home in Eastbourne

for tired businessmen. You wouldn't call that libellous?"

"Extremely," Bobby smiled. "If there was such a place."

"What about the photograph of Lord Paddington?"

"A hired model. There is no such person as Lord Paddington."

Dagobert was overcome with admiration. Bobby, pleased, enlarged.

"*Home Truth*," he said, "has the reputation of being the most daring publication in England. Sometimes its revelations shock even me, though I write them all myself. Actually we print nothing but fiction, interspersed with normal gossip-column stuff. Our really hot feature articles expose people and institutions that do not exist. Our readers are naturally eager to believe the worst and never doubt the authenticity of what we write. . . . Our readers are also very, very eager not to be mentioned in *Home Truth* themselves."

Dagobert, impressed by such ingenuity, filled Bobby's glass again. "And that's how we make our 'undeclared' earnings," he nodded.

"You mean," I said, "people pay *not* to be talked about in *Home Truth*?"

"According to their means—and of course according to what they have to hide," Bobby said.

"And how," Dagobert asked, "do we collect our 'unpublished' material?"

"The public is most co-operative," Bobby said. "People practically queue up to expose their neighbours. Then we get thousands of anonymous letters, generally valueless, but sometimes containing nuggets of gold. You learn to smell them."

"Whom does *Home Truth* belong to?" Dagobert asked.

"At the moment H. H. owns the controlling interest. He bought it with a job lot of other periodicals which were on the rocks and has never grasped its potentialities. I send him quarterly cheques, representing fifty-one per cent of our profits—our declared profits, of course. It struck me he might be willing to let his share go."

"Fairly cheap," Dagobert suggested.

Bobby grinned. "What with his new interests—Tabarca, marrying royalty . . ."

"Before leaving London," Dagobert said, "you spoke of not being able to 'guarantee' the wedding."

"People change their minds," he said. "The Princess Juana, for instance. One can't be too cautious."

"What's H. H. like?"

"You know how these eccentric millionaires are," Bobby said vaguely. "Er, eccentric."

"No," Dagobert said. "How did he make his money?"

"According to the official press-release—written, very badly, by himself—he sold papers as a barefoot orphan in the streets of Quebec, saved every penny and fought his way to the top, the old corny story. In reality he was born in Liverpool and was taken to Canada by his parents to avoid the war. Some valueless land they got hold of turned out to contain uranium and brought in millions. These he shrewdly invested and during the post-war boom made a fortune. He changed his name, added the Junior to make it sound more convincing and built up this legend of publicity-shunning mystery. Six or seven years ago he hadn't a penny."

"Have you ever met him?"

"Well, actually, no. I haven't met a lot of people whose biographical details I am familiar with. I leave personal contacts to my, er, trusted colleagues."

"Like Dagobert," I said.

"Just so." Bobby nodded smugly. "Incidentally England and Tabarca have no extradition treaty, so once we arrive the British authorities won't be able to touch you. You're travelling on a false passport, of course. Have a cigar."

He produced one, smaller than his own, but, he assured Dagobert, of similar quality. Dagobert pricked the end with a toothpick and put the toothpick in his mouth.

"I don't see anything very unpublishable in what you've told us about H. H.," he said.

"I've skipped one or two details."

"I was afraid of that. Assuming that the British authorities can't touch me, what about the Tabarca authorities?"

"We needn't worry about them."

"You needn't," I said.

"A medieval dungeon," Dagobert mused, lighting his toothpick, "would be interesting to study from the inside. . . . What were the details you skipped?"

"Let's hope you can keep it vague and friendly," Bobby said. "I loathe scenes. You could, when talking of this and that, tell him he reminds you of a man you knew eight years ago in Quebec, a man named, let's see, Howard Turner . . ."

"Was that H. H.'s name?"

"That was the name he once absent-mindedly used to endorse a cheque I sent him," Bobby said. "He had scored it out and re-signed it Henry Howard Hutton. Which started me thinking—and checking up. A long and costly process, involving a trip to Canada."

"But rewarding," Dagobert said.

I asked: "And had Howard Turner a criminal record?"

"He had," Bobby smiled briefly, "a record."

Dagobert frowned and said: "She will have changed in eight years. What if H. H. doesn't recognise her?"

Bobby toyed with his sapphire ring. "We might have another bottle of champagne," he said. "Yes, there is that."

"You could prod his memory."

"If necessary, *you* could," Bobby said quickly. "If he pretends not to know what you're talking about . . . er, what are you talking about?"

"Pete," Dagobert said.

"That's what I thought. Is that drink coming?"

"Pete who?" I said. "Not—you don't mean—not Flossie's son! The one Bobby wanted to bring to the wedding!"

"To his father's wedding—a sentimental touch on Bobby's part," Dagobert suggested.

"H. H. is Pete's father? But Flossie has never even heard of Henry Howard Hutton."

"She's heard of Howard Turner."

"And they knew each other eight years ago in Quebec?" I asked stupidly.

"Since they had a child," Bobby said, "yes, they presumably knew each other."

"The record you mentioned?" Dagobert said. "Oh, I see. They were *married!*"

"At a registrar's office," Bobby nodded. "H. H. disappeared a week or two afterwards and Flossie never saw him again. Just in case he's forgotten the incident . . ." He fumbled in his wallet and took out an elongated strip of paper. "A photostat copy of the marriage certificate."

He hesitated and gave it to Dagobert. He seemed relieved to get it off his person—like a housebreaker ridding himself of incriminating tools.

"Don't use it unless he gets tough."

"There was no divorce?"

Bobby shook his head. While the bartender uncorked a second bottle of fizzy wine I tried to digest this. Flossie, then, was still married to Henry Howard Hutton, ne Turner. Fantastic as this seemed, it cleared up a couple of puzzling points.

It explained why Flossie's photograph in *Home Truth* had been blurred: H. H. might otherwise have recognised her. It explained Flossie's determination to continue living in what she called sin. Though Jim Martin didn't know it their marriage was not, of course, legal.

The wine was luke warm, but Bobby didn't notice. As a rule he drank little and didn't know one wine from another. He refilled his glass, in an expansive mood.

"Don't look so troubled, dear boy," he said to Dagobert. "We are really bringing joy and light to one and all. Soon H. H. will be the happy, though strictly speaking illegal, consort of the lovely Princess Juana, while Flossie can go on living in blissful bigamy with her Jim and the kiddies. *Home Truth* will have a new owner which will permit me to offer you—if you handle this little affair tactfully—a suitable reward. Even Jane—we'll find a place for her on the staff. Vetting anonymous letters, perhaps. Alas!" he remembered with genuine regret, "the story of Enrico El Loco—Whose Wife Watched Him Wed Another—must remain locked in our hearts. You will make it clear to him tomorrow that it is *Home Truth*'s dearest wish that not a word of all this should be even hinted at in print. Drink up, dear boy."

Next door our party remained unaware of our absence. For the third time that evening we all had our shoes cleaned. I thought of Flossie waiting up until Bobby returned to the yacht. Had something given her a clue to the plot in which she was being used?

I thought in an equally muddled way of Saunders' telegram about Dagobert. I knew there must be a rub somewhere; but when the Civil Guard glanced into the door again I held my breath until he walked on. Dagobert too seemed subdued. Bobby, on the other hand, was full of confident euphoria. His cigar was burning beautifully and he looked every inch the successful young executive.

The commissionaire from the night club next door entered the bar and approached us. Bobby waved him grandly aside.

"Can't one have a moment's peace?" he said. "Let them look after themselves for a while. I think, dear boy, that more or less covers the background of the affair we were discussing. I want you to feel you have my full backing. That's why I have been so frank. What we have said here has been in the strictest confidence. I know, of course, that I can trust you."

He paused as though to allow an invisible secretary to complete shorthand notes.

"And so," he concluded, "if there are no further questions, perhaps we should . . . What's this fellow want? Why does he keep jabbering in dago?"

It was still the commissionaire from the night club and he wanted a word with Bobby. Bobby flicked the ash of his cigar at him and rose, stepping delicately onto the bootblack who had begun on his left shoe. He tossed the boy a coin and flicked a hand towards the bar.

"Settle for the drinks, will you, dear boy?"

The doorman at last made it clear that he had a message for Senor Marcovitch which must be signed for. Bobby tried to extricate himself from the clutches of the bootblack who was loudly protesting that he did not do single shoes for half price. Bobby remained gracious but harassed.

"Jane," he said, "you might sign for it, if you will be so kind. If the matter requires my personal attention do not hesitate to let me know."

The message, a telegram, had been brought to the night club from the Ritz-Carlton where the movements of the *Home Truth* party were known. Dagobert began to intervene, but decided to let me open it. Bobby, recovering suddenly from his illusions of grandeur, kicked the bootblack out of the way and snatched it from my hand. I had just had time to see it was, as usual, signed Saunders.

We all crowded round. The telegram meant little to the bootblack, the commissionaire and the bartender; but its effect on Bobby was immediate. He bolted through the door with it and was sick in the street.

What it said was:

"George and Margaret Faversham Repeat Faversham Stop No Repeat No Details yet re Dagobert Brown."

Chapter 19

"I'M GLAD THERE'S no extradition order out against you," I said to Dagobert, "though it's a pity about the several thousand pounds in notes and negotiable securities. They'd come in useful if you have to go on paying for Bobby's drinks."

But Bobby did no more drinking that night. We found him outside, an ashen and sober figure, squirming with (among other things) humiliation at being discovered in such a condition by Albert who stood regarding him with repugnance.

"Unfortunately," Albert said, "some people do not behave like gentlemen."

Margaret, who was with him, sensed that the moment was not one for pleasantry.

"Anything serious?" she asked me.

"I don't know," I said. "Was your married name Faversham?"

"Faversham?" the Colonel said. "I once knew a chap named Faversham. Athenaeum Club, I fancy."

Bobby at that moment recovered the use of his legs and muttering something about "arrangements" hurried off. Halfway to the Rambla he broke into a run.

Dagobert strode after him. At the corner of the Rambla a

cruising taxi slowed down and Bobby with remarkable agility wrenched open the door and jumped in. I found Dagobert wildly signalling for another taxi. By the time it arrived Bobby's taxi had disappeared around the statue of Columbus.

"Where are we going?" I asked as I was jerked back onto the seat beside Dagobert.

"I'd like to be there when he sees Flossie," he said.

We were held up by the guards at the dock gates. They recognised me, but wanted to see Dagobert's passport. It was, I observed, in his own name. I was still unused to the idea that he was not a fugitive from justice.

"Saunders' telegram giving your alleged criminal record," I said. "Oh, of course, you composed it yourself and sent it this morning from Toulouse."

"I telephoned London and had it sent from there. It seemed a good idea at the time."

"It was a quick way of getting friendly with Bobby," I agreed. "Pity the telegram he's just received had to disillusion him. What does he do next?"

"What," Dagobert said, "do *we* do next?"

"Mind our own business?"

The suggestion clearly tempted him. "Keep the taxi," he said, jumping out. "I'll be back shortly."

He was back sooner than he had expected. The yacht's gangway had been raised. The crew on deck had received instructions from Bobby to lower it only for members of the *Home Truth* party.

A light in Flossie's cabin was still burning. It went out as I watched and a moment later a light in the royal suite—Bobby's quarters—went on. Dagobert was prowling around the moored yacht, eyeing hawsers. An armed dockguard paused and eyed Dagobert. I volunteered to go aboard alone.

"From now on," he said, "we travel together—preferably on the scooter back to London."

He gave the taxi-driver, however, the address of the Sol y Sombra, the final night club on our advertised programme.

The more I considered our position the more inclined I felt to take a chance on the scooter. Not that our position wasn't strong; it was merely hopeless. Bobby had shown us every card in his hand, and there was nothing we could do about it. Or rather, anything we did would make matters worse.

We could—and probably ought to—tell Flossie precisely why Bobby was taking her to Tabarca, if she didn't, by now, know. This would mean the end of her idyll in Lathomstowe, of Jim and the children, followed by a divorce from H. H. which as a Catholic she wouldn't consider valid. It might mean criminal proceedings against her for bigamy.

We could give Henry Howard Hutton the photostat copy of his marriage certificate. This would effectively destroy his prospects of marrying Princess Juana, unless it landed us in the medieval dungeon Dagobert had mentioned for attempted blackmail.

We could go to the police and explain what Bobby proposed to do. But he hadn't done anything yet and would simply deny the whole story. He wasn't carrying H. H.'s marriage certificate. We were.

The only positive result of such action would be to prevent Bobby from becoming sole owner of *Home Truth*—a minor satisfaction. The price would be disrupting the peace of the Martin family, and, for all we knew, the happiness of H. H. and the Princess Juana. It hardly seemed worth it.

Our simplest course seemed to be to disappear, leaving Bobby to do his own blackmailing. Alternatively, Dagobert said without enthusiasm, we could hang around and do a little blackmailing ourselves; in view of what we knew Bobby would certainly offer us both a free trip to Tabarca.

I told Dagobert what Margaret Penrose had told me this afternoon. Her husband George was evidently the hero of one of those "unpublished" stories Bobby kept locked in his safe. George—the Reverend George Faversham—had contributed to *Home Truth*'s "undeclared" profits until, bled white and driven insane with worry, he had finally shot himself.

It shed a lurid light on the ingenious activities of *Home Truth's* editor. Bobby, it was true, would never have dared to publish George Faversham's name, address or description. But, we later learned, *Home Truth* had printed an article shortly after George's financial contributions ceased, and shortly before he killed himself. It was entitled: This Choirboy Had the Face of an Angel—Who Fell! And he could have been *Your* Son!

We wondered what other stories remained locked in Bobby's safe? Was there, for instance, anything about Juan Roig? Or about any of the other members of the so-called Lucky Seven?

On the surface it seemed unlikely that Bobby would choose for companions people he was blackmailing. But did he necessarily know his victims by sight? We knew he did his blackmailing through third parties, "trusted colleagues" as he had called them when he believed Dagobert to be his man. The method spared his delicate nerves. In fact he was frightened to do the dirty work himself. As he had explained, many people whose biographical details he was familiar with were personally unknown to him: H. H. for instance.

It seemed an odd set-up—blackmail by those who were themselves being blackmailed—as odd and contradictory as Bobby himself who was both criminally ruthless and emotionally soppy. Though he could stomach murder—at second hand —he was sentimental and probably even sincere when he attacked genuine or imagined abuses in the pages of *Home Truth*. Bobby was one of those persons who didn't let his right hand know what his left was doing.

He certainly didn't know what he was doing when he gave Margaret Faversham a prize. Her entry form had been signed with her maiden name of Penrose and her address was given as Reading, instead of the Cornish village where her husband had committed suicide.

I, too, had won by chance. But the Colonel? Derek? Ninette?

"He can't be blackmailing everybody who reads *Home Truth*," I said.

"No," Dagobert agreed. "But everybody he's blackmailing is apt to read *Home Truth*."

Thus confused, we reached the Sol y Sombra. Our inclination to find the motor-scooter and return to London had waned. I too wanted, in Margaret's words, to see "if Mr. Marcovitch would venture out of his depth." I had gone off Bobby since I learned how George Faversham had died.

Dagobert dismissed the taxi with regret.

"You're worried about Flossie," I suggested.

"No, not about Flossie. I'm worried—" and the thought seemed to cheer him—"I'm worried about Bobby Marcovitch."

I recalled his theory that Bobby was not the kind of person who killed, but the kind who got killed. I hoped, in a way, the theory was sound.

Chapter 20

As Dagobert paid off the taxi it was claimed by a man who emerged from the night club. It was Derek Upjohn. Derek didn't see us and I wondered how much more brandy he had drunk.

We paused to listen as he told the driver to take him to the Estacion de Francia. It was the railway station for Paris and London. He seemed to be in a hurry. As he got in Dagobert said:

"It's only a quarter to three and the first train doesn't leave until half past seven."

"Oh," Derek said. "Oh, hello . . . Some business suddenly cropped up. . . . In London, you know. Nuisance."

"Besides, your luggage is on the yacht."

"So it is." He looked foolish but not in the least intoxicated. "Then I have plenty of time to pick it up. Thanks. You might make my apologies to the others."

Dagobert kept a hand on the taxi door. "What are you frightened of?" he said.

"Frightened? What an extraordinary idea. Why should I be?"

"Perhaps I should say, what are you running away from?"

Derek, in spite of his obvious haste to catch a train which didn't leave for nearly five hours, reflected a moment before he said:

"Jane will be able to give you a clue. I spent an evening in Chartres boring her on the subject. Now do forgive me." He closed the taxi door and leaned forward to speak to the driver. "*Allons!* What are we waiting for? *Vamos!*"

The car lurched forward. We stepped back and collided with a blind lottery-ticket seller who was attached by a string to a small mongrel dog. The dog had been sniffing at the front tyres of the taxi. When the wheel caught him there was a piercing howl. The taxi-driver cursed and swerved to the middle of the road. The sound of grinding gears did not drown the blind man's wail or the animal's crazed yelping. It had snapped the fragile leash and was writhing in pain in the road.

Dagobert caught it while I restrained its owner. The dog

twisted and bit him. As Dagobert caught him again Derek Upjohn reappeared. He had jumped from the taxi and run back.

He took the dog cautiously but firmly from Dagobert's arms and said: "Is there a chemist open somewhere?"

There was a *Farmacia de Guardia* which stayed open all night in the next street and by the time we reached it the animal was whimpering less hysterically.

"A shot of morphine and then we'll have a look," Derek said.

He spoke to the animal in a canine language it seemed to understand; already its amber eyes—in colour not unlike Derek's—regarded him with less suspicion. It was a sort of smooth-haired terrier and between occasional snarls it made a halfhearted attempt to wag its docked tail. The blind man too calmed down, as though he sensed the *animalico* was in good hands. I had forgotten Derek Upjohn was a veterinary surgeon.

The dog's front leg was broken. The chemist, a brisk and sensible man, suggested it should be put out of its misery. It was, after all, a mongrel of no value, and twenty-five pesetas would be liberal compensation for its owner. The blind man, grasping that the dog was to be killed, began to whimper again; the dog at once joined in. Derek cut short the discussion.

"Splints," he said. "We'll give him a moment for the injection to take effect." He glanced at the clock over the chemist's counter, but there was no longer any impatience in his manner.

We went into the back room where there was a two-hundred-watt lamp. I don't know how much brandy Derek had drunk that night, but as he set the broken leg his hand was as steady as it had been in Chartres when he built the pagoda of dominoes and sugar cubes. Even the chemist was impressed by the deftness and certainty of those blunt fingers.

It was a quarter past three when we walked back to the Sol y Sombra. Dagobert asked Derek if he wanted another taxi, but Derek shook his head. The impulse to run away seemed to have died down. The last half hour had left him dull and listless.

He revived for a moment when he fell back to have a word with the blind man who was clutching the dog in his arms. I heard them arguing about the animal—the man in Spanish which Derek didn't understand and Derek in English which the man didn't understand.

At the door of the Sol y Sombra my heart sank at the sound of castanets. One more flamenco ensemble was more than I could face. Dagobert, who is made of tougher fibre, went in. I waited for Derek. He had drawn the blind man into the shadow of a doorway where the argument continued. Derek was thrusting something into the man's hands which he seemed unwilling to accept. I saw what it was and realised that Derek was not so sober as he appeared.

He had given the man the entire contents of his wallet.

"That was quite a liberal compensation," I said as the blind man grumbling about "locos" stumbled off. "Have you left yourself enough for a ticket back to London?"

He looked shamefaced. "It wasn't much actually," he said. "I've a traveller's cheque. Where's Dagobert?"

"In the Sol y Sombra," I said. "Can you take it again?"

"*Olé*," he said ruefully. "Why not?"

I took his arm. It was shaking. "I don't pretend to know what is wrong," I said, "but it can't be as bad as all that."

"No," he agreed. "The old boy and his dog upset me rather. It's nothing really—nothing that dozens like him don't cheerfully put up with. Lead the way."

But he still hung back.

"Odd," he murmured, trying to smile. "I mean Dagobert asking me what I was frightened of. Did it show so badly?"

"You seemed to be in a preternatural hurry," I said. "Any particular reason?"

"One gets in a panic sometimes." He sensed I was watching him and made an effort to return my glance. He gave it up suddenly and groped for the door.

"All right, yes, I was frightened," he said. "The trouble is I still am. You see, Jane, I'm . . . well, I'm going blind."

Chapter 21

At the Sol y Sombra ("Barcelona's most sophisticated night club, a favourite haunt of the smart international set") we were promised a glass of champagne—"a sparkling climax to an enchanted evening, after which, exhausted but happy, seven lucky people would retire to dream of tomorrow's thrilling arrival in Tabarca."

Only three of the seven were there when we came in; they looked exhausted but not very happy. The glass of champagne—arranged and paid for that afternoon by Bobby—had long since been consumed and waiters, despairing of further business at our table, had cleared away the empty glasses in a marked manner.

Margaret sat alone at the table, chain-smoking. Ninette and the Colonel danced together like people who were running short of conversation. At the bar Albert tried to keep the party spirit alive. Two bouncers watched him hopefully.

At least the castanets had stopped. The Atomic Dixieland Chicos were playing "Oh My Papa" while the smart international set shuffled round or sat, in souvenir hats, yawning. I recognised the man from New Jersey who was telling one of the hostesses about button-processing. He wasn't yawning.

Derek drifted towards Albert at the bar. I heard him order soda-water. Dagobert had already joined Margaret. He rose as I approached, but Margaret didn't see me.

"No," she was saying, "why should I? It's the only thing I've ever had out of *Home Truth* and I wouldn't miss a moment of it."

"Jane has decided to go home," Dagobert said persuasively. "And so has Derek. I suspect Ninette may also drop out. Flossie too, if—"

"They will do exactly as they please," she said. "I shall miss them of course, but I am going to Tabarca. I propose to see this thing through to its—" she smiled pleasantly but firmly —"to its bitter end."

Like Bobby, I was beginning to find Margaret's heavily equivocal remarks unnerving. Dagobert clearly did too; for when the waiter cynically inquired what—if anything—he wanted, he lost his head and ordered a magnum of Veuve Cliquot.

"Expense account," he said as the waiter and I both raised eyebrows. "Er, Bobby . . ."

"Where is Bobby?" Margaret asked idly.

"On the yacht."

"Recovering from the shock," she nodded. "How did he find out I am Margaret Faversham?"

"A telegram from a man called Saunders."

"I seem to remember the name. One of the men George had to see during his trips to London. Jane has told you about George?"

"Yes."

"Then I needn't."

He held a match to her cigarette. "You've never told the police?"

"No," she said. "I've often considered it. Blackmail, I understand, is hard to prove, especially when it is done through third parties who are probably victims of blackmail themselves. Besides, the penalties, though severe, are not severe enough."

"Twenty years?"

"Not enough," she repeated. "Mr. Marcovitch is rather more than a blackmailer, you see . . . Here comes the champagne you ordered—why, I wonder? Hoping to make us all miss the boat?" Her smile flickered and vanished. "He is a murderer," she said.

With the champagne Ninette and the Colonel also arrived. Ninette was flushed and bright-eyed and she wore a comic paper hat which made her look more than ever like the picture of Yvonne on the beach at Ostend. Hugo, she said, had been telling her about Shepheards Hotel in Alex or was it Gib, and about the time young Bingo . . .

The Atomic Dixieland Chicos broke into a rock 'n' rumba. I recognised the questing look in Hugo's eye and hastily agreed when Ninette suggested that we retire to repair our make-up.

"Young Bingo," she rasped, clutching my arm a little hysterically. "Now there was a lad—old Wessex's boy, don't you know? The time he slipped the meringue glace down the French Ambassador's wife's back—cashiered, of course." She gave up the attempt to mimic the Colonel's voice. "Excuse me for a moment while I scream!"

For a second I was afraid that was literally what she was going to do, but instead she sank down on the bench before the glass in the cloakroom. She looked at herself in the paper hat and burst quietly into tears.

"Well, Jane," she said. "I finally screwed up my courage . . . and did it."

"Did what?"

"Proposed to him."

"Oh, I see."

"I wish he didn't peer at you in that shy, half-savage way. I wish his hands weren't so blunt and strong. I wish he didn't look like Mel Ferrer. I wish I was dead!"

She caught sight of herself again in the glass. She looked bruised and crushed and uncommonly pretty. Struck by the picture of desolation she presented she watched the tears roll like glycerine down her cheeks. It was a moment in a Class B film, but no less painful for that.

She essayed a weary smile and said with a catch in her throat, not unworthy of her favourite film actress: "Yes, I—I proposed to him, Jane. I told him I was all his, to do with as he wished —and he fled howling into the night!"

"He came back again," I said. "At this moment he's at the bar drinking soda-water."

"Really?" she said with interest. "I didn't see him. Why didn't you tell me? Gosh, what shall I do?"

"You could start by washing your face," I said. "Dash cold water over it. The shock will do you good and prepare you for another shock. There's a reason why Derek ran away like that."

"I know," she said bitterly. "Yvonne. He's still in love with her."

"I wasn't referring to Yvonne, or to anything as far-fetched as his still being in love with her," I said impatiently. "Derek Upjohn is going blind."

"Oh that," she said. "Yes, I know."

"You know . . . I mean you knew before you asked him to marry you?"

"I guessed ages ago. And made him more or less admit it. That's when I decided to marry him."

I looked at her with admiration, awed that such determination and silliness should co-exist. "Have you," I asked, "thought what being married to a blind man would mean?"

She nodded. "Anyway lots of great men have been blind—like Beethoven," she said. "Besides, there must be something that can be done about it. He says not, but that's because he's defeatist. He just doesn't *care*."

"Perhaps," I said sentimentally, "you can make him care."

She looked doubtful, but went to work on her face nevertheless. "He *did* come back tonight," she said practically. "There must be doctors and Derek must know who they are. After all, he was a medical student himself once—until he suddenly threw it up and became a vet. It's all part of his running away from things." She bit her lip and gave herself a jab with the powder puff. "Yvonne," she said in a harsher voice, "was a nurse."

"Yvonne," I reminded her, "is dead."

"Yes, that's the trouble." She sounded hopeless again. "What can I do? You see, I remind him of her. Every time he looks into my eyes he sees her. When I lie in his arms he feels *her* heart beating against his. . . ."

"Is that what he says?"

"No," she said truthfully. "As a matter of fact I've never lain in his arms—or in anybody else's. But if I did that's what would happen. I know it. Oh Jane! What chance have I got against a rival who is dead?"

Looking at her critically I felt she had a pretty good chance. Derek wasn't so blind he couldn't see how extraordinarily lovely she was. The important thing, I said, was to find out exactly what could be done about his eyesight.

"When did it start?" I asked. "How long has he known about it?"

"A couple of years, I think," she said. "He won't talk much, but . . . well, he gave up medicine when he came back from some sort of holiday in Ostend."

"With Yvonne."

"He went with Yvonne," she winced, "but he came back alone. Yvonne died suddenly in Ostend. She was eighteen, just my age."

"What did she die of?"

"I didn't dare ask. He said it was the first time he'd faced the fact his eyesight would fail him. He was going to be a surgeon. When he came home, instead of going to see a specialist, he just threw in his hand, and ever since has been waiting for it. . . . He won't even wear proper glasses, only those dark things because, he says, light is sometimes suddenly unbearable. He treats approaching blindness as though he *deserved* it—as though it was a kind of punishment from on high. At times, I think, he's worked himself up into believing he was responsible for Yvonne's death. How mixed-up can you get?"

I was rather mixed-up myself by this time; but, like Ninette, I felt that Derek had enough to worry about without such morbid fancies.

We found him at the bar, still toying with his glass of soda-water. Ninette, suddenly very shy, asked him to dance. He put down his glass and went with her quietly.

"Like shleep to the shlaughter," Albert commented. "Have a drink. They're on Dagobert's expense account." He lowered his voice. "We're all going to get pie-eyed and let the yacht sail without us—over the briny deep. Mine's whisky."

Dagobert, I gathered, had no plan whatever for that night apart from supplying the seven of us (for in spite of defections we were with himself and Albert still seven) with drink. His policy—if it could be called a policy—was to keep the spirit of mutiny alive and if possible make us all miss the boat. He knew that this was unlikely as well as pointless. Bobby would not sail without us. And even if he did nothing would be solved.

At any moment we expected Bobby to arrive in a pet and

order his wayward flock on board. The captain's orders were to sail at five o'clock. It was already past four and there was no sign of our shepherd. If Bobby was asleep, would the captain simply follow instructions and sail without us?

I had a feeling that even Margaret no longer cared. She had stopped glancing at her wristwatch. For Ninette time had no existence. She danced continuously with Derek who, though he showed no ardour, betrayed no impatience. Possibly he still intended to catch the train from the Estacion de Francia at seven-thirty.

It is hard to avoid attributing your own feelings to others. I began to imagine that we all shared my own reluctance to return to the yacht.

Dagobert several times reverted to the subject of my dropping out of the party. He had friends (I had never heard of them) on the Costa Brava nearby who would be overjoyed to have me as a guest for a few days. What worried him was that I knew far too much about Bobby and his plans.

I reminded him that we were from now on travelling together.

"See what I mean?" said Albert, who had caught this much of the conversation. "Not a chance."

"Not a chance of what?" Dagobert asked.

"Getting away from her. As it says in that article: 'Strong-minded, gets her own way.' I escaped for a couple of weeks once," he added wistfully, and with a scowl finished his drink. He caught Dagobert's mildly speculative eye and said: "Let's show them how to dance, Jane." He hiccupped and politely covered his mouth with his forefinger. "I beg your pardon. May I have the honour?"

Albert was going through one of those phases when the ghostly influence of his mother's restraining hand was slight. A fine woman, he told me, and very brainy; she drove Pop off his rocker. She had great ambitions for Albert, her one and only. If, he added with satisfaction, she could only see him now!

Albert didn't dance very well—Mother had not approved of dancing—but he did his best to make the time pass interestingly. I think Dagobert had enlisted his aid. Where the rest of us sat back and vaguely hoped the yacht would sail without us, Albert put his heart into the business. For some reason he too seemed to dread the end of the evening.

At a quarter to five he discovered that I had no comic hat, which would never do. He returned to the table a minute later with one, followed by a hatless *Guardia Civil*. I suspected he was about to be given another night's free accommodation in the local jail.

"All my life I've dreamed of pinching a copper's helmet," Albert told me, deeply disappointed that the *Guardia* treated the incident as a joke. Indeed the *Guardia* was the only one who laughed.

It was ten minutes to five.

I saw Dagobert's eyes stray towards the door. There was no sign of Bobby. Margaret too followed his glance. She looked at her wristwatch, but made no comment. Derek and Ninette rose to dance again, Ninette like a child who at bedtime evades adult attention, Derek as though the matter had long since been taken out of his hands.

Albert dug the *Guardia* lustily in the ribs and pounded on the table for more champagne. All that happened was the soft-footed approach of a waiter with the bill.

"I told the fellow to keep an eye on the time," Colonel Warrington explained. "It's H minus 10, you know, and we mustn't miss the boat, what? These sailor types are very keen on punctuality."

Hugo had also told the waiter to call taxis. We all allowed him to herd us in like—Albert, pleased with the phrase, repeated—"like shleep to the shlaughter."

The journey back to the docks was enlivened by Albert's effort to get a small donkey into our taxi, but otherwise it passed in silence. Possibly the others were dreaming of tomorrow's thrilling arrival in Tabarca. Personally, I was praying that the yacht had sailed.

Chapter 22

IT HADN'T, of course.

When instinct warns me of impending drama, nothing ever happens. I wondered what I had expected: an ambulance? A cordon of police? The yacht to be on fire?

It was moored at the dock exactly as we had left it some hours before. Even the single light in Bobby's quarters was still on, though Bobby himself did not emerge to greet us.

The crew had lowered the gangway and the duty officer welcomed us aboard. I waited for him to challenge Dagobert; to my disappointment he didn't. I had looked forward to making a scene and refusing to sail without him. Bobby must have changed his mind about allowing only members of the *Home Truth* party to come on board. Even Albert, to his visible embarrassment, was smartly saluted.

The diesel engines were already softly throbbing. It was exactly five o'clock and the Colonel seemed pleased with our timing.

"Two bells," he said. "Dog watch—time we were all in our hammocks. Can I give you a shakedown?" he said to Dagobert. "A bit cramped, but . . ."

He was grateful when Ninette said she would move in with Margaret, letting Dagobert share the cabin with me. So was I, though Margaret seemed less pleased. In any case we were all too tired to argue.

Albert disappeared and Bobby remained in retirement. There was a sign on Flossie's door saying "Please do not disturb." Flossie, we felt, had been disturbed enough for one night and Dagobert decided to postpone seeing her until the morning.

No one stayed up to watch our departure. I saw the lights of Barcelona slowly recede from the porthole of our cabin. When we had been under way for about twenty minutes I crept down the passage in my dressing gown. All was quiet except for the steady churning of the engines and the creak of timbers as the ship met the swell beyond the harbour. I paused outside Flossie's door and heard the springs in her bunk complain as she tossed and turned over. I wondered if she were really asleep and gently tried the handle of the door. Somewhat to my relief it was locked on the inside.

At that moment I heard a footfall behind me. My heart went into my throat and I spun round. It was Dagobert. Apparently he had padded down the passage after me. Ever since we had come on board he had kept an unobtrusive but constant eye on me.

I went back to our cabin with him and watched him slide the bolt home. It was the last of my self-engendered frights that night. The bunks were narrow but we managed to sleep in only one of them.

Five or six hours later, when we were finishing breakfast, the seat at the head of the table was still unoccupied. Bobby was given to excessive heartiness at breakfast and no one greatly regretted his absence. Only Margaret glanced speculatively from time to time at the empty chair.

Albert, with his hair slicked down and his protuberant ears pink from soap and water, had worked his way through several plates of bacon and eggs which, to the steward's delight, he delicately ate with his knife. Albert seemed to provide unfailing amusement for the crew.

"The condemned man," he said, mopping his face with the napkin tied around his neck, "made a hearty breakfast."

The steward grinned and Ninette blanched. The sea was not rough, but she had merely toyed with her grapefruit. "Why do millionaires," she wondered, "buy yachts when they can afford to stay on land?"

Derek assured her that he had already caught a glimpse of Tabarca on the horizon. Though his appetite was unimpaired he seemed to share her impatience to reach shore.

Hugo Warrington had slept like a top and done his constitutional ten times around the deck. He was keenly looking forward to meeting this fellow H. H. It might turn out they had friends in common.

"Or it might turn out," Dagobert said conversationally, "that you've already met him."

"What's that? How do you mean?"

"You've met so many people," Dagobert explained politely though, I thought, disingenuously.

He returned to his toast and marmalade. Like Ninette Dagobert had eaten almost nothing.

Margaret said in an aside to the steward: "Has Mr. Marcovitch had his breakfast yet?"

I may have imagined that the entire table seemed to wait upon the steward's reply.

"No, Senora," he said, and hastened with toothpicks to Albert who was in difficulty with a back molar.

The wireless officer came in with a message for Bobby.

"We'd better knock him up," Colonel Warrington said. "It might be important."

It wasn't important. It was a message of general welcome from the Princess Juana in Tabarca addressed to Bobby but intended for all of us.

"Better knock him up anyway," the Colonel insisted. "We'll be there in half an hour."

Bobby's instructions had been that no one should disturb him until he rang. The wireless officer knocked on the door of the royal suite nevertheless. We heard him try the door, rattle it, then bang on it loudly. By this time most of the breakfast party had risen and gone out into the passage.

Dagobert lingered, for the first time pretending interest in his cup of coffee. I heard someone—I think it was the Colonel—saying: "Then, by Jove, you'll have to break the door in."

I hovered between Dagobert and the group outside. He had lighted a cigarette and immediately put it out again in his saucer. His hand was shaking.

"What's the matter?" I whispered. "Don't you feel well?"

He swallowed with an effort. "I feel," he said, "like . . . a murderer."

"What have you done?"

"That's just it—nothing."

By this time someone had obtained permission from the Captain to break the door in. I heard the thud of heavy shoulders and the sound of splintering wood. The door burst from its hinges and feet trampled forward, deadened by the thick carpet of the blue and gold drawingroom.

I wavered for another moment, then joined the others. I felt Dagobert's hard, restraining grip on my arm. He was just behind me. It must have struck him, as it struck me, that this crowd milling through the royal suite would effectively obliterate traces of previous visitors—if such things should later prove important.

Dagobert did nothing. The Captain wasn't there and Hugo Warrington seemed to be in charge. We did not interfere.

The wide gilt doors leading into the bedchamber were ajar but the brocade curtains were drawn. The pink-fringed lamp, embroidered with the arms of the Branzas and intertwined H. H.'s, was still alight, as it had been last night when the yacht was in Barcelona harbour.

The soft pink glow disclosed the inert mass which lay athwart the bed. It looked like a bolster, beaten out of shape, and so small compared with the vast oval of the bed that it seemed incredible it should be a human body—and a rather plump human body at that. Mercifully it was covered from our sight by the bedclothes with which it had evidently been strangled or smothered. There were signs of a struggle, but the body now lay very still. Even before Colonel Warrington gently prodded it we knew that it was lifeless.

No one screamed, not even Ninette. She had hidden her face in Derek's arms. I saw Margaret avert her eyes. Margaret and I had once watched Bobby bouncing with pleasure on this same oval bed, as though with a foretaste of proprietorship. Margaret seemed loth to see that bitter end she had promised herself.

I dared not look at Dagobert. I understood how he felt: like —as he had said—a murderer by default. He had lightly foretold Bobby's fate. It was Bobby he had been worried about. Bobby, he had said, was the kind of person who gets murdered; and he had done nothing to prevent it.

Colonel Warrington cautiously drew back the bedclothes which covered the body. I looked away.

As I looked away I saw standing among the little group in the door, I saw—and, blinking my eyes, continued to see—Bobby Marcovitch.

This time someone did scream.

Colonel Warrington had just exposed the face of the corpse; and the face was Flossie Martin's.

Chapter 23

THE PERSON WHO had screamed was Bobby. The Colonel scowled at him and said:

"Let us not lose control. This is a job for the skipper. Where is he?"

Captain McNaughten, an elderly Scot who under the pretext of duty avoided passengers as much as possible, was on the bridge. We were approaching the narrow harbour entrance where navigation required his attention, but the radio officer went in search of him.

"Meanwhile you, Marcovitch, should strictly speaking be in charge," the Colonel said. "Where have you been?"

Bobby had put a fist into his mouth to prevent a second shrill of hysteria. His blue eyes were glazed with fright.

"I," he stuttered, "I, ah . . ." He bit his hand, as though to assure himself he was actually awake. He found, to his evident distress, that he was. "Since you ask, I," he said, "I, as a matter of fact . . ." He stopped, perhaps aware by the set of our faces that we all knew he was about to lie. "As a matter of fact," he repeated with a trace of his normal cockiness, "if I'm in charge here I do not answer questions. I ask them."

"Just as you wish," the Colonel said stiffly. "Carry on."

Carrying on was the last thing Bobby was capable of. It was obvious where he had been. He had just dragged himself out of bed. Margaret gave him a glass of cold water. He gulped it down, caught sight of Dagobert and begged faintly for a second glass. He made a feeble gesture towards the oval bed and said:

"Who is it?"

The Colonel bit his lip, but kept his temper. "As you must have seen, Mrs. Martin," he said patiently.

"Yes, of course," Bobby nodded. He found a silk handkerchief in the pocket of his dressing gown and caressed his brow cautiously.

"I mean, is she . . ."

"She is dead."

"What's she doing in here?"

"A penetrating question," the Colonel said. "The first question, I imagine, the authorities will ask."

Bobby, rattled, cried with a return of hysteria: "She took an overdose of barbitone!"

"There is a bottle of barbitone on the bedside table," the Colonel said. "Remarkably observant of you to have noticed."

"She did it on purpose! Out of pure spite! Against me!"

He was nearly screaming again. Dagobert winced and tried to catch his eye. Our sympathy for Bobby was limited, but it is unpleasant to watch even a rat blunder into a trap.

"Perhaps," Dagobert said, "we'd better wait for Captain McNaughten."

The Colonel said: "If, Marcovitch, you are suggesting that Mrs. Martin committed suicide you are mistaken. She was smothered, possibly while asleep, perhaps after taking a sleeping draught. Post-mortem will tell us. In any event it is obvious she was murdered."

This succeeded where the glass of cold water had failed. The animal stupidity on Bobby's face gave way to animal alertness. "Aren't you—aren't we jumping to conclusions?" he said, forcing himself to approach the oval bed. "Please stand back, everybody, until the skipper . . . Er, Colonel Warrington, you might, if you don't mind, just . . ."

Colonel Warrington pulled the bedclothes over Flossie's head and shoulders again and re-arranged them much as they had been when we first saw her.

Over her nightdress she was wearing the pink fluffy dressing gown. She had not removed her make-up. Rouge, powder and lipstick had been smeared together and over the sheet and pillows.

Bobby breathed more easily when the open eyes no longer stared at him. He said: "Yes, we mustn't jump to conclusions, must we? I mean why should one, I mean anyone, murder Mrs. . . . er, Martin? We all know she was highly strung, given to fits of depression—witness her behaviour after dinner last night when she refused to join us at El Rincon. She slept with the aid of, ah, let me see, was it barbitone . . . ?"

Moving now with greater confidence he had strolled over to the bedside table where there was a tumbler half full of water and the bottle of pills. All of us, except Colonel Warrington, had drawn back as Bobby had told us to do. He reached casually for the bottle of pills. Colonel Warrington at once intercepted him.

"We won't touch anything further, if you don't mind," he said.

Bobby shrugged, but continued to eye the pills. "I was under the impression I was in charge until the Captain arrived," he said, removing the silk handkerchief again.

"Fingerprints," the Colonel explained.

"I know all about fingerprints," Bobby said crossly, but the Colonel continued to prevent his touching the bedside table.

Bobby dried his hands on his handkerchief. They had begun to perspire.

"It is," he smiled brightly, "even possible that my own fingerprints will be on that bottle. You see, I fetched the barbitone at her own request from her cabin."

"Keep it for the Captain," Dagobert advised.

"Which," Margaret pointed out, "will give you a moment to compose yourself and to make your story consistent."

"I am composed!" he snapped. "I merely exchanged rooms with Flossie last night. She was restless and didn't like her own cabin, so naturally I offered her mine. I slept in her cabin."

This, I knew, could be true. Last night when I paused outside Flossie's door I had heard someone tossing on the bunk inside. I naturally assumed it was Flossie, but it could equally well have been Bobby.

He continued to smile at Margaret and with deliberate insolence added: "Fortunately *I* have nothing to hide."

He thrust the handkerchief back into his dressing-gown pocket. As he did so he went rigid. His eyes started and sweat broke out on his forehead. His small mouth began to work.

"I don't feel well," he stammered. "If you'll . . . excuse me, please," and he turned to the door.

Again the Colonel anticipated his movement.

"If you don't mind," he said, "none of us will leave this room until the skipper comes."

Bobby blundered on, but came up against Albert who, instinctively taking his orders from Colonel Warrington, barred his passage.

"I'm in charge here!" Bobby shouted. "Take your hands off me! I'm—I'm not well, I tell you. I'm the one who gives orders, d'you hear?"

Albert did not hear. He glanced at the Colonel inquiringly and continued to hold Bobby by the scruff of the neck.

"Let me give you another glass of water, Mr. Marcovitch," Margaret said. "You'll feel better in a moment."

Bobby subsided onto a straight chair, panting. His face went a greenish tinge and I thought he really was ill. The Colonel looked impatiently at his wristwatch. The engines had gone into reverse and we could feel the yacht trembling as it manoeuvred through the breakwater and into the harbour. The radio officer appeared for a moment at the door to say that Captain McNaughten was coming.

Dagobert said to Colonel Warrington: "Why did you break the door in?"

"Had to. It was locked."

"Didn't the steward have a key?"

"There's apparently only one key."

Dagobert was examining the outer door which had been smashed in. The Colonel joined him.

"By Jove!" he whistled. "I see what you mean."

The door had been locked. If Flossie had locked it the key ought to have been on the inside. It wasn't.

"Could you get into this suite without a key?" Colonel Warrington asked the steward.

"No, senor. You could perhaps crawl through a porthole, but they are all locked. We have the air-conditioning."

Dagobert and the Colonel began to search for the missing key, Colonel Warrington methodically, Dagobert going through the motions. Bobby watched them dully while Albert and a steward stood over him.

If—as Bobby suggested—Flossie died from an overdose of self-administered sleeping pills, then she had presumably locked the door of the suite herself, and the key ought to be somewhere inside. If someone had murdered her the murderer must have locked the door and taken the key with him.

"He may," said Margaret, eyeing Bobby, "have tossed it overboard."

Captain McNaughten, red in the face, arrived to apologise for having been so long. There was a band on the quay below and the royal party was waiting to welcome us. Would we all adjourn to the saloon while the owner's suite was sealed and left under guard?

Bobby, protesting at being forcibly detained, demanded to be allowed to return to the cabin where his clothes were.

"By all means," Captain McNaughten agreed, appalled to find our group leader still unshaved and in pyjamas.

Albert said hesitantly: "Shouldn't we all be searched or something first?"

"What for?" the Captain said nervously. "Yes, of course, if you think so."

"There was something about a key," Margaret said.

The Captain did not know what she was talking about, but the Colonel—and a second later the rest of us—remembered Bobby's singular reaction a moment previously when he had thrust his handkerchief into his pocket. Colonel Warrington grasped Bobby's right hand as it plunged again into his dressing-gown pocket.

Bobby was still clutching the key when Colonel Warrington forced his hand open.

The Colonel was a judicious man. Before speaking he tried the key in the Yale lock of the broken-in door. It fitted, and when turned, smoothly worked the lock.

"Before we land, sir," he said to the Captain, "I must give Mr. Marcovitch formally into your custody. The charge is that he murdered Mrs. Martin."

Chapter 24

COLONEL WARRINGTON'S MANNER was grave and authoritative. It impressed even Captain McNaughten who was unused to having his passengers charged with murder. It deprived the rest of us, including Bobby, of speech.

But for all his air of reluctantly performing an unpleasant duty I thought Hugo Warrington had accused Bobby with a certain complacency. I waited for Dagobert to object, but he merely murmured: "Bright idea of Albert's." That key—if it was the only key with which the murderer could have entered the suite—would be difficult for Bobby to account for.

Hugo Warrington explained its meaning to Captain McNaughten as we went into the saloon. The Captain, who had not followed very carefully, drew a sudden breath of relief. The yacht had just nudged against the dock.

" 'Fraid the matter's no longer under my jurisdiction," he said. "We are in Tabarca. What you'll have to do is to see Mr. Hutton. . . ." He glanced round in a harassed way as though expecting Henry Howard Hutton himself to come to the rescue. "Or, of course, the Princess," he added.

He repeated his orders to the steward that no one was to enter the royal suite, promised to summon a doctor and excused himself. The Colonel, protesting, followed him. The others, finding nothing to say, filed out onto the deck.

Bobby watched them escape from the saloon in a daze. He seemed grateful that we had lingered behind.

"What do I do?" he asked in a small voice.

"Nothing," Dagobert advised. "If you have the good fortune to be arrested, go quietly."

"Whose side are you on?"

"Yours for the moment. I may change sides later."

"Mine!" Bobby sneered. "How did that key get into my pocket? It's a frame-up!"

"Possibly," Dagobert said. "Still the safest place for you is jail."

"Leaving you to turn the screws on H. H.?" Bobby said. "While I'm safely locked up, you cash in. Yes, I see the game."

His hangover, followed in brutal succession by violent death and an accusation of murder, had dulled Bobby's normally sharp intelligence. For the moment he failed to grasp that no game was now possible. H. H. could not be blackmailed for concealing a legal wife who was no longer alive. Flossie's death had removed the sole impediment to the marriage of Henry Howard Hutton and Princess Juana.

"Hey!" Bobby woke up suddenly. "That proves it!"

"What?"

"Why should I kill her? She was money in the bank to me. Use your head."

"Tell me what happened last night and I'll try to," Dagobert promised.

"I've told *you* too much already. That was a lousy trick, by the way, that telegram!" he added with grudging admiration. "D'you know, we could work together at that."

"What on?"

"Well, *somebody* killed her," he said.

"The popular opinion seems to be that you did. When you came back to the yacht last night at half past two she was waiting up to have a chat with you, wasn't she? She turned off the light in her cabin and came into the owner's suite. I imagine there was an argument."

"If there was," Bobby said, "no one heard it. The place is soundproof."

"What was the row about?"

"Who said there was a row? On the contrary—"

"Perhaps," Dagobert interrupted, "you'd rather explain it all later to Mr. Hutton. Let's go, Jane."

"Wait a minute!" Bobby said. The band on the quayside had broken into the Tabarca national anthem and the sound distracted him. He tried to concentrate. "Okay," he said, "there was a kind of scene. She had some crazy idea that her first husband—Howard Turner, as she called him—was catching up with her, closing in, as she called it. Hound of Heaven stuff. I calmed her down."

"With the barbitone?"

"I fetched the barbitone later—when I took my night clothes to her cabin. No, I calmed her down by saying he wasn't closing in on her: she was closing in on *him!*"

"You told her Howard Turner was H. H.?"

"Maybe stupid of me, but I decided it was time to take her more or less into my confidence. By keeping her mouth shut, I explained, there was money in it for us both. I put it very tactfully. After all, he'd left her flat eight years ago—and why shouldn't Pete, his kid, get something out of it? A couple of thousand, I suggested. I'd handle it for her."

"How did she take the suggestion?"

"Not very reasonably," Bobby admitted. "She said that would be blackmail. She threatened—very unfairly, I thought—to leave the yacht then and there. That's why I had to lock her in."

"What did you do with the key?"

"That's just it!" Bobby squirmed. "Like a fool I left it in the door. But who's going to believe that?"

"Oddly enough, I am," Dagobert said.

Bobby looked relieved though disappointed at Dagobert's credulity. Dagobert added:

"I saw it in the door when we all came on board last night."

"Then why didn't you say so when that fool Colonel—"

"It seemed a better idea to get you arrested."

"But I'm obviously innocent."

"One is always suspicious of the obviously innocent," Dagobert said sententiously. "Why did you leave the key in the door?"

"Just as I was locking it I heard your taxi arrive. I didn't want to see any of you so I dashed down the passage and shut myself in Flossie's room, clean forgetting the damn' key."

"You remembered it later."

"Naturally. But by that time people were crashing around. I thought I'd wait a while and when everybody was asleep go back and have a further word with Flossie. I reckoned the two thousand I'd offered her wasn't enough and was going to raise it a bit."

"What did she say to that?"

"I didn't go back. And don't try to trick me into admitting I did! When it got quieter—about half an hour out—I did put my head into the corridor for a moment. But somebody was still hanging around."

"Who?"

"That fellow Albert. How did *he* get on board anyway?"

"In the usual way. You didn't notice anyone else?"

"You and Jane, about ten minutes earlier, muttering outside my door. Like a dope I fell asleep when—" he reproached himself bitterly—"when by keeping an eye peeled . . . I say! If we could find out who really *did* kill her . . ."

"It would make good 'unpublishable' material for *Home Truth,*" Dagobert agreed.

"Yeah," said Bobby thoughtfully. "Let's narrow it down. It

must have been one of you . . ."

"Unless post-mortem establishes death at *before* five o'clock —in which case it narrows down even further—in fact to you."

"Don't be ridiculous! She was alive until five o'clock. I was with her. I left the key in the outside of the door—where *you* saw it, remember, and where," he conceded fairly, "anybody could have used it."

"But it was found on you."

"Yes," he said. "That was a plant—and I suspect you know it. We'll have to work on fingerprints and so forth in the royal suite."

"Unhelpful. We all swarmed in before the murder was discovered."

"That was bad luck."

"If it *was* luck," Dagobert said.

"Anyway post-mortem will prove she was still alive at five which means anybody could have killed her. Including, if it comes to that, you."

"We shall see."

Something in Dagobert's manner disturbed Bobby. "What do you mean?"

"You're forgetting that the doctor who will do the post-mortem will be from Tabarca."

"What's that got to do with it?"

"His professional opinion may be influenced by—shall we say —considerations of state."

Bobby went pale. "I don't get it."

"Your popularity with the local authorities will be slight."

"After all the good publicity I've given the place? Why?"

"Roughly because Henry Howard Hutton is well aware of your plan to blackmail him."

"Christ!" Bobby gasped. "How could he be?"

"When I gave him that photostat copy of his marriage certificate," Dagobert said, "I told him about it."

Chapter 25

"THAT," I SAID to Dagobert as we reached the deck, "effectively flattened Bobby. It also flattened me. How could you have told him?"

Dagobert smiled, enjoying his little moment. "I sometimes dabble in amateur detection," he said. "This is Tabarca. You know, the place we're always talking about."

Below us the entire population of the island—two thousand, six hundred and one, plus cats, goats and burros—seemed to have gathered round the small harbour, shouting, waving flags and letting off fireworks. I saw banners with the words: WELCOMB HOM TRUT and heard cries of "Viva Enrico El Loco!" The band, dressed in rope-soled shoes, black velvet berets, red sashes and brand-new blue jeans with the manufacturer's labels still intact, had finished the national anthem and was playing "Oh My Papa."

The Castillo, a Moorish tower in crumbling stone, dominated the village which tumbled in precipitous cobblestoned streets to the crescent Esplanade, lined with palm trees, fishing nets and public conveniences. A baroque church, its dome of bright blue *azulejos* glinting in the sun, rose from the central mass of pink-tiled rooftops.

Behind, like an ancient backcloth, an extinct volcano extended its wrinkled flanks. It was the volcano which had destroyed Tabarca nearly two thousand years ago, but was now tamed and terraced with vineyards. Above the vines grew carefully tended olives and above the olive groves, straggling halfway up the mountain, carob trees disputed the sparser ground with esparto grass.

I saw Dagobert's eye straying up towards the rocky summit, doubtless surveying the possibilities of a stone hut or cave for us among the outlying goatherds' dwellings.

"Isn't it heaven!" Ninette exclaimed.

To my surprise Albert, clutching the rail beside her, agreed. I had not suspected Albert of appreciating the picturesque. He continued, with the rapt gaze of the romantic, to study the jumble of colour-washed houses, the scarlet bougainvillaea which gushed from crevices in the Castle walls, the neat, curved line of terraces, here and there interrupted by disorderly spikes of aloes or an untidy riot of prickly pear. There was a faraway look in his eyes as though the scene were comforting and familiar to him—or as though it fulfilled some secretly cherished dream.

"It's all right," he said. "Kind of unspoiled, what you might call peaceful."

The word "peaceful" was lost in a crackling explosion of fireworks and renewed cheers for Enrico El Loco. Mooring ropes had been cast to the dock and paper streamers were being flung back by the mob on shore. The band was playing again, but we couldn't hear what. Three or four policemen, their white duck uniforms wilting, struggled to keep a space clear just beneath us. It was occupied by a sedate group of people who were obviously not villagers.

"The nobs," said Albert glumly, retiring from the rail.

The portrait of Princess Juana on the cover of *Home Truth* had been idealised, but I instantly recognised her. She was a small, sensible-looking woman of about thirty. She wore a grey flannel suit, well-cut though a little tight, high-heeled court shoes and a hat which might have been bought at Debenhams. She had dark, restless eyes and seemed unamused by the hubbub around her. Albert saw me watching her.

"Now there's one," he grinned unexpectedly, "who *does* remind me of Mother."

At the Princess's side, deferential though resplendent in a frock coat plastered with medals, a fat man fretted at the delay and glowered at the children who broke through the police cordon. Behind him, yawning delicately, stood a tall, languid young man in a lavender bush shirt and a deep purple silk scarf knotted round his Adam's apple.

An elderly gentleman with a walrus moustache and the Branza hooked nose hovered at the edge of the group. His attention was distracted by a group of gypsy girls who were tittering and sticking out their tongues at him.

"Looks like old Don Carlos," Colonel Warrington said. "Heard they'd had to lock him up—D.T.s among less respectable complaints."

"Which one is Henry Howard Hutton?" Ninette asked, eagerly scanning the group.

"Yes," I said, glancing suspiciously at Dagobert.

"H. H.?" said Dagobert airily. "Oh, he's already on board."

"Already on board? How could he be?" Hugo Warrington demanded. "They haven't got the gangway down yet."

They got it down at that moment and Princess Juana swept forward. She ignored the police force who stiffened to attention. Someone was trying to unroll a red carpet, but she briskly kicked it out of her way. When she reached the deck the crowd began to bellow again for Enrico El Loco.

She paused briefly and turned to wave a gracious though admonitory hand. Then, brushing Captain McNaughten aside, she made straight for Dagobert.

She smiled with sudden charm and held out her hand. Dagobert, startled, leaned over it with an ease which gratified me.

"You are of course Mr. Marcovitch—and these are your Lucky Seven," she said with almost no accent. "Welcome to Tabarca. This is indeed an occasion for us. We think of you as pioneers, discoverers, the first, we hope, of the many. As you point out in your letters—and I must say I entirely agree—our little island has been neglected far too long. I trust you have brought photographers with you and a journalist or two." The smile vanished. "Where," she said, "is Mr. Hutton?"

Behind me on the deck there was a shuffling of tennis shoes. I glanced round nervously to see Albert slinking off. The Princess followed my glance.

"Henry," she said.

She didn't raise her voice, but Albert stopped dead in his tracks.

"Henry," she repeated gently. "Please stop being absurd and come back at once."

Albert came back at once.

Chapter 26

PRINCESS JUANA NOTICED our stricken faces.

"He does this sort of thing constantly," she explained to Dagobert. "I hope you haven't minded."

She regarded Albert with indulgence. Colouring slightly, she turned her cheek which he dutifully pecked at, to the renewed applause of the crowd below. We continued to gape.

"They adore him," she said not without pride. She straightened his collar and glanced at the tennis shoes with distaste. "And what role are we playing today, Henry?" she asked. She didn't wait for him to say, but returned to Dagobert. "One of my ancestors, Alfonso the Childish, used to trade clothes with a footman and insist on waiting at table—so Henry will be in the best Branza tradition."

"Well I'm dashed," the Colonel murmured mildly.

"Incognito!" Ninette whispered.

"A passion of his," the Princess nodded. "Of course everyone recognises him at once, but the islanders are simple folk and find it amusing."

I remembered the amusement Albert had caused among the yacht's crew and Captain McNaughten's pink face in his owner's presence. I also remembered that last night Albert had come aboard without anyone lifting a finger to stop him. He had come to breakfast this morning from the Captain's quarters where he must have spent the night.

One or two incidents were in retrospect less diverting: Flossie's attack after dinner at Caracoles last night. "I get spots before my eyes," she had told me, "and imagine things."

One spot before her eyes could have been a fleeting glimpse of Albert who, with Dagobert, had escaped up an alley as we all came out of the restaurant.

Then in Toulouse the night before when she had retired to her room without dinner. She had, she complained, a feeling of being "closed in on." Had she glimpsed Dagobert's pillion rider and, though not actually recognising him, been reminded of the Howard Turner she had married eight years previously in Quebec? The marriage, according to Bobby's reports, had lasted two weeks—perhaps those same two weeks to which Albert had wistfully referred: when he "escaped from Mother."

"Yes, Henry's mother," the Princess was telling Dagobert, "was a remarkable woman. It was her shrewd sense, he tells me, her genius for speculation, which created the H. H. legend and financial empire. She bought Tabarca and, if one must put it very, very crudely, the Branzas. . . ."

She indicated her kinsmen coming up the gangway, as though in acquiring them the late Mrs. Hutton had made her one shaky investment.

"A truly remarkable woman," she repeated with a sigh. "Henry is lost without her. She had such fresh, New-World ideas about our future: a casino, fashionable beaches, an advertising campaign. She will be hard to live up to. . . . But I mustn't exhaust you with all this now, Mr. Marcovitch. We shall have plenty of opportunity to discuss it at leisure. You must present your Lucky Seven—an idea, incidentally, worthy of Ethel Hutton herself! Come, Henry, introduce your new friends to me."

"In the first place," Albert said, "the one you're talking to isn't Bobby Marcovitch. It's Dagobert Brown."

This did not register. Though the Princess frequently addressed her fiance she rarely waited to hear what he replied. She had seen Ninette.

"And who is this?" she asked Dagobert.

"May I present Miss Ninette Nixon," Dagobert said. "Her Highness—"

"You are extremely pretty," the Princess interrupted. "We must keep you away from— Ah, here he is: my cousin Don Carlos de Branza. Don't curtsey, my dear. We are very democratic in Tabarca." She gave Ninette her hand, a warm smile and passed her on to Don Carlos who could in his excitement only babble in French. "We shall have a publicity poster made of her in a bikini," she told Dagobert, "as soon as we get the beach cleaned up. And this?"

Dagobert presented Colonel Warrington who said he had once had the honour of meeting her father, Prince Jaime, at Cowes.

"I remember the occasion perfectly," said the Princess with her most charming smile; and introduced him to the fat man in the bemedalled frock coat.

He was the Mayor of Tabarca and had once, she explained, worked in London where he took advantage of the excellent evening courses at the University.

"Senor Sans," she said, "has arranged a strict schedule for our entertainment. I don't know what I should do without him. Could you," she said to him, "stop that music for a moment so we can hear ourselves speak! Mrs. Hutton," she continued when the Mayor had gone to shake his fist at the band-leader, "thought we should outline the *Castillo* in neon strips of blue and gold, the colours of the royal arms. What do you think? Do try to persuade Henry. I don't think I've met this young woman, have I?"

She was looking at me. She didn't see me, but her smile was so winning I had the illusion I had made a good impression. Dagobert said I was his wife. She pressed my hand cordially, passed me on, and promptly forgot me.

The person she passed me on to was, inevitably, the languid young man in the lavender silk bush shirt. He was her cousin Alonso Duque de Finestrat.

"Crikey," he sighed, "will she never stop talking?"

She was telling Dagobert she had been in touch with the Pepsi-Cola people warning them of the sudden demand they might shortly expect in Tabarca for their product. She had also written to a firm in Chicago about the installation of juke-boxes.

Captain McNaughten managed to approach her to say that a doctor was required on board. She told him of "Henry's" plan to transform the yacht into a passenger boat giving regular, daily service for tourists between Barcelona and Tabarca. Captain McNaughten caught Albert's eye, hastily agreed with the Princess and withdrew.

A few minutes later I saw him hurrying up the gangway with two uniformed policemen and a man carrying a black bag. They went towards the royal suite. Shortly afterwards Senor Sans followed them. Princess Juana was discussing a miniature-golf course.

"The people we must aim at," she told Dagobert, "are the new ruling class—the family with a fortnight's holiday on a travel allowance. Isn't that so, Henry?"

Henry nodded.

"I suppose Juana knows what she's doing," my companion murmured. "She keeps quoting the Hutton woman. Poor H. H."

"I can't," I admitted, "get used to the idea that he is H. H."

"No. Neither can he. Between ourselves," he added confidentially, "I didn't think Henry would come back. I imagine Juana was a bit nervous too. Perhaps that's why she's talking her head off now—with relief, as it were."

"Didn't you expect him?"

"Not until we received his radio message from the yacht this morning."

"Where has he been?"

"Nobody knows. On a prolonged binge, I suspect. He may have been more upset by his mother's death than he pretends. He *said* he had to get away for a bit—think things over. In his own words: 'learn to stand on his own feet, like an ordinary bloke.' His plan to hitch-hike seems to have been uncommonly successful. A couple of weeks ago Juana had a picture postcard from Quebec where, he claims, he once sold newspapers. A very romantic type, Henry."

"Then it will be nice for him to marry royalty," I said.

"It will be nice for the Branzas," he said modestly.

Finestrat, from which he derived his title, was, he told me, a fishing village on the other side of the island. After the wedding he hoped to have a bathroom installed in the ducal hovel.

"People normally call me Finny," he said. "Clients especially."

I wanted to talk about H. H., but I said encouragingly: "Clients?"

Before his credit had been unfrozen by rumours of the forthcoming alliance between the Branzas and the Huttons he had, it seemed, acted as chauffeur-interpreter to transatlantic ladies visiting European cultural centres like Monte Carlo, whose democratic inhibitions only allowed them to call him Duke behind his back.

"That's how I first met Mrs. Hutton," he said. "She was in Nice with a view to buying the Promenade des Anglais. In a careless moment she once tipped me a hundred francs. Mama always kept Henry short so we split it to play the fruit machines. Now I think of it," he said, "Henry won the jackpot."

Later the Huttons visited Tabarca where Ethel had been quick to see investment possibilities.

"Juana took to Henry at once," Finny said wonderingly. "There's something defenceless about him which appeals to strong-minded women. They enjoy bullying him. Mama Hutton bullied him into buying Tabarca. The price, incidentally, so terrified Henry that the original figure had to be slashed in half before he stopped shaking with fright."

"Wasn't the money his mother's?"

"In practice, yes. But it was in his name. He had to sign the cheques, though it was she of course who wrote them out. She made the decisions. Henry meekly did what he was told. All things considered," he reflected, "Henry did all right."

"Surely it was *his* decision to marry your cousin."

"Don't you believe it," Finny said. "Mama and Juana fixed it up between them and 'consulted' Henry after it was settled. Henry put up a token resistance and as usual signed on the dotted line. It was the last big deal the old warhorse pulled off before high blood pressure claimed its own. The theory was that the decadent house of Branza could do with a shot of New-World vitality. Look at 'em."

I saw what he meant. Juana was flushed and alive with animation. Albert or—as I tried to think of him—Henry paled into insignificance in her background.

"He has, however," Finny reminded me, "some hundred million dollars."

This sobered us both and we fell into respectful silence, inwardly contemplating this awe-inspiring sum. It cast an aura around the homely figure of Albert, transmogrifying him, so that all which remained visible through the golden haze was the dim, legendary outline of H. H.

I shook myself before the vision became too concrete. I was beginning to observe a physical change in him. The others—Margaret, the Colonel, Derek and Ninette—had slowly recovered from their first shock of disbelief and were studying him in silent wonder.

They, too, were conscious of the metamorphosis. Some hundred million dollars had been added to his stature.

Chapter 27

BOBBY, HOWEVER, DIDN'T notice it.

"Psst!" he said, squeezing under the lifeboat against which Henry was leaning.

Two policemen rounded the deck after him. They pulled up

uncertainly, wondering whether amidst the fireworks anyone would notice if they fired revolvers.

Bobby tapped Henry on the shoulder. "Psst!" he repeated urgently.

Henry edged away from Juana who was telling us about arrangements to floodlight the church. Bobby whispered to him reprovingly:

"That's the Princess you were talking to. Look, I want to see H. H., and," he added as Senor Sans reappeared, "I want to see him quick."

"About anything special?" Henry said uneasily.

"Don't ask questions. I'll make it worth your while. Which one is—Take your hands off me!" he squeaked as Sénor Sans put a vast genial arm around his shoulder.

The police closed quietly in. Henry returned to Juana.

By this time everyone—except Juana—was aware of the scuffle beside the lifeboat. Bobby had evidently decided to ignore Dagobert's advice about going quietly.

"They can't do this to me!" he shouted. "Stop them somebody! I demand to see the British Consul!" His voice rose with indignation. "I am an Englishman—not a filthy dago!"

This, audible even to the crowd below, evoked a rousing cheer. Bobby, heartened, continued.

"Wait till this gets into the press! Wait till I see H. H. Hutton. Wait till—"

"And who," asked Juana, "is this? Have I met him?"

"It's Bobby Marcovitch," Henry said.

"Don't be silly, dear. Can't you see I'm talking to Mr. Marcovitch?"

She continued to regard Bobby with friendly curiosity, taking him for one of the more erratic members of our party. Bobby had stopped in mid-career. He blinked at the Princess and then at Henry. He tried to speak, but only gurgling sounds came from his throat.

"You'll join us, I hope," Juana said, putting him at his ease. "We are walking in procession to the Castle between loyal, cheering crowds—Senor Sans' idea."

"He can't," Henry said. "He's going to jail, as soon as you give orders to have him arrested."

She smiled at Bobby as though to beg his indulgence for this whimsical remark; but Bobby hadn't heard it. He was still goggling at Henry.

"Who's that?" he said.

"Haven't you met Mr. Hutton?" Juana said. "Let me introduce you . . . I'm afraid I didn't hear your name."

Bobby swallowed. "He . . . do you mean . . . Albert?"

"Yes," she sympathised. "Isn't it trying of him?"

"Albert . . . is H. H. . . . ?"

"I'm so sorry," she apologised.

Bobby took comfort in Senor Sans' supporting arm. "Who," he said weakly, "is nuts around here anyway?"

The word was familiar to the Princess and gave her a clue. The doctor had come out on deck and she recognised him with relief. She assumed he must be in charge of poor Bobby.

"Come now," she urged us all briskly. "Isn't that the national anthem? We must go. Will you take my arm, Henry?"

"Marcovitch," Henry said, "is accused of murder."

"You can tell me all about it later. Meanwhile we must not fail Senor Sans."

She turned away, graciously indicating that the rest of us should follow. Bobby made a frantic effort to free himself from Senor Sans' embrace.

"Hey! Just a minute!" he blurted out. "What about Flossie?"

"And who is Flossie?" Juana paused to inquire. "Must we wait for her too?"

"You'll have a long time to wait," Bobby said.

Juana looked hopefully at the doctor as though she expected him to administer something soothing like an injection or a

strait jacket. She asked Senor Sans absently:
"Where is she?"
"In the royal suite, ma'am."
"What is she doing there?"
"She's dead," Bobby said.
"What can he be talking about, Henry?"
Henry looked as though he didn't know. Senor Sans gave Bobby's arm a friendly twist.
"About Flossie," Bobby said doggedly.
"I'm sorry to be dull-witted," Juana said, "but will someone be good enough to explain what all this is about?"
"Why doesn't Your Highness ask H. H.?" Bobby said.
He tried to catch Henry's eye, but Henry was nervously studying his fingernails. Henry had shrunk again. Albert himself could not have looked more crestfallen or inadequate. Even a burst of cheers for Enrico El Loco failed to restore his self-confidence. Juana gave his hand a reassuring pat.
"Perhaps if the rest of you went ahead," she suggested. "You're hurting the poor fellow," she said to Senor Sans. "Henry will look after him if necessary. Now . . . ?"
No one moved and Bobby was suddenly conscious that he was the centre of attention. He lingered over the moment like a man poised for a spectacular high dive.
"I could be wrong about Flossie," he temporized. He saw he was holding his audience and said: "Maybe a word in private with H. H. would settle the matter. Otherwise," he paused, but Henry still avoided his eyes, "otherwise," he repeated, creeping nearer the edge of the diving-board, "it becomes my duty, my painful duty to inform Your Highness that Flossie . . ." he drew a swift breath, "that Flossie was—well, as a matter of fact, she, she was . . ."
And then he lost his nerve.
Henry looked up awkwardly from his fingernails. "I think he wants to say," he murmured, "that Flossie was my wife."

Chapter 28

I WAITED FOR the reaction to this sensational revelation, but there wasn't any. Most of the people who overheard Henry's confession understood no English. Those who did wore expressions of polite incredulity. Members of our own party, who had known Flossie and heard so much about Jim and the children in Lathomstowe, decided that Henry as well as Bobby had gone out of his mind.

It was hard to tell whether Juana had taken it in or not. She smiled vaguely and said: "Poor fellow."

Whether she meant Bobby or Henry I couldn't be sure. Both looked in need of comfort. Henry's ears were pink, Bobby's blue eyes were popping. He would have denied everything had anyone been willing to listen.

From the theatrical point of view the moment had fallen flat. As Dagobert said, Henry's genius for underplaying his part amounted to ability. He resembled a shamefaced schoolboy who had spoken out of turn.

Juana treated the incident as though—if it had really occurred—it was an error in taste which, though in itself trivial, required tactful smoothing over. She chatted animatedly with Henry about a proposed monument of Ethel, his mother, in the guise of Ceres spilling prosperity from an overflowing cornucopia. Senor Sans feared there would be a revolution unless the procession to the Castle began at once.

He exchanged a word or two in rapid Catalan with the Princess and herded everyone towards the gangway. The band began the national anthem for the third time and led the way up the steep central street towards the plaza. The loyal, cheering crowds, unrestrained by the police force—most of which remained on the yacht—mobbed the group enthusiastically and strewed the path with flowers and seasonal fruits. Rockets spluttered, fire-crackers exploded, dogs barked and churchbells pealed.

It was relatively peaceful on board the yacht. In the confusion Dagobert and I had managed to get left behind.

Bobby tried to join us, but one of the guards cracked him smartly on the head with the butt of his revolver. We joined him instead.

"I'm making notes about this," he said. "Wait till they see the next issue of *Home Truth*!"

"H. H. says there isn't going to be a next issue," Dagobert said. "He was very upset to learn it was a blackmail sheet."

"I bet he was. But not as upset as he's going to be."

Dagobert lighted a cigarette and handed it to him. "You know that safe of yours in London—full of unpublished stories. Does Saunders know the combination?"

"No one knows it except me."

"Then you'd better tell me what it is, fairly quickly."

"Look, I know I've behaved like a fool," he said patiently, "but . . . shall we talk about something else?"

"I'm talking about who murdered Flossie—and Juan Roig."

Bobby inhaled his cigarette. "I've got theories about that."

"For your sake let's hope they're wrong. What is the combination?"

"You weary me, dear boy. That safe is my insurance against a destitute old age."

"You may not have an old age," Dagobert said; but Bobby wasn't listening.

He was watching the gangway with an expression of complacence. "I thought so," he said smugly.

Henry had come back.

Bobby stubbed out his cigarette and rose. The policeman tapped him on the head again.

"See what I mean?" Dagobert said.

Henry was alone and I wondered how he had escaped from the procession. Perhaps Juana in her absent-minded fashion had mislaid him. He glanced briefly in our direction and slouched along the other side of the deck.

"You two better run along," Bobby said. "He wants a word alone with me. Oi! H. H.," he called.

The second policeman, feeling out of things, punched him in the ribs. Henry disappeared into the saloon. Bobby, unperturbed, recovered his breath.

"They'll regret this," he said. "I'll have another cigarette, please, while H. H. plays hard to get. He hopes to reduce the terms. I don't mind. I've plenty of time."

"But no more cards," Dagobert reminded him.

"One more," Bobby said.

"I wonder," Dagobert mused, "if they have a torture chamber in the Castle dungeon. . . . They might persuade you to remember the combination of that safe."

"He harps, doesn't he?" Bobby said to me.

"For some obscure reason," I said, "he's trying to save your life."

"Just leave that to Bobby," Bobby said. "And to Albert. Incidentally, how did you twig him? I'll be frank and admit I didn't. That accent and appearance—okay, maybe. But his manner, even his sentiments were pure depressed masses."

"From which, as you pointed out, Howard Turner rose less than seven years ago."

"Seven years is a long time. You may not believe it, but I was a bit of a Teddy-boy myself seven years ago," he said. "It changes you, being Henry Howard Hutton Junior."

"Henry Howard Hutton Junior was a character invented by his mother. According to him she had the brains, drive and ambition. She made him what he is today, he tells me. And, between ourselves, I'm not quite sure what that is."

"One of the richest men in the world," Bobby said.

"Since his mother's death, the Princess says, Henry has been utterly lost. He doesn't know a stock from a bond. Since his mother's death, I may add, shares in H. H. Hutton Holdings Inc. have risen phenomenally."

"It could be luck."

"Like getting a lift with me outside Boulogne," Dagobert said.

"I see what you mean," Bobby said. "It was also lucky reaching Tabarca to find there was no longer anything to prevent him marrying Princess Juana. Maybe his luck won't hold."

"It held long enough for him to find someone convenient to accuse of murder," Dagobert said grimly. "You. Now what's the combination of that safe?"

"Is it important?" asked Henry, who had stepped out of the saloon behind us.

He moved so quietly in his tennis shoes that we were momentarily unaware of his presence. Standing there with his hands in his pockets and Albert's expression of modest resignation it required an effort to remember he was the H. H. Hutton we had been discussing. Dagobert said:

"Marcovitch's life probably depends on it."

"Oh, then it isn't important," Henry said, and strolled over to the railings to watch the last of the procession in the plaza.

"Hey!" Bobby said, scrambling to his feet. "H. H.! Just a sec." He added, when Henry ignored him: "Sir."

We walked over to Henry. Bobby would have come with us,

but one of the guards kicked him gently in the shins.

"*Dejalo,*" Henry said. It meant: "Leave him alone," but Bobby, taking no chances, sat down again. Henry greeted us moodily.

"Did you notice Juana when I told her?" he said. "She didn't believe a word of it. None of them did. Enrico El Loco—they smile—what will he say next?"

"The art of being unconvincing," Dagobert nodded. "It has its value."

"I heard Finny betting Don Carlos the next thing I'd say was that I murdered her myself," he said. "Anything for a laugh."

"And did you?"

"I'm the only person with an obvious motive, but Senor Sans won't listen. He says Marcovitch did it. That key . . ."

"Yes," Dagobert said. "I was there when you had him searched."

"Then the time of death . . ."

"Don't tell me that's already been decided."

"These people work quickly when they want to. I don't understand the technical details, something about relative temperatures, but it works out so that, er . . ."

"None of us was on board at the time of death?" Dagobert suggested.

"That's right," Henry said. "Only Marcovitch. He was alone with her about the time she was smothered. The rest of us were on that pub-crawl and Senor Sans is satisfied with our alibis. Except, possibly, with yours. You and Jane, they say, visited the yacht at about the right—or should I say the wrong—time. No one seems to know whether you came on board or not. But don't worry about it."

The dock was nearly deserted now. A few stray dogs and a gypsy family were watching stores being brought aboard the yacht. A couple of guards rolled cigarettes and spat occasionally into the water. Fireworks were running short and the band sounded fainter as it climbed up to the Castle. Above the Castle a slight breeze caught and unfurled the royal standard. In the clear sunlight we could distinguish the golden sardines of Branza quartered with heraldic H. H. H.'s picked out in bright scarlet. Dagobert admired the effect.

"Mother's idea," Henry explained.

"Like the new issue of postage stamps with your profile superimposed on Juana's," Dagobert said drily. "Your mother didn't know you were already married?"

"I was afraid to tell her. It would have killed her. In fact when I finally had to—after she'd arranged for me to marry Juana—it did."

"Very interesting," Bobby remarked.

Henry continued not to hear him. Bobby, encouraged by no longer being struck every time he moved, edged nearer. Henry murmured:

"I've just seen her. Flossie, I mean. I used to call her Flo. She was a maid in a house across the street from the boarding-house Mother used to run in Quebec. She had no family. Mother couldn't stand her. She was a thin, pathetic little thing always shivering with the cold. She's changed more than I have in these last eight years. I wouldn't have recognised her."

"Why didn't you get a divorce?" I asked.

"I thought she was dead."

"She is now," Bobby pointed out.

Henry said to me: "I only discovered quite recently when I went to Quebec that she was alive and happy and living in Lathomstowe. I returned to London, but didn't have the courage to see her. I saw Pete once—on his way to school. I didn't have the courage to speak to him either. Mother hadn't told me about Pete, though she *must* have known."

"Pete, yes," Bobby said. "How are you going to talk yourself out of him?"

"Then I learned that Flo was coming to Tabarca," Henry went on. "I arranged to cross the channel on the same boat, hoping to have a word with her—to explain things if I could. Anyway to ask her for a divorce. When I heard there was a free seat in the Rolls-Royce I tried to thumb a lift. Your driver nearly ran over me. Dagobert was more generous. Except for occasional glimpses from a distance I didn't see Flo until this morning and she—"

"What time this morning?" Bobby interrupted.

". . . and she was dead," Henry said.

"So your problems were solved," Bobby nodded, propping himself comfortably against the railing beside us. "Sad, but let's look on the bright side. Listen, H. H. You're probably in a hurry and we can skip these delaying tactics." He jerked a thumb towards the policemen. "Those baboons, I take it, don't understand English. You can speak freely in front of Jane and Dagobert. They're more or less working with me. Okay. I've been thinking it over. You didn't know who Flossie was. The first time you saw her was this morning when the Colonel broke in the door. Right? Last night when you came on board you went straight to bed. Captain McNaughten will swear to that—or if he won't I will. Now how did Flossie die? Simple: she took an overdose of barbitone as I first said. Let's say she did it by accident. Something upset her at dinner—maybe a touch of ptomaine—and she didn't realise how much she had taken. That tame doctor of yours had better find a trace of ptomaine, together with a sufficient amount of barbitone, when he does the autopsy. I'll speak to him, if you like. About Pete—I suggest an allowance, given anonymously, through me. Finally about yours truly: in short, Bobby himself . . ."

"I haven't told you," Henry said to Dagobert. "The yacht is sailing at two-thirty, in about half an hour. The first port of call is Southampton."

"Good idea," Bobby agreed. "I'll be delighted to see the end of the Lucky Seven and the cruise will do me good. Half an hour just gives us time for a spot of business. If you'll step down to my cabin, H. H., I've a couple of papers for you to sign. They authorise certain minor changes in the management of *Home Truth*."

"Juana," Henry added tentatively, "wondered if you and Jane might enjoy the voyage."

"Glad to have them with me," Bobby said. "Any company is better than none."

"Captain McNaughten will make you comfortable," Henry said. "I hope you'll decide to go."

"They will, H. H. Don't worry. Just leave them to me—Who," he broke off, "is this?"

It was Senor Sans who had changed his mayoral frock coat for the more martial uniform of Chief of Police, a position he also held. He came puffing up the gangway, followed by a squad of men with rusty bayonets.

"What's he want?"

Henry seemed to notice Bobby for the first time. "He wants you," he said.

"Listen, H. H. Let's get this straight."

But Henry had lost interest. Or perhaps he was genuinely distressed when Senor Sans seized Bobby. He winced and walked off.

"Stop them, H. H. Tell them it's all a mistake. Tell them how we've fixed it up—like men of the world—between us." His voice cracked. "I'll keep my mouth shut, H. H. I didn't see you last night in the passage. Mr. Hutton," he whispered. "Sir. Just a minute."

Henry wiped the sweat from his forehead with the sleeve of his flannel blazer. It was sweltering in the midday heat. Even the dogs and the gypsies had gone. There were no witnesses to the solitary procession which crossed the Esplanade and vanished in the rabbit-warren of clothes-hung alleys below the Castle.

At the last moment Bobby's effrontery had failed him. Perversely I felt a pang of regret. All we heard as Senor Sans' men marched him down the gangway was a bleating sound.

" 'Not with a bang but a whimper,' " Henry quoted unexpectedly. "As Mother used to say . . . It's Senor Sans first real murder case. Sorry you'll miss it."

"We'll read about it in the papers."

"I doubt if it will get into the papers. Senor Sans hopes to deal with the matter quietly—so as to cause the minimum fuss and worry for Juana."

"Wouldn't it cause less fuss if you simply sent Bobby back to England?" I asked.

"I wish it had been possible," he said. "But the crime took place on a boat flying the Tabarcan flag. They tell me the trial must therefore take place here. What could I do?"

"You could, for instance, tell them—whoever 'they' are—to go to blazes," Dagobert said.

"But in Tabarca, you see, I'm only a simple, private citizen."

"Who owns the place," Dagobert said.

"Juana gives the orders, I'm afraid," he said. "Which reminds me—I'd better go. Not that anyone will have missed me." He glanced at his cheap wristwatch and extended an apologetic hand. "You sail in twenty minutes."

"Juana's orders?"

"Our, er, invitation," he smiled diffidently. "A slight return, I hope, for your kindness in giving me a lift on the motorscooter. As they say," he grinned, slipping into Albert's familiar diction, "one good turn deserves another. *Bong voy-aage,* Jane. Cheerio, cock."

Dagobert spent the twenty minutes before the yacht sailed composing a lengthy telegram to Saunders. I entertained the wireless operator while Dagobert sent it off.

We hurried down the gangway just as the ship's siren announced our departure. Two of Senor Sans' men, the only people on the dock, stared at us uncertainly. Dagobert handed them our suitcases to carry. They followed, muttering, as we climbed the broiling flagstones which led up to the plaza.

I clung rather closely to Dagobert. I still thought we were making a mistake in not accepting Henry's kind invitation. When Dagobert told me why the invitation had been so cordial I knew we were making a mistake.

"That key which was found in Bobby's pocket," he said. "I saw how it got there."

"How?"

He stopped to look round for our luggage. The yacht was nosing its way out through the breakwater. Flossie's body was still on board. Arrangements had been made for it to be shipped back to England and a cable sent to Jim Martin expressing the Princess' deepest condolences. Dagobert said:

"And Henry saw that I saw."

"Who?"

"Henry, of course," he said. "He slipped the key into Bobby's pocket himself.

Chapter 29

We missed luncheon but, as Juana said, we had probably been wise. It was, she explained, an informal affair, arranged by

Senor Sans and eaten in haste in order to give us ample time for the afternoon's programme: a visit to the new ice plant, a recital of Catalan poetry and folk dance, an address of welcome by the president of the Sardine Packers' Syndicate.

Juana assumed we had lunched at leisure, perhaps in one of the proposed but as yet inexistent luxury restaurants on the Esplanade. She had forgotten—if she had ever known—that we were supposed to have sailed on the yacht.

Henry, too, received us without surprise. He merely looked as though he felt (as I did) that we had made an unfortunate decision. He showed us to a room and told our armed porters to leave our suitcases there. Their disappointment was visible: they had hoped to deliver our luggage to a cell in the Castle dungeon.

"Perhaps later," Dagobert said, as he over-tipped them.

Senor Sans, who had a sense of humour, laughed heartily —for the first time since our arrival. Senor Sans had greeted us coldly. Bobby had told him that Dagobert was a famous detective.

As promised by *Home Truth*, the Lucky Seven (or rather the five of us who remained) were lodged in the Royal Palace. This turned out to be a large suburban chalet built in the twenties by Juana's father. The furniture had come from England and was in pale fumed oak. There were three-piece suites in shadow-repp with tassels, a cocktail cabinet with a mirrored interior which lighted up when opened, an electric clock which didn't go. There were nests of tables, tea-trolleys and, on the walls, copper warming-pans, views of Tower Bridge, Highland cattle and a signed photograph of the Prince of Wales. A cabinet with leaded panes contained Don Carlos' billiard trophies. Finny told us that every bedroom had a tiled shower-bath, a radio and a plug for electric razors. Henry loathed the place and Juana, who normally lived in a hotel in Cannes, didn't see it.

"It isn't *exactly* what you'd expect, is it?" Ninette said as we sipped coffee on the verandah. "Of course it's very comfortable and," she added with more warmth, "you can see at once that Princess Juana is a lady, but . . ." She glanced doubtfully at Don Carlos, gently snoring in his wicker rocking chair. He had been delegated to entertain us and we were otherwise unchaperoned.

"I gather," said Colonel Warrington, "that Marcovitch's quarters are more picturesque—if less comfortable."

Through the view-finder of his Leica camera he continued to study the Castle which rose above us. It was the first time anyone had mentioned Bobby, but everyone knew where he was.

The Castle had been more photogenic from the deck of the yacht. From the chalet verandah the massive stone walls of the square dungeon were oppressive. They were pierced only by a minute window or two and by a low postern-gate which communicated with the chalet garden by means of a humpbacked stone bridge which crossed a narrow gorge choked with prickly pears.

At one of the high windows hands gripped the rusting bars and a face briefly appeared. The prison quarters were in an upper storey of the great tower. The face could not be identified and there was no reason to suppose it was Bobby's. Finny had told us there were workmen in the *Castillo*. Henry's mother had wished to make it habitable again, though no sane member of the Branza family had lived in it since the seventeenth century. Men were also at work in the great hall clearing out the goats and gypsies, in preparation for tonight's banquet at which—it was general knowledge—Juana would officially announce the date of her marriage to Henry.

Margaret averted her eyes as the Colonel snapped the blurred face at the barred window.

"What did Mr. Hutton mean," she asked me, "about Mrs.

Martin, Flossie, having been his wife?"

"It seems our host specialises in outrageous remarks of the sort," the Colonel said. *"Pour épater la bourgeoisie,* as my friend Louis de Bourbon used to say. His own eccentricity was to—"

Ninette sighed deeply. "Poor Bobby," she said.

"We must not be sentimental," Margaret said impatiently. "He richly deserves whatever punishment he receives." She rose abruptly. "I think I'll miss the ice plant and have a siesta instead. Will you make my excuses?"

She retired, leaving her coffee untouched.

"Mrs. Penrose," Ninette explained, "had almost no sleep last night on the yacht. She got up a dozen times."

"Did she leave the cabin?" Derek asked.

"She walked around the deck, I think." She ate Turkish Delight thoughtfully. "Is Finny really a duke? I wonder if he's married?"

"What," Derek said to Dagobert, "are we going to do about him? Marcovitch, I mean."

"There's nothing much we can do, is there," Hugo Warrington said practically. "Senor Sans assures me he'll have a fair trial. Of course it's a bit embarrassing that a chap we've all known . . . I once met that fellow Heath, as a matter of fact, in an R.A.F. mess. You'd have taken him for a gentleman. Don't know what the world's coming to. Wonder what old Prince Jaime would have said if he'd known his only daughter was going to marry, er . . ."

His voice trailed off discreetly. Don Carlos continued to snore and we remained unattended. Finny, pleading work of national importance, had crept off for a nap. Juana and Henry had promised to join us shortly.

"If you mean Mr. Hutton," said Ninette who alone among us sometimes gave way to impatience with Colonel Warrington, "I think she's jolly lucky to get him."

"The *mariage de convenance* is, of course, not uncommon among—"

"What's more," she interrupted, "the Princess is in love with him! I've seen them together and I know."

"My dear young lady, I'm not for a moment suggesting that—"

"And another thing! Mr. Hutton is in love with her. I don't know what a marriage of convenience is, but I do know when a man and a woman are really in love with each other!"

She shot Derek a look which I couldn't interpret and walked over to the balustrade, giving us a view of her shapely back. Derek said:

"Bravo!" and to Dagobert, more seriously: "If only we could get permission, at least, to see him."

"He must," I agreed, "have proper legal defence."

"Senor Sans has already laid that on," the Colonel said. "Marcovitch will be defended by his brother-in-law."

"And prosecuted by another brother-in-law," I said. "Senor Sans himself will act as judge. And the jury, I understand, are also all relatives."

"Then what chance has he got?" Derek demanded.

"None, I should think," Hugo Warrington said calmly. "As Mrs. Penrose just said, let us not be sentimental. Mr. Marcovitch was a blackmailer."

Ninette spun round. "How do you know?"

"Margaret, Mrs. Penrose told me."

"But that doesn't make him a murderer," she protested.

"It makes him something far worse," he said. "Incidentally it makes him a murderer too. Or at least responsible for a man's death—her husband's."

"Did she," I asked, "did she tell you about George?"

"There was no need to," he said shortly. "I once met the Reverend George Faversham. Shall we discuss something more agreeable?"

"Catalan poetry," Derek suggested. "Have you met many eminent Catalan poets, sir?"

"Mistral I knew slightly," he said, unaware that the query was ironic, "though strictly speaking he wrote in Provençal."

Dagobert smiled, doing a quick mental calculation. Hugo Warrington surprised me again by chuckling.

"He's checking up on me," he said. "Yes, Mistral died in, was it, 1914? A sly one, your husband, Mrs. Brown. I suspect he's seen through me—just as he saw through Albert, eh?"

"Yes, I think I have," Dagobert said.

"How did you guess Albert was actually this H. H. Hutton?" the Colonel said. "Always interesting to hear how you sleuth chaps work. When did you spot him?"

"A couple of nights ago in Toulouse."

"I suppose he gave himself away in his cups?"

"The more he drinks, the less he gives himself away," Dagobert said.

"Remarkable. Then how did you draw your conclusions?"

"It was obvious," Dagobert said modestly. "The more one thought about it the more obvious it became. Albert *had* to be Henry Howard Hutton Junior."

I regarded Dagobert with pride. Even Derek was impressed by the subtlety of his deductive processes.

"Gosh!" said Ninette.

"Especially," Dagobert explained, "after I caught a glimpse of his passport in the Toulouse police station. I put two and two together."

"Deucedly clever," Hugo said. "What did it say?"

Dagobert grinned. "It said Henry Howard Hutton Junior."

Margaret Penrose came out of the house, complaining that she could not sleep. I suspected the cause of her insomnia was the sight of Senor Sans coming down the path from the Castle. He had gone up to make sure that Bobby was "comfortable." Margaret, like the rest of us, was less indifferent to news of

Bobby than she pretended. But only Ninette had the courage to stop Senor Sans as he hurried importantly across the verandah.

"What's happening to Bobby?" she demanded.

"The uncertainty," Colonel Warrington said. "If you could tell us exactly what and, er, when . . . it would be a relief to one and all."

"At least to one," Dagobert said.

"Uncertainty?" said Senor Sans, puzzled. "Oh, you mean the confession."

"Has he confessed?" Margaret asked.

"My men work on that now, Senora," he assured her. "At first, sometimes, they are ashamed and do not like to confess."

"But if he didn't do it!" Ninette cried.

"I tell him he did do it," Senor Sans explained.

"But surely there will be an investigation," Derek said. "Witnesses, statements and so on."

"A thorough investigation," Senor Sans agreed. "In fact I have already made it. He is guilty."

"But a trial . . ."

"He gets that too. All very fair and scrupulous. Then . . . ssst!" He drew an eloquent forefinger across his throat.

"And you're going to hang him—just like that?" said Margaret, appalled.

Senor Sans was equally shocked at the suggestion. "No, Senora, certainly not. We are not so uncivilised that we hang him. We . . ." He looked round in search of something to illustrate his point. He found Finny's discarded silk scarf and made a loop in it. "We garotte him." He jerked it suddenly into a tight knot. "So! The executioner," he added wistfully, "is the doctor's son, my nephew Paco."

"When does the show take place?" Dagobert asked.

"Ah, that is to decide," Senor Sans said. "Tonight at the banquet in the Castle the Princess graciously announces the date when she gives her hand to Mr. Hutton. This, between ourselves, is for Sunday, in three days. For three days there will be fiesta. So I think—not to spoil the good time—we garotte the Senor Marcovitch quick—tomorrow morning when the sun rises. That will suit?"

He paused at the door to remind us that the tour of the ice plant began in a quarter of an hour, gave Don Carlos' rocking chair a prod with his boot and went inside. Dagobert said:

"That doesn't give us much time, does it?"

"W-what for?" Ninette stammered.

"To decide which one of us killed Flossie," Dagobert said.

Chapter 30

WHICH *one of us* killed Flossie . . .

Having tossed this lightly into our midst Dagobert disappeared for the afternoon. He was not, he said, one of the Lucky Seven and therefore had no right to share the entertainments prepared for us.

He rejoined us, however, in the plaza at about half past seven during the recital of Catalan poetry. I could see that his afternoon had been as frustrating as our own. Every attempt he had made to see Bobby had failed: Senor Sans had been obstructive, Henry remained a simple, private citizen without authority, Juana knew nothing about the matter.

"Anyway you missed the Sardine Packers' Syndicate," I said.

Margaret was more sympathetic. "Does it really matter?" she asked him anxiously. "Yes, I suppose it does."

Dagobert seemed grateful for the assurance, halfhearted though it was. He too had debated the problem: did it matter who killed Flossie? Everyone in Tabarca knew that Bobby's execution was fixed for dawn tomorrow. Everyone who knew Bobby knew he deserved to die. Even if he hadn't killed Flossie, even if he hadn't killed Juan Roig, he had murdered George Faversham with a weapon crueler than smothering or drowning: blackmail.

And why, after all, should we assume he had not killed Flossie? And Juan Roig too? Merely because of a vague theory that Bobby wasn't the killing type? I began to feel a little impatient with Dagobert's theories. I felt impatient, probably, because deep down I agreed with him.

"And yet," I said, "there's no proof that he *didn't* do it."

"The point is," he reminded me sombrely, "there's no proof that he did."

"He *could* have."

"So," he said remorselessly, "could everybody else."

"Not Juan Roig," I said illogically.

"We were all on the channel ferry."

"But Margaret saw Bobby go out on deck with him."

"It was a big deck and Margaret . . ."

He concentrated on Catalan poetry, pretending an interest in it which, for all I knew, he may have felt. I guessed what he had been about to say: Margaret saw what she wanted to see. Anyone, who was a good enough sailor, could have followed Juan Roig out on deck—includng Margaret herself.

While he thumbed through the Catalan dictionary he had bought that afternoon, I evaded the issue—the physical reality of Bobby Marcovitch in a prison cell awaiting death—by idle speculation.

Flossie had been smothered. That much of the doctor's report we all accepted.

When? Senor Sans said the doctor had determined the time at approximately two-thirty a.m. This was when Flossie had gone into the royal suite and Bobby had told her why he was taking her to Tabarca. We were on the dock at that time and all other members of the party including Albert were together in a night club.

The doctor was yet another of Senor Sans' brothers-in-law and in fixing the time at two-thirty he was plainly acting under instructions. Whose instructions—Henry's or Juana's? Bobby said Flossie was alive at five a.m. when, hearing our taxi arrive, he hastily left her, turning the key but leaving it in the door. Dagobert had seen the key in the door. Had anyone else seen it? And later used it to enter the suite?

Bobby himself *could* have come back. Then, Ninette had told us, Margaret had slept badly and left the cabin they shared to walk around the deck. Bobby said he had seen "that fellow Albert" lurking in the passage. Whether anyone else—Derek Upjohn, Hugo Warrington or indeed Ninette herself—had wandered during the night we didn't know. The crew had not been questioned and they were now many leagues out to sea.

In brief, anyone could have entered the royal suite and killed Flossie.

I wasn't getting very far by examining opportunity. I considered character, like Dagobert eliminating the "non-killer types." I thus eliminated myself and, for no very clear reason, Ninette, which narrowed down the Lucky Seven group to three: the Colonel, Derek and Margaret.

Could Margaret kill anybody? Possibly Bobby, but not Flossie whom she liked nor Juan Roig whom she didn't even know. I still remembered the chill loathing in her voice when she told me that forgiveness came hard to her.

Derek Upjohn, with his sense of guilt and bouts of drunkenness, was certainly a complex character—rather more than the "crazy mixed-up kid" Ninette once called him. To be sure, going blind was something to be "mixed-up" about. Then he was good with dogs, I remembered inconsequentially, and were not murderers traditionally fond of animals?

Hugo Warrington was too true to type to be anything but bogus. This, however, did not necessarily make him the type that kills. His satisfaction at the prospect of Bobby's execution *could* be explained by a desire to see rough justice done. It could also be explained another way: with Bobby dead the case would be closed and no more questions asked.

The trouble with my short list of suspects was, of course, that not one of them had a motive. Before the trip none of them had known Flossie. Juan Roig they had barely met.

But Bobby could have known Juan Roig, or at least known about him through an intermediary like Saunders. I had an idea that Dagobert's telegram to Saunders might concern the possibility of Juan Roig's having been a contributor to *Home Truth*'s undisclosed earnings. I had not seen the telegram and Dagobert was uncommunicative, having, I suspected, little faith in its results.

It was possible, then, that Bobby had been blackmailing Juan Roig. It was possible that Juan Roig had been difficult and that Bobby in a fit of panic had pushed him into the channel.

Could he not have had similar difficulties with Flossie? She had threatened to leave the yacht. She had refused to play her part in his blackmailing plan. Couldn't he have smothered her in an access of uncontrollable rage?

I thought of Bobby and knew he couldn't. Bobby didn't lose control where money was concerned and, as he had said, Flossie alive was money in the bank to him.

I watched the recital. The bard, to everyone's relief, was refreshing himself from a leather bottle while a pair of earnest young clerks from the post office demonstrated the traditional Tabarcan sword-dance. The orange trees around the plaza were festooned with small children hoping to see the dancers impale themselves.

Dagobert, unaware that the poetry had ceased, remained absorbed in his dictionary. On the outskirts of the crowd three or four of Senor Sans' men remained absorbed in Dagobert.

Juana watched the spectacle with apparent interest. Henry watched Juana as though only she in all that multitude existed.

Henry . . .

I looked away and murmured: "There isn't anyone else."

"No," Dagobert agreed. "And yet I don't think he did it."

I sighed with patient exasperation, half expecting this preposterous defence of his late pillion rider. No, I thought wearily, it couldn't (in Dagobert's estimation) possibly be Henry! Henry was merely the sole person who had a reason for killing Flossie! He was merely, in case the obvious needed underlining, the one who had planted the key in Bobby's dressing-gown pocket. With Henry's tacit agreement—if not on his active instructions—Bobby would be punished for a crime which only Henry himself could have committed.

But this wasn't good enough for Dagobert! I tried to be reasonable.

"No one else gains by it," I argued.

"If you must introduce the profit motive," he said, "there's something in it for Juana too—about a hundred million dollars, in fact."

Chapter 31

Bobby left notes of that night's state banquet. He wasn't there, but I have borrowed freely from his description.

In the draughty hall of the *Castillo*—still smelling faintly of disinfectant—we were "whisked back" into the Middle Ages. Bobby's pen, doubtless inspired by the rich odour which rose to his solitary cell above, dwells wistfully on the royal feast set before us.

The banquet table "literally groaned" with good things—and before they were half finished Don Carlos was beneath it. Foie gras and caviare had been brought from the mainland; there were roast partridges, pheasants and turkeys on spits, York hams and pale pink hams cured in snow from the Sierras. Massive dishes of lobster and langouste, of shrimps and prawns under piles of golden mayonnaise, stood like set pieces on the sideboards. In our honour a monstrous baron of practically raw beef was served with mint sauce. There were casks of claret, barrels of burgundy, magnums of champagne and jeroboams of ancient brandy.

Flossie would have enjoyed it; so would Bobby. But the rest of us picked our way cautiously through this gargantuan and interminable feed. The Branza tribe, however, fell to as though they hadn't eaten for weeks. Finny admitted that the tradesmen had been a little restive during Henry's prolonged absence.

Tonight's blow-out, be confided, had set the royal exchequer back about two years' revenue.

"Not to mention the family jewellery," he added, "which Juana will now be able to get out of hock."

Yes, I reflected, a hundred million dollars ought comfortably to redeem Juana's jewellery. . . .

Juana, meanwhile, sat beside Henry on a raised dais at the head of the table, regal in green velvet and paste copies of her pawned jewellery. In the candlelight she more nearly resembled the official portrait of herself which had been reproduced on the cover of *Home Truth*.

She was not exactly "beautiful"—as Ninette insisted she was—but you couldn't take your eyes off her. Although she was tiny—a head shorter than Henry—she possessed something of the robust quality of her ancestors whose portraits lined the freshly whitewashed walls: the aquiline nose, the stubborn chin, the commanding glance—qualities which had kept her family afloat through centuries of rough weather. Generations of Branzas had fought, schemed, intrigued, married for survival. In a sense the acquisition of the Hutton millions was the continuation of an historical process.

Ethel Hutton may have bought Tabarca. Juana de Branza had only to announce her marriage to Henry to have it back again.

And so the Branzas ate with good heart. Their appetite would have been less keen perhaps had Flossie been there. . . .

In addition to ourselves there were nearly fifty at the long trestle table—relations, legitimate and, according to Finny, otherwise, Senor Sans with other island notables and, below the salt, the commercial ragtag and bobtail. Beyond, glimpsed through low stone arches, crowded entertainers, retainers and anybody else who could push in, commenting freely on the appearance of the guests, watching every mouthful we ate. It was, as Bobby wrote, "feudal magnificence torn from the illuminated pages of a medieval manuscript." At any moment we expected jongleurs and minstrels.

Even Colonel Warrington's memories did not go far enough back to recall a similar affair.

"Extraordinary," he said to Senor Sans, who had arranged it.

Senor Sans, pleased, explained that it only revealed the savagery and primitive conditions which made Tabarca the scandal of the civilised world.

"It fills me with shame, sir," he said, letting his belt out a notch or two, "to think that while we gorge ourselves those poor people outside are starving like dogs. Tomorrow, when you come to my office, I show you the malnutrition statistics." He belched genteelly. "A little more brandy, sir? It aids to digest."

After two or three hours the table had begun to look like a battlefield. Lobsters and spilt red wine made colourful splashes on the once-shining napery. In the shambles half-devoured carcasses of kid and lamb loomed beneath guttering candles. Casualties among the wine glasses were greeted with cries of delight. On the rush-strewn floor cats fought for bones. The servants had given up trying to restore order and were openly snaffling sweetmeats from the sideboards.

Henry regarded the confusion with the chastened air of one who will eventually have to pay for it. The untouched wine in his champagne glass had lost its effervescence. Beside him Juana surveyed the company with abstract benevolence. Her smile, I thought, had become slightly fixed. I saw her hand suddenly reach for Henry's beneath the tablecloth. Both flushed at the contact.

The silence which had fallen over the top of the table spread slowly down its length. Senor Sans glanced portentously at his watch. It was midnight.

Juana laid aside her table napkin and Finny whispered: "Here it comes." The mob beyond the arches abruptly stopped chattering. Don Carlos woke up with a snort and gazed round with bleary eyes. From somewhere in the distance came the heart-broken bray of a solitary burro.

There was a rustle of expectancy as Juana rose and a corporate breath of relief when she smiled and indicated that we were to keep our seats. Her female relations looked coy and mysterious and Don Carlos winked salaciously at no one in particular. Servants began cautiously to refill champagne glasses.

Even before Juana could announce the happy date the loyal masses were straining at the leash. After the wedding, Senor Sans had promised, taxation would be abolished and, if he was re-elected, profits from the proposed Casino would be distributed quarterly among deserving electors. All were prepared to shout themselves hoarse in honour of Enrico El Loco whose marriage to their Princess would bring these good things in its train.

They were even prepared within reason to listen to Juana.

She spoke with commendable brevity. She welcomed the *Home Truth* party to Tabarca and trusted that our short visit to the island would be enjoyable. In a few minutes, she believed, there would be a display of pyrotechnics. The band would provide music for dancing in the plaza, and until dawn the taverns would at her own expense serve all comers.

No one at the table was very interested in this and I heard Finny mutter: "Get on with it." I was watching Henry. His ears had gone a dull pink. Juana continued to smile pleasantly while she thanked us all for having made the evening such a success. Her only regret, she said, was that a headache prevented her from taking part in the remaining festivities. She would therefore, with our kind permission, say good-night.

Before anyone quite realised her speech was finished she inclined her head gracefully and turned from the table. She had spoken in English and the crowd, who hadn't understood a word, roared gratefully for Enrico El Loco. Henry remained seated, apparently deaf and dumb.

"What about the wedding?" Finny called.

This was translated to Don Carlos who immediately had a coughing fit and had to be removed from the table. By this time everyone had grasped that the expected announcement had not been made. Uneasy silence gave way to the scraping of chairs, muttered queries and finally open growls of resentment.

Juana's black eyes were cold as she faced the table again. The smile was still on her lips but something in her bearing quelled the company. She did not have to raise her voice.

"Perhaps I should explain," she said, "that Mr. Hutton and I have decided not to be married after all."

Senor Sans bit through his unlighted cigar.

"But he's got to!" he choked. "He signed a contract."

"I have destroyed the contract," the Princess said.

And before anyone could speak again she quietly withdrew.

Chapter 32

THE BAND STRUCK up a ragged version of the national anthem which was drowned in the pandemonium that broke out the moment the Princess left the hall. Finny's mother, the Dowager Duchess of Finistrat, had hysterics and fled after Juana to comfort the "*pobrecita.*" Don Carlos, who grasped the situation with difficulty, spoke of family honour and called for pistols. The mob outside, more practical, burst in and fell upon what was left of the banquet.

Henry sat alone on the raised dais before his flat champagne, unconscious of the hubbub. Senor Sans tried to approach him but receiving no response marched off, fiercely rebuttoning the jacket of his uniform. He slipped through a narrow aperture in the thick stone wall and a moment later I could hear him puffing as he climbed the steep spiral steps which led up to the prison cells. Doubtless he proposed to take it out on Bobby. Dagobert said to Henry:

"Shall we go up and help Senor Sans encourage Bobby?"

"Why?"

"It might throw light on who killed Flossie."

Henry's interest in the subject was evidently exhausted. "That's already been decided," he said.

"Quite."

Henry, misunderstanding the dryness of Dagobert's tone, said impatiently: "Marcovitch will get fair treatment, if that's what you're worried about. Tabarca's not so Ruritanian as it appears. Finny—and Sans himself—like to give the impression the place is run on comic-opera lines. As a matter of fact its chief magistrate is far from uncivilised."

"And who's that? You?"

"Juana," he said shortly.

"Why did she break off the wedding?" I asked.

Apparently he didn't hear the question. Most of the guests had now dispersed and the marauding hoi polloi cautiously avoided the head of the table. Ninette approached and plucked at Dagobert's sleeve.

"Finny and Derek and I are going down to the plaza to dance," she said. "Coming?"

We said we could come in a minute. She shot a look of compassion at Henry and retreated. Henry, addressing his glass of flat champagne, repeated:

"Why did she break off the wedding?" No one spoke and Henry regarded the dim portraits on the wall as though Juana's ancestors might supply an answer to the question. "That one," he mused. "Alfonso the Fiery slaughtered three thousand Moors in the sack of Hadjez-el-Bab in 1489. The bearded type next to him, Pedro the Hasty, found his wife in bed with a page and tossed her out of an upper window of the Castillo. But none of them, Juana tells me, was cowardly enough to smother a defenceless creature in cold blood and arrange for the crime to be pinned on someone else." He seemed suddenly to remember our presence. "Ninette and the others," he said, "are waiting for you."

We joined them at the door which led out to the ramparts.

"What went wrong?" Ninette whispered. "Ought we to leave him? Poor Albert! Gosh, I mean H. H. Fancy feeling sorry for a millionaire. But you can't help it, can you?"

"Yes," I said to Dagobert some time later, "on the whole I can help it."

We had remained alone on the castle ramparts to watch the last of the fireworks. The crowd had been through the great hall like locusts; the candles had burned down, flickered and gone out.

But the distant plaza was bright with coloured electric bulbs and noisy with dance music amplified through loud-speakers. Shouts of revelry reached us, as they must have reached the upper regions of the dungeon where, outside Bobby's cell, we could hear the measured tread of sentry's boots.

Just below us the chalet gardens nestled round the base of the Castle. The house was dark except for a corner on the first floor—Juana's rooms—and a wrought-iron lamp on the verandah.

"Certainly I can help it," I repeated, perhaps raising my

voice, for I felt warmly on the subject. "What are the unvarnished facts about Henry? He played fast and loose with the affections of a wretched child and married her in secret. He gave her a baby and promptly deserted her. While Flossie worked in a cheap cafeteria to support his son, Henry became one of the richest men in the world. Years later he contracted a brilliant match. Though he had carefully changed his name it occurred to him that an abandoned wife might prove embarrassing. He had to do something about it. . . . Well, he did something, and she died. Wedding bells could ring and everyone was happy. Now, suddenly, there's a hitch. His fairy Princess tears up the contract and refuses to fall into his arms. And we," I concluded angrily, "we are *sorry* for him!"

"Extremely kind of you," Henry murmured. "I'm sort of sorry for myself."

I caught a glimpse of amusement on Dagobert's face. He had let me rave on knowing that Henry lurked in the shadows behind me. I said sharply to Henry:

"What are you doing there?"

"As a matter of fact," he said, "I was contemplating a swift jump from the ramparts. Not very seriously," he added sadly.

"I thought you'd gone down to the chalet to have it out with Juana."

"I had it out with Juana this afternoon," he said.

"Did you," I asked, "did you hear . . . everything I said?"

"Yes. It was a pretty fair account of my career. One or two details could be corrected, not that you'd believe me if I corrected them. Juana didn't."

He leaned against the balustrade beside us and gazed down at the shingle beach. I followed his gaze and drew back an inch or two. The drop was even more vertiginous than I had realised.

"Correct them anyway," Dagobert said.

"Why waste your time? I cut a sorry figure any way it's told."

Dagobert asked: "How could you marry Flossie without your mother knowing it?"

"Being a coward I couldn't marry her any other way. I waited until Mother was out of sight."

"The famous fortnight when you got away from her?"

He nodded. "She'd gone to Alberta about some wasteland which was left to us by an uncle. As soon as she was gone I persuaded Flo to marry me. For a couple of weeks it looked as though things were going to work out. We found a room on the other side of Quebec and, though Mother always said I was too delicate to work, I found a job. I was coming home that night to tell Flo the good news when a truck ran me down. I woke up in hospital about a week later. In my wallet they had found Mother's address and she was there. Flo wasn't."

"And," I suggested, "you'd lost your memory?"

"Nothing so convenient," he said. "Flo was the first person I asked for. Mother began to cry. When I asked her why, she said Flo knew all about my accident, but refused to see me. A weakling and an invalid—probably permanent, she hinted—was no use to Flo. Flo had once called me a mother-ridden nonentity, and it had the ring of truth.

"I was another month in hospital and Flo never turned up. She didn't know where I was, of course. Mother told her we were moving to Alberta and that I'd already gone ahead. Flo was too frightened of Mother to say we'd been married. So was I—especially when Mother told me Flo had run off with a flashy travelling salesman in a Chrysler convertible.

"You didn't know Mother, and neither did I—then. She could make the most far-fetched story sound convincing. And, well, she was very maternal and understanding. We would go to Alberta, she said, perhaps sell some of our land and farm the rest—I'd soon forget about Flo. . . .

"I was on crutches when I got out of hospital and too weak, or, if you like, too weak-minded to argue about it. I went to Alberta, but I didn't forget Flo. We sold a few acres of land for a few hundred dollars and then uranium was discovered nearby. The next few acres fetched a few thousand. Mother wanted to sell the lot, but I got cautious. We leased a bit more and sat on the rest. At the end of eight or nine months royalties began to pour in—in hundreds of thousands.

"The more money I got my hands on the more I missed Flo. I wanted to show her I wasn't the feeble cipher she thought I was. I wanted to make her regret her travelling salesman and his Chrysler convertible. I bought a Rolls-Bentley and decided to drive back to Quebec to find her. I didn't tell Mother what I proposed to do, but she must have guessed. She remarked casually one morning at breakfast that she'd heard from the people across the street from our old boardinghouse in Quebec. Flo and her boy friend, it seemed, had been killed in a plane crash.

"I don't think I seriously suspected that Mother was lying; but I drove to Quebec anyway. She came along, partly to show off in front of our former neighbours, but chiefly to keep an eye on me. I didn't find Flo. She'd long since left the room where we lived and they didn't know where she was. Actually by this time she was in hospital herself—in a charitable institution for destitute mothers. I discovered this only last month when I returned to Quebec. They told me at the hospital that my son Pete was born there.

"The point is," he continued listlessly, "why didn't I find out all this years ago? I could have, of course; and the fact that I didn't makes me all the things Jane thinks I am. I still felt bitterly humiliated because I thought Flo had left me flat. Then, to be honest, I had other distractions: money. The land we still owned turned out to contain one of the richest uranium deposits in Canada. The thousands became millions. We changed our name to Hutton and began to branch out. Mother became a great lady. I faded tactfully into her background, her colourless and semi-invalid son. As a matter of fact the manipulation of vast sums has its charms and, well, for years I didn't think of Flo—or of any other woman."

He let the stub of his cigarette slip from his fingers. I watched the glowing tip on its interminable journey to the beach below. He said:

"Then I met Juana. . . ."

"And your mother," I prompted, "arranged for you to marry her."

"Mother arranged nothing!" he said harshly. "She was—heaven forgive me . . . and her!—a silly woman whose limited intelligence was concentrated on one object: to keep me attached to her apron strings."

"And yet she bought Tabarca."

"I bought Tabarca."

"But her business genius, her flair for investments—"

"Nonexistent. She did the talking. She said exactly what I told her to say. Ethel Hutton was the terror of the financial world while I was her rather simple-minded appendage. I enjoyed playing the fool . . . until today when I realised I really was a fool. . . . I believed Juana was fond of me. She isn't."

In a lull in the music from the plaza we could hear the sea stirring the shingles on the beach. The sentry's tread outside Bobby's cell paused, then began again. Dagobert asked:

"Did Juana know you'd been married before?"

"Yes, I told her the whole story."

"But her reaction when she heard of Flossie's death!" I objected.

"Juana does not have reactions—at least not in public," he said. "Yes, she knew why I went to Canada. We both agreed that I had to find out where I stood. You see, I'd begun to suspect Mother's story of the plane crash. If Flo was still alive I hoped she'd release me. If necessary Juana said she'd wait till I was divorced. You know the rest."

"Bobby killed Flossie," Dagobert said, "and a divorce was not necessary. . . . Only Bobby did not kill Flossie."

"So I have heard," Henry said indifferently.

"Do you know who did kill her?"

"I know who *you* think did. And," he added wearily, "who Juana thinks did."

"Then can you blame her for calling off the wedding?" I asked.

"No. In fact I'd blame her if she hadn't. The trouble is there's nothing I can do about it."

"You can," Dagobert said, "find out who did murder her. Unless you already know."

Or, I thought, unless Juana's right and you did it yourself.

Dagobert said:

"That key which was found in Bobby's pocket."

"You saw me plant it on him, didn't you?"

"Yes, but where did *you* get it?"

"I found it in the door of the suite."

"*After* Flossie had been killed?" Dagobert said.

"Yes."

"You saw she was dead, locked the door and took away the key?"

"Yes."

"Why?"

"I wanted time to think things over."

"And to remove any awkward evidence which might lead us to the real murderer," Dagobert suggested. "The murderer, it would seem, was too hurried, or too flustered, to lock the door."

"I suppose so."

"What frightened him—or her—away? Seeing you?"

"In any case," Henry shrugged, "I didn't see her. Or him."

Dagobert seemed unimpressed by this curious word order. He had grown increasingly restless during the past few minutes and only half-listened to what Henry said. He was fidgeting near the edge of the ramparts, alternately consulting his watch and the stars, apparently seeking inspiration from them. It was contagious and I too stared up as though awaiting some last-minute revelation from the skies. I began to imagine a faint throbbing in my ears. Dagobert said suddenly:

"A little over twelve hours ago I sent an urgent radiogram to Saunders."

Henry had evidently heard about Dagobert's first telegram sent from Toulouse and he grinned, glad to change the subject.

"Whose name did you use this time?" he asked. "Bobby's?"

"No," Dagobert said. "I signed it Henry Howard Hutton Junior."

"You signed my name?" Henry sounded puzzled and a little annoyed.

The buzzing sound in my ears increased. Dagobert continued to prowl around the ramparts. At first I thought the red and green lights blinking on the horizon were belated pyrotechnics. Henry said:

"Looks like an aeroplane. What did the radiogram say?"

"In it you offered Saunders the editorship of *Home Truth,* plus a handsome block of shares," Dagobert said. "You also authorised him to charter a seaplane and come to Tabarca. You instructed him to bring certain documents from Bobby's private safe and if he couldn't open it, blow the safe open. You hinted that speed was vital and that if he and the documents were not instantly forthcoming the police would seize both them and himself. It was an elaborate variation on the old theme: 'Fly at once. All is discovered.' "

"W-what's discovered?" Henry asked, trying to keep up with Dagobert who was halfway down the steps which descended towards the village. The plane was already circling the harbour.

"I don't know," Dagobert said, "but Bobby has promised us some fascinating reading matter."

Chapter 33

BOBBY HAD PUT it mildly.

For nearly two hours we sat in the ill-lighted customs shed poring over the contents of the three bulging dispatch cases Saunders had found in Bobby's private safe.

Dagobert at first encouraged me to lend a hand; but glancing over my shoulder at the manuscript I was engaged in diciphering he took it from me and hastily burned it. Brandy was sent for to revive me and from then on I squirmed patiently in a corner with Saunders while Henry and Dagobert did the research. Both, on occasions, had recourse to the brandy to prevent sudden surges of nausea.

The arrival of a seaplane in the middle of the night caused a certain stir, though most people believed it had something to do with the festivities. Dancing had been resumed in the plaza, the loudspeakers were going full blast, children were screaming happily, courting couples argued, youths waged gang warfare with stones and water pistols filled with red wine, the taverns rocked with song and battle, and some enterprising person had broken into the new ice plant and discovered how to work the siren.

Saunders was convinced he had arrived in the middle of a revolution, but Henry said the islanders were taking the fiesta with unusual apathy.

Saunders was a small, nervous man in a bowler hat, who persisted in thinking that Dagobert was H. H. He seemed happier when the file devoted to himself was handed over, unopened, and added to the burning heap in the middle of the concrete floor.

We never learned what hold Bobby had over Saunders. In view of the speed and efficiency with which he produced Bobby's dispatch cases possibly he had been a professional safe-blower.

Henry was studying a folio marked *Harrington*. The name was evidently unfamiliar, but as he read it he frowned. He slowly scanned it again and passed it over to Dagobert.

"Could be," he said.

"Could be what?" I asked, noticing Dagobert's glazed expression. "Who's Harrington?" Both ignored me.

"What you expected?" Henry muttered.

Dagobert nodded and continued to study the dossier without elation. He rose finally and put it carefully on the bonfire. As an afterthought he finished off the brandy. He dumped what remained in the dispatch cases unread into the flames. Apparently Harrington's dossier had told him what he wanted—or didn't want?—to know. Though the night was mild he hovered around the blaze as though grateful for its warmth. I too had begun to shiver. Henry said finally:

"What do we do?"

Dagobert betrayed signs of ragged nerves. "You own the place," he said. "Do as you damn' well please."

"Nothing?" Henry suggested hopefully.

Dagobert was also tempted. "Do nothing," he said, "and in

a couple of hours Marcovitch will be dead." He gave the fire a vicious kick with his foot. "Suit yourself. Come on, Jane. Let's go out and celebrate."

Henry fell into step beside us outside the customs shed. Saunders remained on a bench in a corner of the shed, perhaps waiting for immigration officers to examine his passport.

Henry said quietly: "You'd better come with me. Strictly speaking Juana ought to be informed. But first we might check with Marcovitch. The laws of Tabarca, I imagine, can be redrafted so that he spends, say, the next twenty or thirty years in jail. I'll have a word with Senor Sans. What," he resumed, after we had climbed for a while in silence towards the Castle, "what about . . . about Harrington?"

"Never heard the name," Dagobert said.

"Marcovitch, however, has," said Henry.

"You wouldn't," I said, "care to tell me what it's all about?"

"No," both replied simultaneously.

We avoided the plaza and skirted the chalet garden. Juana's lights were still on and Dagobert, forgetting his recent proposal to celebrate, suggested that I should go to bed. I ignored this and we regained the Castle ramparts. In the east the sky was paler but below us the fiesta raged with unabated fury.

We walked through the banquet hall, disturbing thirty or forty cats and, by the light of Henry's pocket torch, climbed the spiral stairs of the dungeon. The guards outside Bobby's cell were dozing over a bottle of anis. They pulled themselves together at the sight of Henry and began excitedly to gesticulate and talk in Catalan. In the light of their storm lantern I saw that Dagobert's face was tense.

"Escaped?" he interrupted.

"No," Henry said. "He was released—as I should have anticipated—on Juana's orders."

"When? Where did he go?"

"They don't know. He pushed off about an hour ago, I

gather, laughing his head off. They think he must have joined the fun in the plaza."

"In that case he'll run straight into . . ."

He didn't finish the phrase. Henry too saved his breath. I scrambled after them down the spiral staircase.

"Straight into what?" I panted.

No one enlightened me.

This time when we passed the chalet Dagobert's suggestion that I go to bed was repeated in a manner I dared not disregard. He kissed me good-night and pushed me gently but firmly through the gate. Henry closed it behind me.

I waited until they disappeared, comforting myself with bitter reflections about "man's work" and how "the little woman must at all cost be spared."

"Straight into *Harrington,*" I thought, and realised I had said it out loud.

Instead of following them as I had meant to do, I raced along the path towards the chalet as though my own life, instead of Bobby's, were at stake. My teeth were chattering and my knees knocked together.

I recognised these exaggerated symptoms with dismay. I was simply and shamelessly and for no reason at all scared out of my wits.

He rose in my path before I reached the verandah steps. He had been sitting on a stone bench beneath a mimosa and at first I only saw that his shoulders drooped like the mimosa branches and that his tall angular body moved with an effort.

"Youth, what a fine thing it is!" he said. "How I envy you your energy, my dear. I'm afraid I found the fiesta too much for my old bones."

"After last n-night . . ." I stammered.

"Two nights in a row—quite so," he agreed. "Unless, Jane, you are in a hurry to be off again, perhaps you will smoke a final cigarette with me."

He produced his thin gold case. The feeble glow from the wrought-iron lamp over the verandah caught the yellow metal. Though I had seen his cigarette-case a dozen times I had never before noticed the worn Gothic initial: a single H.

I must have stared at it with peculiar stupidity; for he looked at me curiously and asked:

"Is there anything odd about the initial?"

"It stands for . . ."

"Hugo, of course," he said with a smile. "What else?"

Chapter 34

HUGO WARRINGTON STOPPED smiling.

"You're shivering," he said with solicitude. "Selfish of me to keep you standing here. One forgets that it's late October, nearly dawn and—if one may say so—you are charmingly decollete. Perhaps a turn around the garden?"

Gently he took my arm. I was conscious for the first time that it was bare. His hand was firmer than it looked.

"I'm rather worried about Marcovitch," he said. "The Princess, you know, suddenly decided to release him—none of my business, but a mistake, I think. I daresay Dagobert is looking for him."

"He's in the plaza," I supplied.

"I very much doubt if he'll find him in the plaza," he said. "As a matter of fact, Marcovitch did put in an appearance there about an hour ago—as bumptious, and objectionable, as ever. But something occurred which seemed to shake his self-assurance. I'm not quite sure what. Could it," he paused to watch my face, "could it be connected with the arrival of that seaplane which deprived us of your company for so long?"

He waited, but this time I supplied no information. He politely overlooked my silence and went on.

"Whatever it was, Marcovitch again deserted us, rather abruptly. I imagine he saw something—or rather someone. Or perhaps I should say . . . *someone* saw him. I have seen frightened people before—you, for instance, a moment ago." There was a glint in his eye which could have passed for a twinkle. He seemed to assume, falsely, that I had regained my poise. "But never anyone quite like Marcovitch. I even heard him abjectly begging Senor Sans to lock him up again! Poor Sans is convinced that all Anglo-Saxons are quite mad. I wonder if we are. . . ."

This reflection seemed to divert him more than it reassured me; for he laughed briefly. I tried very cautiously to withdraw my arm from his. I don't know whether he felt me holding back or not. He leaned against me, not heavily, but like an old man who is grateful for support. I wondered what would happen if I attempted to bolt, and hadn't the courage to try.

"For instance," he said, "we pride ourselves on our love of fair play and boast of our peaceful, law-abiding habits. Yet in wartime our enemies complain that we stop at nothing, and our normal Sunday entertainment is to stretch our legs out before the fire and gloat over newspapers filled with arson, rape and murder. Our friend Marcovitch makes a living by catering to such tastes."

"When he left the plaza," I said, "where did he go?"

"Marcovitch? Where do frightened rats usually go? They scamper back to their holes, I imagine."

He measured with a speculative eye the Castle which loomed

over us. The machicolated battlements were dimly outlined against the opalescent glow of dawn, but we stood in the black, obliterating shadow cast by the blank wall of the dungeon.

I was shocked to find we had strolled so far from the chalet verandah that even the dim rays of the wrought-iron lamp were no longer discernible. The lights in Juana's quarters had gone out and I was aware of something new and strange in the atmosphere.

It was a moment before I realised what it was: silence. The loud-speakers had stopped.

"The fiesta seems to be over," I said.

"Almost over," he nodded.

"If," I murmured, "you don't mind, I think I shall . . ."

"No, of course not, my dear."

He wasn't listening, nor did he release my arm when I tried to draw back. We had reached the cactus-fringed edge of the garden where it tumbled precipitously into the narrow gorge which served as a moat at the back of the castle. A hump-backed bridge spanned the gorge and connected the chalet garden with the postern-gate from which we had watched Senor Sans emerge this afternoon. It had once been a drawbridge, but had long since ceased to function. Thyme and rosemary had taken root in the crevices of its crumbling parapet.

"Marcovitch was released through that gate about an hour ago," Hugo Warrington mused. "He would naturally return by the same route, the one he was familiar with. Always study the psychology of the animal you are stalking, my dear."

"We're not, you're n-not waiting for Bobby!"

"No," he said, "not for Bobby. Bobby passed this way some time ago. Shall we draw a little nearer?"

I dug my heels in like a donkey and refused to budge another inch. We had already reached the bridge.

"I once did a spot of tiger shooting in Burma, did I ever tell you? Waiting hour after hour in the jungle one develops an extraordinary faculty for sensing the approach of the big fellow. So," he chuckled softly, "does the tethered goat—who is incapable of even attempting to defend herself."

I knew how the goat felt and bleated stupidly: "What b-big fellow?"

"The big cat, of course. You feel his presence in the darkness like a tingle in your spine, even before you see or hear . . ."

The stone which rolled with faint, diminishing reverberation down the ravine may have been dislodged by one of us. After an eternity it came to rest among the prickly pears.

"The tethered goat," he resumed, "is, of course, our friend Marcovitch. The cat, I may say, is . . . already with us."

I stared sightlessly into the darkness before I realised he was probably referring to *himself*.

"But what, what will you . . . What," I corrected, "can he do? I mean, Bobby must be safely in his cell again."

"No," he said gently. "The rat-hole is stopped up. The postern-gate is padlocked. Come, look for yourself . . ."

His eyesight was keener than mine. His right hand felt for the parapet of the bridge; his left hand gripped my wrist. I felt his thin bony fingers tighten.

"Hark!" he whispered.

I heard him catch his breath, but otherwise the silence was broken only by the far-off bark of a dog and the distant laughter of belated revellers in the village streets. Then I heard a vague rustling on the far side of the gorge, as though the breeze had stirred in the bougainvillaea which grew from chinks in the dungeon walls.

But there was no breeze.

I thought the soft metallic screech was the sound of grating teeth, his or possibly my own. But it came from somewhere ahead of us, just beyond the bridge.

My eyes by now were more accustomed to the darkness and,

though the rising hump of the bridge obscured part of what lay beyond, I could distinguish the iron grille of the postern-gate. Someone was clutching the bars, not, I saw, in order to get out but in a frantic attempt to beat his way in. He clawed at the rusting iron and rattled the grille in a crescendo of panic. A sapphire ring flashed from one of his fingers.

"Bobby!" I whispered.

"One shouldn't talk," Hugo Warrington said, "though our prey, I fancy, cannot escape."

"You, you followed him here?"

"But of course, my dear," he said mildly. "Sport—especially blood sport—has always attracted me."

Bobby may have heard us, for he spun round. His back was flat against the padlocked grille and I heard him panting. His face was a pale smudge in the darkness. His eyes seemed to take in the vertiginous drop to left and right and measure the narrow bridge which was his only line of retreat.

"Sometimes when cornered they're dangerous," Hugo Warrinton whispered, and, as Bobby suddenly charged us: "Careful!"

The warning was unnecessary. I lurched back as he let go of my wrist. I tripped and fell, and for a long moment wondered impersonally if I was part of the debris of masonry which crashed and continued to echo in the chasm below.

Bobby had nearly regained the central hump of the bridge before his assailant closed with him. I caught a nightmare glimpse of the two black shadows locked in each other's arms. I saw them grapple and sway on the narrow hump and heard their feet scrabbling for purchase on the loose stony surface. Then, above his enemy's low snarl, I heard Bobby shriek as the parapet gave way. The scream rose to an intolerable pitch until, indefinitely prolonged, it filled the night; and then . . . well, Dagobert pretends I fainted.

True, it was lighter when I regained my faculties and I may

have missed a moment or two of the drama. But the one who seemed nearest to fainting was Dagobert himself.

Henry too was in a bad state. With Senor Sans' aid he and Dagobert had combed Tabarca for Bobby. Only after half an hour's fruitless search had they guessed—as the killer, who had stalked him, knew—that Bobby must have returned to the Castle. Like the frightened rat Colonel Warrington called him he had scurried back across the drawbridge to the postern-gate—to find it barred, and the cat close on his heels.

"What frightened him back?" Margaret Penrose asked.

"One of our party, Senor Sans says," Henry said. "The murderer believed that Marcovitch was safely locked up and would be dead by dawn. When he unexpectedly appeared in the plaza and boasted that he was free the murderer gave himself away. Marcovitch suddenly realised he was next."

"Why didn't he simply accuse the murderer then and there?"

"He lost his head and panicked. You all saw him bolt. The murderer not only saw him, but followed him."

"Why did he panic? I mean, why did he realise he was next?"

Henry shrugged and Dagobert said: "Marcovitch finally understood something which has been obvious all along: the deaths of Juan Roig and Flossie Martin were accidental."

"Accidental?"

"The murderer planned to kill only once. He planned to kill Bobby Marcovitch."

"But poor Flossie . . ."

"He expected to find Marcovitch, not Flossie, in that oval bed. Under the clothes he didn't recognise her. He didn't know she and Marcovitch had changed cabins for the night."

"And Juan Roig?"

"You remember how Marcovitch followed Roig out on deck during the channel crossing. The murderer followed Marcovitch, but in the fog pushed Roig overboard instead. They were about the same size and both were wearing mackintoshes. In the dark just now—his eyesight was more trustworthy."

It was no longer quite dark, but the gorge was still deep in shadow. I peered reluctantly over the edge. A dozen of Senor Sans' men had managed to climb down among the prickly pears. They were carefully lifting two bodies onto makeshift stretchers. One was still alive: Bobby. He lingered for half a day and died without regaining consciousness. The other was dead.

Ninette did not begin to cry until Senor Sans' men had signalled this information up to us.

"His name was Harrington," Dagobert said. "But it was easy to spot him from the information in his dossier. It's hardly necessary to add that Marcovitch was blackmailing him. I've just read his story."

"I don't think we need hear it," Margaret said, and led Ninette back to the chalet.

We turned to Dagobert again when they were out of earshot.

"Ninette," he murmured, "might have prevented Flossie's death—if I hadn't put my foot into it. Thanks to Ninette Harrington nearly lost his nerve and returned to London. Thanks to me he changed his mind. I accused him of running away. I didn't know he was running away from his own compulsion to kill. Harrington," he resumed in a brisker voice, "spent much of his depleted means on winning a place among the Lucky Seven. Saunders tells me he sent in several hundred entry forms. It was the gamble—he once told Jane—he won. The one he lost was Yvonne."

"What's the story?" Colonel Warrington asked.

"He operated on Yvonne and she died. To be exact, he re-operated on her. A Belgian quack, unlicensed, had previously bungled the job and John Harrington really had no alternative. Incidentally the Belgian spent a year in jail and when he got out he sold the details to *Home Truth*. They were just up Marcovitch's street."

"What was the operation? Oh, I see, er, quite," Hugo Warrington added hastily, thinking I was still capable of emotion.

"Yes, Yvonne was pregnant," Dagobert said. "They were not married and she had gone to Ostend especially to see this quack. John Harrington followed her. I imagine he meant to marry her; his dossier didn't say. Anyway he was forced to operate—and when she died he felt obliged to give up his career. His eyesight rapidly deteriorated. He became a vet and changed his name to Derek Upjohn."

"Didn't Marcovitch know his new name?"

"No. Derek was small fry. Saunders collected the blackmail on Marcovitch's behalf."

"Which makes him a blackmailer too," Henry said. "What do I do about him?"

"That's your problem," Dagobert said. "He acted on Marcovitch's instructions. Marcovitch had something on him and he had no alternative. But Saunders knew who Derek really was and, I suspect, was not unamused by the fact that Marcovitch was innocently travelling with one of the firm's victims."

"Don't know who this Saunders is," the Colonel said, "but I'm glad he kept his mouth shut. Marcovitch got exactly what was coming to him."

"Yes, we gathered you did little to prevent his, er, execution," Henry said drily.

"None of my business, was it?" the Colonel grunted. "I saw Upjohn on his trail and came along to see what would happen. Hypocrisy to pretend the result wasn't satisfactory, eh?"

Dagobert said: "Any more questions?"

"Yes, you claim you spotted me," Hugo Warrington said. "How? Or should I say what for?"

"For exactly what you appear to be," Dagobert said with a

wan smile. "You, sir, were so consistently in character, if I may say so, that you *had* to be genuine."

The Colonel chuckled appreciatively. I didn't join in his mirth. A ray of sunlight had pierced the gorge. It glinted on a piece of broken glass caught in the prickly pears halfway down the slope—all that remained of Derek Upjohn's dark spectacles.

Chapter 35

MYSTERY STILL SURROUNDS the fate of my mink coat. Henry, I understand, insisted that Margaret and Ninette should keep theirs—though why they want fur coats in Tabarca I cannot imagine. The last I heard of Margaret and Ninette they were still there. They run a small lending library in the plaza and give English lessons under royal patronage.

Dagobert and I flew to Barcelona that same day with Henry in the seaplane. Henry was disinclined to talk of recent events, but he admitted that he had at first suspected Margaret of killing Flossie in mistake for Bobby. That was why he had taken the key and later planted it on Bobby Marcovitch.

Henry left us in Barcelona and flew on to London with Saunders to wind up certain unspecified business. We returned to London in a more leisurely fashion on the motor-scooter. It was between Toulouse and Chartres when the weather broke that I began to think nostalgically of the mink coat, though (as

Angela handsomely said) riding pillion through driving sleet in Dagobert's mackintosh was doubtless good for my complexion.

It is distressing how petty one is: I can never regard the publicity photograph of Ninette in bathing-dress and wild-mink coat taken on the sun-drenched battlements of the *Castillo* without a stab of envy.

We, however, had our perks too. Mr. Jenkins gratefully presented us with the motor-scooter Dagobert had tested. Dagobert has become expert in dealing with its tendency to wobble on corners and I have recently been trying to interest him in crash helmets.

Last week we joined the Bank Holiday exodus to the South Coast, penetrating towards nightfall as far as Dorking where we discovered a jolly little Tudor inn with a huge, inglenook fireplace, low oak-beamed ceilings and shining pewter. The place was crowded with happy faces all silently glued to the television.

We watched with awe. I thought our roving camera had at least been in for the aftermath of that afternoon's appalling motor-coach crash ("Starlet Flings Pet Rabbit to Safety"), but it was the finals of a Spelling Bee for children under eleven in Leeds.

During an intermission, while a muted chorus of angelic voices sang sweetly of a new laxative ("It Works Three Ways"), we caught the barmaid's attention. We retired with hushed voices to a corner settle where we tried—quite unsuccessfully—to ignore the twenty-one-inch screen. Our roving reporter's dimpled chin at once reappeared.

"And now, yet another scoop," he said. "You have already heard how this morning a Princess and a millionaire were quietly married in a private chapel in Cannes. No cameras recorded this simple ceremony, but we can be permitted to wish Juana de Branza and Henry Howard Hutton Junior all happiness. The film that you will now see has just been flown from Tabarca and shows us another wedding, in its way equally romantic. The Bride? Ninette Nixon of Twelve Victoria Crescent, Wolverhampton."

The plaza of Tabarca flickered across the screen and for a moment the dignified atmosphere of the Dorking Arms was disturbed by strange Catalan cries, fireworks and pealing bells as Ninette, radiant in white chiffon and orange blossoms, appeared on the steps of the church on the arm of her husband.

"The groom? The lucky man is none other than Don Diego Sans who has just been triumphantly re-elected Mayor of Tabarca. Ah me, some men have all the luck! 'Bye, Ninette . . . I hope one of those kisses you're throwing is for me. . . . And now back to Lincolnshire where dogs are out again, on the trail of the Man with the Squint. . . ."

"Once knew this fellow Sans," said a tall man in a Norfolk jacket to his neighbour at the bar. "Matter of fact I helped him a bit last year—spot of bother with a killer at large on the Island. I was staying with the Princess at the time. Did I ever tell you?"

Evidently he had, for his neighbour edged away and bore his gin and lime towards our settle where there was a better view of the television. Colonel Warrington, unperturbed, buttonholed someone else.

"Extraordinary chap, this H. H. Hutton, you know. I knew him quite well. Used to delight in getting himself up like a hitch-hiker, run around incognito. I remember once in Barcelona . . ."

The man with the gin and lime appealed to us for sympathy.

"He expects us to believe all that," he sighed. "Between ourselves, doubt if he's ever been out of Dorking."

We finished our half pints and joined the record-breaking crowds on their return to London, refreshed by our day in the country.

I bought a copy of *Home Truth* the other day for sentimental reasons. It has apparently changed its policy. The new emphasis is on domesticity and our newsagent reports that its circulation has dropped alarmingly. It contains such useful articles as "Baby's First Tooth" and "How to Transform that Old Cupboard Under the Stairs into an Amusing Den for Him." Gloria Saunders contributes a knitting pattern for a Balaclava Helmet for the Outdoor Man which Dagobert wants me to try. This year's thrilling competition offers a prize to the person who sends in the best recipe for a Budget Cottage Pie: a week in Bournemouth at an hotel guaranteed to be within five minutes' walk from the sea-front. Dagobert is already busy on it, experimenting with capon livers, truffles and kirsch.

We called on Jim Martin in Lathomstowe yesterday, but found that he had moved to the Bishop's Avenue in Hampstead. During the last year Jim Martin has, according to his former neighbours, had nothing but luck, landing contract after contract. At the moment his firm is constructing the new H. H. H. Building on the Embankment and it is rumoured that his son Pete has already been entered for Eton.

Our own luck has been variable. We sold the shares we purchased in H. H. Hutton (London) Limited just before they soared, and reinvested the money in Jenkins' Scooters which has recently suspended production. Dagobert has practically stopped reading the *Financial Times.* To be sure, the Jenkins shares represent all there is between us and work, but, as Dagobert says, a philosopher rises above such trivialities.

THE PERENNIAL LIBRARY MYSTERY SERIES

Delano Ames

FOR OLD CRIME'S SAKE — P 629, $2.84

MURDER, MAESTRO, PLEASE — P 630, $2.84

"If there is a more engaging couple in modern fiction than Jane and Dagobert Brown, we have not met them." —*Scotsman*

E. C. Bentley

TRENT'S LAST CASE — P 440, $2.50

"One of the three best detective stories ever written."
—Agatha Christie

TRENT'S OWN CASE — P 516, $2.25

"I won't waste time saying that the plot is sound and the detection satisfying. Trent has not altered a scrap and reappears with all his old humor and charm." —Dorothy L. Sayers

Gavin Black

A DRAGON FOR CHRISTMAS — P 473, $1.95

"Potent excitement!" —*New York Herald Tribune*

THE EYES AROUND ME — P 485, $1.95

"I stayed up until all hours last night reading *The Eyes Around Me,* which is something I do not do very often, but I was so intrigued by the ingeniousness of Mr. Black's plotting and the witty way in which he spins his mystery. I can only say that I enjoyed the book enormously."
—F. van Wyck Mason

YOU WANT TO DIE, JOHNNY? — P 472, $1.95

"Gavin Black doesn't just develop a pressure plot in suspense, he adds uninfected wit, character, charm, and sharp knowledge of the Far East to make rereading as keen as the first race-through." —*Book Week*

Nicholas Blake

THE CORPSE IN THE SNOWMAN — P 427, $1.95

"If there is a distinction between the novel and the detective story (which we do not admit), then this book deserves a high place in both categories." —*The New York Times*

Nicholas Blake (cont'd)

THE DREADFUL HOLLOW P 493, $1.95
"Pace unhurried, characters excellent, reasoning solid."
—*San Francisco Chronicle*

END OF CHAPTER P 397, $1.95
". . . admirably solid . . . an adroit formal detective puzzle backed up by firm characterization and a knowing picture of London publishing."
—*The New York Times*

HEAD OF A TRAVELER P 398, $2.25
"Another grade A detective story of the right old jigsaw persuasion."
—*New York Herald Tribune Book Review*

MINUTE FOR MURDER P 419, $1.95
"An outstanding mystery novel. Mr. Blake's writing is a delight in itself." —*The New York Times*

THE MORNING AFTER DEATH P 520, $1.95
"One of Blake's best." —Rex Warner

A PENKNIFE IN MY HEART P 521, $2.25
"Style brilliant . . . and suspenseful." —*San Francisco Chronicle*

THE PRIVATE WOUND P 531, $2.25
[Blake's] best novel in a dozen years . . . . An intensely penetrating study of sexual passion. . . . A powerful story of murder and its aftermath."
—Anthony Boucher, *The New York Times*

A QUESTION OF PROOF P 494, $1.95
"The characters in this story are unusually well drawn, and the suspense is well sustained." —*The New York Times*

THE SAD VARIETY P 495, $2.25
"It is a stunner. I read it instead of eating, instead of sleeping."
—Dorothy Salisbury Davis

THERE'S TROUBLE BREWING P 569, $3.37
"Nigel Strangeways is a puzzling mixture of simplicity and penetration, but all the more real for that." —*The Times Literary Supplement*

THOU SHELL OF DEATH P 428, $1.95
"It has all the virtues of culture, intelligence and sensibility that the most exacting connoisseur could ask of detective fiction."
—*The Times* [London] *Literary Supplement*

Nicholas Blake (cont'd)

THE WIDOW'S CRUISE P 399, $2.25

"A stirring suspense. . . . The thrilling tale leaves nothing to be desired."
—*Springfield Republican*

THE WORM OF DEATH P 400, $2.25

"It [The Worm of Death] is one of Blake's very best—and his best is better than almost anyone's." —Louis Untermeyer

John & Emery Bonett

A BANNER FOR PEGASUS P 554, $2.40

"A gem! Beautifully plotted and set. . . . Not only is the murder adroit and deserved, and the detection competent, but the love story is charming." —Jacques Barzun and Wendell Hertig Taylor

DEAD LION P 563, $2.40

"A clever plot, authentic background and interesting characters highly recommended this one." —*New Republic*

Christianna Brand

GREEN FOR DANGER P 551, $2.50

"You have to reach for the greatest of Great Names (Christie, Carr, Queen . . .) to find Brand's rivals in the devious subtleties of the trade."
—Anthony Boucher

TOUR DE FORCE P 572, $2.40

"Complete with traps for the over-ingenious, a double-reverse surprise ending and a key clue planted so fairly and obviously that you completely overlook it. If that's your idea of perfect entertainment, then seize at once upon *Tour de Force.*" —Anthony Boucher, *The New York Times*

James Byrom

OR BE HE DEAD P 585, $2.84

"A very original tale . . . Well written and steadily entertaining."
—Jacques Barzun & Wendell Hertig Taylor, *A Catalogue of Crime*

Marjorie Carleton

VANISHED P 559, $2.40

"Exceptional . . . a minor triumph."
—Jacques Barzun and Wendell Hertig Taylor, *A Catalogue of Crime*

THE CUCKOO LINE AFFAIR P 451, $1.95

". . . an agreeable and ingenious piece of work." —*The New Yorker*

A HERO FOR LEANDA P 429, $1.50

"One can trust Mr. Garve to put a fresh twist to any situation, and the ending is really a lovely surprise." —*The Manchester Guardian*

MURDER THROUGH THE LOOKING GLASS P 449, $1.95

". . . refreshingly out-of-the-way and enjoyable . . . highly recommended to all comers." —*Saturday Review*

NO TEARS FOR HILDA P 441, $1.95

"It starts fine and finishes finer. I got behind on breathing watching Max get not only his man but his woman, too." —Rex Stout

THE RIDDLE OF SAMSON P 450, $1.95

"The story is an excellent one, the people are quite likable, and the writing is superior." —*Springfield Republican*

Michael Gilbert

BLOOD AND JUDGMENT P 446, $1.95

"Gilbert readers need scarcely be told that the characters all come alive at first sight, and that his surpassing talent for narration enhances any plot. . . . Don't miss." —*San Francisco Chronicle*

THE BODY OF A GIRL P 459, $1.95

"Does what a good mystery should do: open up into all kinds of ramifications, with untold menace behind the action. At the end, there is a bang-up climax, and it is a pleasure to see how skilfully Gilbert wraps everything up." —*The New York Times Book Review*

THE DANGER WITHIN P 448, $1.95

"Michael Gilbert has nicely combined some elements of the straight detective story with plenty of action, suspense, and adventure, to produce a superior thriller." —*Saturday Review*

FEAR TO TREAD P 458, $1.95

"Merits serious consideration as a work of art."

—*The New York Times*

Joe Gores

HAMMETT P 631, $2.84

"Joe Gores at his very best. Terse, powerful writing—with the master, Dashiell Hammett, as the protagonist in a novel I think he would have been proud to call his own." —Robert Ludlum

C. W. Grafton

BEYOND A REASONABLE DOUBT P 519, $1.95

"A very ingenious tale of murder . . . a brilliant and gripping narrative."
—Jacques Barzun and Wendell Hertig Taylor

Edward Grierson

THE SECOND MAN P 528, $2.25

"One of the best trial-testimony books to have come along in quite a while." —*The New Yorker*

Cyril Hare

DEATH IS NO SPORTSMAN P 555, $2.40

"You will be thrilled because it succeeds in placing an ingenious story in a new and refreshing setting. . . . The identity of the murderer is really a surprise." —*Daily Mirror*

DEATH WALKS THE WOODS P 556, $2.40

"Here is a fine formal detective story, with a technically brilliant solution demanding the attention of all connoisseurs of construction."
—Anthony Boucher, *The New York Times Book Review*

AN ENGLISH MURDER P 455, $2.50

"By a long shot, the best crime story I have read for a long time. Everything is traditional, but originality does not suffer. The setting is perfect. Full marks to Mr. Hare." —*Irish Press*

TENANT FOR DEATH P 570, $2.84

"The way in which an air of probability is combined both with clear, terse narrative and with a good deal of subtle suburban atmosphere, proves the extreme skill of the writer." —*The Spectator*

TRAGEDY AT LAW P 522, $2.25

"An extremely urbane and well-written detective story."
—*The New York Times*

UNTIMELY DEATH P 514, $2.25

"The English detective story at its quiet best, meticulously underplayed, rich in perceivings of the droll human animal and ready at the last with a neat surprise which has been there all the while had we but wits to see it." —*New York Herald Tribune Book Review*

THE WIND BLOWS DEATH P 589, $2.84

"A plot compounded of musical knowledge, a Dickens allusion, and a subtle point in law is related with delightfully unobtrusive wit, warmth, and style." —*The New York Times*

Cyril Hare (cont'd)

WITH A BARE BODKIN P 523, $2.25

"One of the best detective stories published for a long time."

—*The Spectator*

Robert Harling

THE ENORMOUS SHADOW P 545, $2.50

"In some ways the best spy story of the modern period. . . . The writing is terse and vivid . . . the ending full of action . . . altogether first-rate."

—Jacques Barzun and Wendell Hertig Taylor, *A Catalogue of Crime*

Matthew Head

THE CABINDA AFFAIR P 541, $2.25

"An absorbing whodunit and a distinguished novel of atmosphere."

—Anthony Boucher, *The New York Times*

THE CONGO VENUS P 597, $2.84

"Terrific. The dialogue is just plain wonderful."

—*The Boston Globe*

MURDER AT THE FLEA CLUB P 542, $2.50

"The true delight is in Head's style, its limpid ease combined with humor and an awesome precision of phrase." —*San Francisco Chronicle*

M. V. Heberden

ENGAGED TO MURDER P 533, $2.25

"Smooth plotting." —*The New York Times*

James Hilton

WAS IT MURDER? P 501, $1.95

"The story is well planned and well written."

—*The New York Times*

P. M. Hubbard

HIGH TIDE P 571, $2.40

"A smooth elaboration of mounting horror and danger."

—*Library Journal*

Elspeth Huxley

THE AFRICAN POISON MURDERS P 540, $2.25

"Obscure venom, manical mutilations, deadly bush fire, thrilling climax compose major opus.... Top-flight."

—*Saturday Review of Literature*

MURDER ON SAFARI P 587, $2.84

"Right now we'd call Mrs. Huxley a dangerous rival to Agatha Christie."

—*Books*

Francis Iles

BEFORE THE FACT P 517, $2.50

"Not many 'serious' novelists have produced character studies to compare with Iles's internally terrifying portrait of the murderer in *Before the Fact,* his masterpiece and a work truly deserving the appellation of unique and beyond price."

—Howard Haycraft

MALICE AFORETHOUGHT P 532, $1.95

"It is a long time since I have read anything so good as *Malice Aforethought,* with its cynical humour, acute criminology, plausible detail and rapid movement. It makes you hug yourself with pleasure."

—H. C. Harwood, *Saturday Review*

Michael Innes

DEATH BY WATER P 574, $2.40

"The amount of ironic social criticism and deft characterization of scenes and people would serve another author for six books."

—Jacques Barzun and Wendell Hertig Taylor

HARE SITTING UP P 590, $2.84

"There is hardly anyone (in mysteries or mainstream) more exquisitely literate, allusive and Jamesian—and hardly anyone with a firmer sense of melodramatic plot or a more vigorous gift of storytelling."

—Anthony Boucher, *The New York Times*

THE LONG FAREWELL P 575, $2.40

"A model of the deft, classic detective story, told in the most wittily diverting prose."

—*The New York Times*

THE MAN FROM THE SEA P 591, $2.84

"The pace is brisk, the adventures exciting and excitingly told, and above all he keeps to the very end the interesting ambiguity of the man from the sea."

—*New Statesman*

Michael Innes (cont'd)

THE SECRET VANGUARD P 584, $2.84
"Innes . . . has mastered the art of swift, exciting and well-organized narrative." —*The New York Times*

Mary Kelly

THE SPOILT KILL P 565, $2.40
"Mary Kelly is a new Dorothy Sayers. . . . [An] exciting new novel." —*Evening News*

Lange Lewis

THE BIRTHDAY MURDER P 518, $1.95
"Almost perfect in its playlike purity and delightful prose."
—Jacques Barzun and Wendell Hertig Taylor

Allan MacKinnon

HOUSE OF DARKNESS P 582, $2.84
"His best . . . a perfect compendium."
—Jacques Barzun & Wendell Hertig Taylor, *A Catalogue of Crime*

Arthur Maling

LUCKY DEVIL P 482, $1.95
"The plot unravels at a fast clip, the writing is breezy and Maling's approach is as fresh as today's stockmarket quotes."
—*Louisville Courier Journal*

RIPOFF P 483, $1.95
"A swiftly paced story of today's big business is larded with intrigue as a Ralph Nader-type investigates an insurance scandal and is soon on the run from a hired gun and his brother. . . . Engrossing and credible."
—*Booklist*

SCHROEDER'S GAME P 484, $1.95
"As the title indicates, this Schroeder is up to something, and the unravelling of his game is a diverting and sufficiently blood-soaked entertainment." —*The New Yorker*

Austin Ripley

MINUTE MYSTERIES P 387, $2.50
More than one hundred of the world's shortest detective stories. Only one possible solution to each case!

Thomas Sterling

THE EVIL OF THE DAY P 529, $2.50

"Prose as witty and subtle as it is sharp and clear. . .characters unconventionally conceived and richly bodied forth . . . . In short, a novel to be treasured." —Anthony Boucher, *The New York Times*

Julian Symons

THE BELTING INHERITANCE P 468, $1.95

"A superb whodunit in the best tradition of the detective story." —August Derleth, *Madison Capital Times*

BLAND BEGINNING P 469, $1.95

"Mr. Symons displays a deft storytelling skill, a quiet and literate wit, a nice feeling for character, and detectival ingenuity of a high order." —Anthony Boucher, *The New York Times*

BOGUE'S FORTUNE P 481, $1.95

"There's a touch of the old sardonic humour, and more than a touch of style." —*The Spectator*

THE BROKEN PENNY P 480, $1.95

"The most exciting, astonishing and believable spy story to appear in years. —Anthony Boucher, *The New York Times Book Review*

THE COLOR OF MURDER P 461, $1.95

"A singularly unostentatious and memorably brilliant detective story." —*New York Herald Tribune Book Review*

Dorothy Stockbridge Tillet
(John Stephen Strange)

THE MAN WHO KILLED FORTESCUE P 536, $2.25

"Better than average." —*Saturday Review of Literature*

Simon Troy

THE ROAD TO RHUINE P 583, $2.84

"Unusual and agreeably told." —*San Francisco Chronicle*

SWIFT TO ITS CLOSE P 546, $2.40

"A nicely literate British mystery . . . the atmosphere and the plot are exceptionally well wrought, the dialogue excellent." —*Best Sellers*

Henry Wade

THE DUKE OF YORK'S STEPS P 588, $2.84
"A classic of the golden age."
—Jacques Barzun & Wendell Hertig Taylor, *A Catalogue of Crime*

A DYING FALL P 543, $2.50
"One of those expert British suspense jobs . . . it crackles with undercurrents of blackmail, violent passion and murder. Topnotch in its class."
—*Time*

THE HANGING CAPTAIN P 548, $2.50
"This is a detective story for connoisseurs, for those who value clear thinking and good writing above mere ingenuity and easy thrills."
—*Times Literary Supplement*

Hillary Waugh

LAST SEEN WEARING . . . P 552, $2.40
"A brilliant tour de force." —Julian Symons

THE MISSING MAN P 553, $2.40
"The quiet detailed police work of Chief Fred C. Fellows, Stockford, Conn., is at its best in *The Missing Man* . . . one of the Chief's toughest cases and one of the best handled."
—Anthony Boucher, *The New York Times Book Review*

Henry Kitchell Webster

WHO IS THE NEXT? P 539, $2.25
"A double murder, private-plane piloting, a neat impersonation, and a delicate courtship are adroitly combined by a writer who knows how to use the language." —Jacques Barzun and Wendell Hertig Taylor

Anna Mary Wells

MURDERER'S CHOICE P 534, $2.50
"Good writing, ample action, and excellent character work."
—*Saturday Review of Literature*

A TALENT FOR MURDER P 535, $2.25
"The discovery of the villain is a decided shock." —*Books*

Edward Young

THE FIFTH PASSENGER P 544, $2.25
"Clever and adroit . . . excellent thriller . . ." —*Library Journal*